# LADY

---

# LAZARUS

# LADY

---

# LAZARUS

A Novel

Cheryll W. Crane

iUniverse, Inc.
New York  Lincoln  Shanghai

# LADY LAZARUS

iUniverse books may be ordered through booksellers or by contacting:

iUniverse
2021 Pine Lake Road, Suite 100
Lincoln, NE 68512
www.iuniverse.com
1-800-Authors (1-800-288-4677)

This is a work of fiction. All of the characters, names, incidents, organizations, and dialogue in this novel are either the products of the author's imagination or are used fictitiously.

ISBN-13: 978-0-595-40608-1 (pbk)
ISBN-13: 978-0-595-84974-1 (ebk)
ISBN-10: 0-595-40608-4 (pbk)
ISBN-10: 0-595-84974-1 (ebk)

Printed in the United States of America

In Memory of Dale M. and Reginald R. Whitelow

# PROLOGUE

People say I let myself go. They are mistaken. I went. There is a difference. After being pushed by one thing and then another, I got out of the way.

In this place we are denied many things, but we are allowed to remember. I remember how I got here. I also remember how and by what miracle my children were saved. When I close my eyes, I see Stranger Woman. Luckily for my children and me, she came along when she did.

In this place, I'm denied many things; however, I am allowed to speak when spoken to. Here we are interviewed, counseled, and examined like specimens. We are encouraged to speak the truth.

Invariably, they ask me the same two questions: whom I intended to blame and what was I thinking? I answer both questions truthfully: no one and nothing.

When Susan Smith killed her children in Union, South Carolina, she blamed their absence on a nonexistent black man. More recently, other women who have committed the most unnatural act have blamed their behavior on their husbands, on their medication (or lack thereof), or on God.

I blame no one. Unlike Susan Smith, I didn't have a plan. The day I took my children to Eloise Lake I didn't even have a car. My children and I walked the whole way, eight miles, to the lake. I assure you that nothing as convenient as a national scapegoat—a bogeyman—danced in my head. My head was empty. My mind was blank.

I was just trying to get away from where I had been.

If there had been a voice in my head, a directive, it probably would have said this: "Go on. You have to do something. Do what you have to do." But as I've said, when I stepped down into the water my mind was blank. When I pushed off, I was deaf to the world.

Right away the cold got my attention. It was a dark surprise. Fall was several weeks away, but the water already felt like it did in deep winter. It chilled my bones and circled my waist like a hand. It rocked me back.

It rocked us back. My baby Diego was riding heavily on my hip. He was thirteen months old and big for his age. By leaning into the push and pull of the water, I managed to keep us upright as I waded out. And I kept going.

When the water reached my chest, I didn't turn back. I could have, but I didn't. Instead, I shifted my son to the front of my body. I held him high, like an offering.

That's when I could have released Diego. All I would have had to do was bend forward and let him go. He would have floated free. Just like that.

My daughter would have been a different story. Quite different. I turned and looked back over my shoulder and saw Suzanne dancing on a big rock in the clearing. She was pretending that she was Sea Dancer, the ancient woman who climbed out of the water at the beginning of time. It has been said that Sea Dancer's hips and her sensual swaying rule the four seasons, the tide, and the mind of one man out of every two. Who wouldn't want to be her?

Suzanne sang out, "I'm Sea Dancer, Mama. Watch me. I'm Sea Dancer."

I was watching her all right. Suzanne's eyes were closed. She was twisting and turning, moving to the beat of her own heart.

I could have startled her on that silver rock. I could have swooped in, gotten the upper hand and given my little girl a real shock, but she's a fighter like my father, Lester H. Moon. The H. is for Hopewell and he lived up to the name; he never gave up hope. He had to fight to get born, fight to stay alive, and, for all I know, he's fighting still.

Suzanne, his first grandchild, is a throwback. If I had grabbed hold of her, she would have fought me for her life. It would have taken all my strength to pull her off that shiny rock and drag her to the water; and that would have been the easy part. Once I got her into the lake, I would have had to plant myself like a tree that shall not be moved. I would have had to pin Suzanne's arms behind her back with one hand and, with my other hand, press flat against her face until she went down. And if she had gone down at all, she would have gone down hard, screaming and kicking the world.

If.

It never happened. Instead, Stranger Woman called me by my name. She said, "Mattie Moon."

I looked around and saw a face that I will never forget. The woman who called my name had smooth dark skin with high cheekbones, brown eyes that shone like burnished coal, a thin nose, and full lips.

Stranger Woman was tall and her African headdress made her appear taller. Her silk dress flowed in the breeze and cast a shadow across the water. She wore gold earrings that brushed against her collarbone. There was gold at her wrist, too. When she held her hand out to me, the yellow circles set off sparks that skipped and hopped across the water and lit a fire in Diego's eyes.

Stranger Woman kept her midnight eyes on me. I knew that she knew me. Twice before she had come to me in times of need, but this was the first time I had seen her up close. This time, before I went down for the third time and for good, she called my name.

She saved my life and the lives of my children.

In this place, we are denied many things, but we are allowed to remember. In this place, we are also allowed to think and even to write. I think about my children all the time. On my good days, I write about them.

# PART ONE

# CHAPTER ONE

My dancing girl has light brown eyes that see everything, and perfectly shaped ears that, at times, she wills not to listen. A miniature woman, she's heard too much already.

In calendar years, Suzanne is nine, but in woman years she's more than three times that. She's pushing thirty at a minimum. Maybe every little girl grows up when she's nine. I know I did.

I was nine years old when I lost my dad. He didn't die, but he went away all the same. One day he walked out of my childhood and ended it. He said he had to go.

It was mid-October. I had run home from school that day. I ran, pranced, and jumped all the way from the schoolhouse down the winding road that led to my front door. Before entering the house, I stood on the porch and waved at Carl, the bull that lived in the field next to our house. "Hi, Carl," I yelled out in a high friendly voice.

Carl ignored me. He always ignored me, but I liked him anyway. I liked his bulk, all that heft and dreamtime darkness. I liked his penetrating eyes that I wanted to see into, but couldn't, as he dropped his head and ignored the likes of me. Most of all, I liked his reliability. Good old Carl was always there, day after day. I counted on him. He was part of home.

When Carl moved off in search of his supper I opened the door and went into the house. There shouldn't have been anyone moving around inside our house that early in the afternoon—both of my parents worked, as had their parents, grands, and greats—but I knew instantly that someone was there. I could feel it. I wasn't scared; I was curious. I asked myself, Who could it be?

I stood still for a moment and listened. Whoever it was must have felt as if she belonged there. She showed no need to rush around, grab something, and get out quickly. Not Aunt Shirley, then. Shirley Lee Taborn was slender and light on her feet. She was always in a hurry, with a hundred and one things on her to-do list, and the hasty pace of someone who didn't have long to get them done.

The thing my aunt didn't have was time. The person down the hall from where I stood did. She (or he) was moving more like Carl—bull-like. Darkly. Precisely. And something was changing in our house.

I looked around the living room. Nothing was out of place, broken, or trampled on, so I tiptoed back to Mama and Daddy's room. The door was open. Daddy was standing by the bed. He was packing.

I had felt my daddy leaving for weeks, but seeing him fold his clothes and stack them in his plaid suitcase made my heart jump nevertheless. I thought: Where is he going? How long will he be gone?

When he took his suit down from the hook on the door, I got my answer. Daddy was going away for good. He had told me himself that he had only worn that suit one time in over a decade. I had never seen him wear the jacket and the pants at the same time. If he was taking them both with him, he was going to be gone for a very long time. I put my hand over my mouth to stop the scream.

Daddy looked up, saw my eyes filling with tears, and said, "Don't look at me like that now, Mattie. I've got to go."

I smeared the water across my face and walked over to the bed. Confused by my feelings and ashamed of them, I sat down and held onto Daddy's torn suitcase. Before I knew it, I started crying like a two-year-old.

Daddy gave me a few minutes to let it out. Meanwhile, he kept on packing. He folded his other pair of dress pants (he had worn them quite a few times), put his good shoes in a plastic bag, and rolled his tie into a tight black ball. Then he wrapped a washcloth around his toothbrush, cleared his throat, and sat down next to me.

Daddy looked like he wanted to cry, too. "I can't stay here, Mattie," he said. "I've got to move on. The truth is, if I don't get away before dark, I'll never leave. And if I don't leave, I'll die."

Daddy rummaged around in his suitcase, found a handkerchief, and handed it to me. I wiped my face again and blew my nose. I tried to sit up straight like a big girl, but I couldn't do it. My back and my spirit were bent.

Daddy patted my arm and tried to explain to me the part I already understood: he and Mama were completely different people. Direct opposites.

"Your mama is real religious," he said. "In her own mind, she's Heaven bound."

I knew that. Mama had been on her way to Heaven as long as I'd known her. As far as she was concerned, both the planet Earth and the people riding on it were a nuisance, something to be suffered through. She couldn't wait to leave.

Daddy, on the other hand, enjoyed his earthly existence and he wanted it to last as long as possible. He had often said it was worth the time and the trouble. He said that even his bad times were better than no times at all. Had to be.

That Daddy was alive at all was considered a miracle by some, but not by him. He didn't believe in miracles. Fate, either. He acknowledged luck, though (he had to). His had been a breach birth. The midwife said he was lucky. She didn't think he would make it, but she hadn't told Daddy and he kept on coming, coming on strong. Once out in the world, he had seizures that went on for the first six years of life. His mother had to hold him down to keep him from hurting himself. He was anemic, too, though thankfully not sickle cell. The tonic they gave him for his blood damaged his teeth, but not his will. He kept on fighting.

Daddy grew up poor, but because he survived a difficult start he believed his luck would improve. In time, and gradually, it did. He left school in the middle of the tenth grade, worked odd jobs, two and three at a time, to help support himself and his family. Then he was drafted. He fought for his life in Viet Nam, and again he was lucky. He marched home from the war and began working in the mines. He was trapped in a mine once, given up for dead. He lived, though. And after that, as he put it, he was fool-lucky enough to be one of the first men to crawl back down when the mine reopened. Daddy believed in good and bad luck; he appreciated the good and dealt with the bad.

The year I was born Daddy and his friends built our house. It leaned a little to the right and it was drafty, but it was ours. The one Daddy made just for us. He rarely complained about how hard it was to heat or how low it was to the ground.

Daddy said that the one thing that kept him going was music. He had an old piano and a harmonica that he loved true. In our homemade living room, he played all kinds of music—delta blues, rock and roll, jazz, and country. And although he had stopped attending church as soon as his parents let him, every now and then he played us the spirituals that he remembered from long ago. Daddy played them real good, too. If my daddy had been a place of business, his sign would have read OPEN 24 HOURS. It would have been lit in neon as bright as Las Vegas. Daddy never closed; he never gave up.

Mama did. She gave up on the present and spent her time looking forward to the future, the promised by-and-by. If Mama had been a business, her sign would have been the flip side of Daddy's. It would have been the one that warned OUT TO LUNCH, or, possibly, CLOSED FOR REPAIRS. Our earthly day-to-day journey was too fly-by-night for Mama. She believed in the eternal—an everlasting life that defeats death. Daddy believed in the chaotic now-and-now. He and Mama were surely opposites.

"Your Mama's idea of living is waiting to die," Daddy said, standing up to stick his comb in his back pocket. "She's killing me. I've got to go."

While Daddy sorted his socks, separating the ones that were worn thin from the ones that were downright hopeless, I tried to think of something to say, something that would hold him in place, keep him where he belonged until his mind changed and he remembered that life with us wasn't so bad, that our times together were better than no times at all. Had to be.

I knew that if I could just say the magic words, I could set time, and Daddy, in reverse. He would empty his cardboard-thin suitcase; put his clothes back wherever they belonged, in the drawers, the closet, and on the hook at the door; play us a tune on the piano; wash up; and arrive home from work dog tired, covered with coal dust. Just like any other day.

For a second I thought I had come up with something. It was October. That meant that Halloween was right around the corner. Daddy carved the best jack-o-lanterns in Crittendon County. I was going to remind him of that, tell him that soon he'd need to get two big pumpkins from the field on the other side of Carl's, prop them up against the shed and have them ready to go. But as soon as I opened my mouth, my thoughts zigzagged and disintegrated. My head hurt. My heart pounded. I couldn't think about the next day, let alone two weeks down the road to All Candy Night.

"Claudette is a fanatic," Daddy said, having to talk for both of us. "It's Jesus she wants. Jesus all day and Jesus at night. I've tried everything I know to please her. Nothing works."

He threw his nightshirt in the suitcase. "God's only son is your mama's best friend," he said. "So you know she's not satisfied with an average black man for a husband. And that's what I am, Mattie. I admit it. I am an average black man. But I am a man. And I've got to go."

He reached way into the back of the closet and got his plastic raincoat. Like his good suit, he never wore that see-through coat, either, but he kept it hanging around. Just in case.

Hearing the sound of that coat crinkling as he stuffed it in the bag embarrassed me almost as much as my tears had. Daddy wouldn't need that thing. He knew he wouldn't want to be seen wearing that.

"Claudette wants me dead," he said, nodding his head like he was winning the argument he was having with himself. "Dead and buried."

The shock of those words set my tongue to work. "Oh, no," I said. "Mama doesn't want you dead, Daddy. She doesn't want you dead."

"Yes, she does, too," he said. "Claudette already sees me, as a dead man, raised up out of my grave, floating around in Heaven somewhere. In other words, no man at all."

He looked me straight in my eye and said, "To her, I'm already a ghost. Or an angel. Call it anything you want to, except a man. Cause there ain't no need for but one man in Heaven. The Man. A fool could figure that out and I'm not a fool, Mattie. What is there left for me to do, but go?"

Right there, Daddy was practically begging me to keep him at home. He was waiting for me to use my magic words, but my tongue sat slack against my teeth, useless. My mouth was full of mush. Daddy heard my silence. He smiled, recognizing the bitter truth: I was a fraud, a dummy-girl, a lifeless doll propped up on a bed. I couldn't perform any tricks. He saw that I was mute, pathetically without magic, and unable to save either one of us.

Hollow and incompetent, I couldn't keep anybody anywhere.

Daddy got his hat, set it on his head, and tipped the brim down over his right eyebrow, exactly like he would have done if it had been any other day.

He looked at himself in the mirror and laughed, but his laugh was harsh. "Funny thing is," he said, snorting, "I knew how Claudette was going to turn out. I knew that someday she was going to end up exactly like she is now, hard-hearted and frightened, denying her own feelings and avoiding mine. Right from the start, every time she allowed herself to be happy it never lasted. She shut down as soon as she could and stayed that way longer and longer each time. I knew someday was coming. I just thought we'd have more time before it got here.

"By then, I told myself, 'Les, Old Buddy, you'll be an old man. You'll be willing to sit on the front porch, blow your harmonica and make do.' Well, someday got here early and I'm not willing to make do."

Daddy let out another tight laugh and we traded places. He became the dummy, the empty-eyed fake man. I stared at him, listening to hear if his new doll-voice had changed, dropped to the floor in a growl, or popped up to the ceiling with a shriek. He said nothing, but his face was a too-early-for-Halloween mask with a plastered-on smile that looked like it was about to break in two like a moldy jack-o-lantern left rotting by the shed.

Smiling his rotting smile, he closed his suitcase and tied a rope around it to make sure it stayed closed. He took eleven dollar bills from his wallet, counted out six of them and placed them on the dresser. And then he stopped smiling. He picked up his bag and walked out of the house.

I followed along behind.

At the edge of the yard, Daddy stopped. We stopped—I'd been riding on his heels. He looked back at the wood-frame house he had mostly built himself. He took in the sight for a good long time. Then he said, "Yes, ma'am. I knew exactly how Claudette Taborn Moon would turn out. I'm the surprise. I never thought I'd leave here walking. I thought I'd be carried out, feet first, wearing that suit. The one they put on you so you're all dressed up with no place to go. They wrap it around you and pin it behind your back, after you've wasted away to a shadow of your former self. The funeral suit that lasts longer than you do. The black suit that covers your bones until even it finally rots away. That suit."

Water stood in Daddy's eyes when he turned back around. He wiped his face with the back of his hand. "I thought I'd live here until the day I died," he said, moving on.

I stood there, looking back like Daddy had, except I was looking to see if there was anybody who could help me keep my daddy at home. Some living, breathing, magic-speaking soul who could help. Anybody. Carl walking upright, maybe, turned into a man with black eyes and a slow steady gait. Aunt Shirley, rushing up to catch Daddy by the collar and help me take him home. Nobody was there. The fields and the road were wide open.

Daddy kept walking on.

"Claudette's people aren't right in the head," he said, as I came up behind him. "You know what her own Mama, Miss Inez, did to her, don't you?"

I nodded. I surely knew.

The day Mama was three months old, Grandma Inez wrapped her in a newspaper and placed her in the pigpen out behind their house. Aunt Shirley, Mama's big sister, eight years old, was jumping rope in the yard. She dropped her rope and came running, screaming and running as fast as her legs would allow. She swooped Mama up at the last minute, snatched her from the pigpen, and carried her to safety.

After saving Mama's young life with her bare hands, Aunt Shirley turned into a young woman. That day. She was strong and handsome, sharp-eyed until (almost) the end.

Mama's older sister had reddish-brown hair with freckled nutmeg colored skin to match. She could have, but never did marry. No quick-stepping man ever caught hold of Aunt Shirley. She never bore children of her own, but she carried with her the knowledge that one day, when she was still a child, she saved her baby sister from two hungry pigs at feeding time. That grew her up fast.

For the next twenty years, Shirley Lee Taborn took care of both Grandma Inez and Mama like they were her own children. Lightning-like, hard-working little woman that she was, Aunt Shirley grew up prematurely, one year ahead of schedule when she was eight years old.

"If it wasn't for Shirley Lee, you wouldn't even be here," Daddy said. "Claudette owes Shirley Lee her life. You do, too. That's the God's truth. Pigs would've eaten her, for sure. But Miss Inez didn't know what she was doing, poor thing. She was touched in the head," he said, tapping his own head at the temple. "That whole family is touched. Everybody but Shirley Lee, that is, and one of her uncles. Out of a whole family. It's called inherited insanity and I believe it. I sure believe it, because in that crazy-ass family it only skipped two. I knew that and I married Claudette, anyway. I gambled and lost. I take full responsibility."

Looking up at the clouds gradually coming together over western Kentucky like one of Mama's handmade quilts, Daddy shook his head and said, "Can't blame nobody but myself."

Mute Girl kicked at some dry leaves on the ground. I hadn't said a word since we left the house, but Daddy read my thoughts out loud.

"Now, Mattie, don't you go worrying that you'll turn out like Claudette's people," he said. "You'll take after Shirley Lee and Simon. Or after my side. We got good sense. Even if we don't always use it."

Daddy and I walked on in silence. I could feel the pressure of the unspoken words building up in my chest. I knew I had to speak or I would explode. I opened my mouth and the words burst forth. "Where are you going, Daddy?" I said, and then I clamped both my hands tight over my mouth, so the pitiful begging—"please, oh please, can I come, too?"—wouldn't escape.

Daddy was a mind-reader, though, a stone heart-reader. He pulled my words out into the air. "There are reasons you can't come with me. I don't rightly know where I'm headed, for one thing, girl. I may go west to the Mississippi and follow it down to Memphis or New Orleans. Then again, I may turn up north; go to Detroit, where my brother, Rob Roy, lives. You remember your uncle, don't you?"

"Um hm," I mumbled, with my hands over my mouth.

Uncle Rob Roy was Daddy's surviving brother. His baby brother, Edward Henry, had died when he was two in a house fire, unexplained to this day. Some suspected that none other than Robert Roy Moon had started it—not meaning to, of course. He was only five at the time.

I adored Uncle Rob Roy. He had dark eyebrows, a dimple in his chin, dark brown skin, and broad shoulders. He was so fine and so funny, and one time when he came to visit he gave me a brand new five-dollar bill. I put it in my pocket real fast, before he could change his mind.

"Course you remember him," Daddy said, moving my hand away from my shut-tight mouth and down to my side. "Who could forget Rob Roy flashing money around like a big businessman and telling just as many lies?"

Knowing there was no point holding back anymore, since Daddy could read my heart and send my words into the wind, I asked him right out, "Are you coming back, Daddy?"

"I've never lied to you, Baby Girl," he said. "No sense starting now. I won't be back this way. Pretty soon, you'll be a young lady," he said, patting my shoulder to soften the blow. "You can come see me. That's the other reason you can't come with me. You have to help take care of your Mama. Somebody has to. She won't let me near her."

Daddy stopped walking. He looked at me like he was fixing to take a picture with his mind. His eyes were the camera's lenses; the memory hidden deep inside his brain was the film. "I'll send you and your mama money as soon as I earn enough to send," he said. "And I'll always remember you exactly like you are now. My dancing girl."

Flash. A promise. And he was gone.

I watched Daddy go down the hill. A minute later, I saw him walking the path between the railroad tracks. Leaning forward slightly, he carried his suitcase with his right hand and he held his left hand out to balance the load.

I stood where I was until I lost sight of Daddy's hat, and then I went back to the house to do my schoolwork and the evening chores.

Near sundown I went back outside. Daddy hadn't come back yet, so I sat down in my tree swing. I swung in the rubber tire and waited for him to return. I knew he was gone; I had seen him go. I knew he meant to stay gone, too. He'd made that clear, but I also knew one other thing: a mind can change. In a split second, a mind can switch tracks. Just like that.

It wouldn't take much, the way I figured it, for a man—an only child's beloved father—to turn around and head back home like a train. On the other hand, in order for that same man to keep walking along the railroad tracks, to walk not only out of his daughter's life but clean out of the state of Kentucky and head southwest or northeast—even he didn't know which way—would take just about everything the man had. Just about everything he had.

So, I waited. I rode back and forth in a tire I called a swing and I waited.

Mama came home from her all-day job and found me sitting in my swing. It was cold and dark. I wasn't swinging anymore, but I was still waiting.

# CHAPTER TWO

I'm the one who told Mama that Daddy was gone. Somebody had to.

I had felt Daddy leaving for weeks; Mama must have felt him leaving, too, because when I gave her the news that he was gone she didn't say anything, not even, "He is?" or "Hmm, is that so?"

She just stood there, silent and still in the dark. I walked over to her, thinking that she might comfort me, give me a quick hug or a pat on the arm, but she moved away from me and went to the edge of the road. With her hands stuck in her pockets, she stared into the distance, where the railroad lay, like a woman watching and waiting for a night-train.

After a few seconds, she turned around, walked past me, and opened the front door. "It's time to get on in, Mattie," she said. "You don't want to catch a cold."

We went into the house and Mama helped me get dinner on the table. I was too sad to eat, but Mama had a complete meal. She ate poke and mustard greens mixed together, buttered cornbread, a piece of chicken, and some hickory-smoked ham. For dessert, she polished off a wide slice of egg custard pie. All without once mentioning her husband's name, Lester Moon.

Some people overeat when they feel lonesome or sad. Others, like me, stop eating altogether. Mama was in the first group. She ate enough for three or four people the night Daddy left home.

Later, while I washed the dishes, Mama threw out most of the personal belongings Daddy had left behind: his old books, a gun that didn't shoot right, and a silk smoking jacket Uncle Rob Roy sent him one year for Christmas, knowing full well that Daddy didn't smoke because of the coal dust that had already settled in his lungs.

Mama didn't throw out all of Daddy's things. She kept his army blanket and his flashlight. When I went to bed, she was sitting on the couch in front of the fireplace, poking the dying fire with a stick. With Daddy's green blanket wrapped tight around her shoulders, she looked like she planned to sit up and stoke that fire all night.

"Mattie."

It was after midnight. I was making such a racket, I barely heard Mama the first time she called my name. She gave me another chance.

"Mattie."

"Yes, ma'am?"

"It's time to stop all that crying. Crying won't help."

I sat up. "I want my daddy back."

"Crying won't bring him back, girl. If he's gone, he's just gone."

"I don't want him to be gone. I want him to come back."

"He may come back," she said, walking to my bed. "May not."

She sat down beside me and stroked my hair. "Basically there are three kinds of men in this world," she told me, "those who stay; those who leave, but come back; and those who leave and stay gone. I'm not going to venture a guess about which of the last two your father is. I never thought he'd leave in the first place."

"He said he had to go, Mama," I wailed, throwing my head against her breast. "But we need him here. We do."

Mama's patience was small, easily lost. She snatched her hand away from my head, pushed me back onto the bed and ran to the light switch. She flipped on the light so I could see her anger as plain as day.

"We need Jesus," she said, through clenched teeth. "Only Christ—and He is always here. He is the True One, the True One who never leaves."

Disappointed in me, she pointed to the space beside me. "He's in that bed with you right now, Mattie Moon," she said. "He's so close, you can touch Him. You can reach out and touch Him."

She turned to go, but then spun back around and said, "And another thing, Miss, there will be no more dancing in this house. Or outside."

"Daddy loved to see me dance," I cried, sitting back up.

She shook her head. "Not another step."

"He said he would always remember me as I am, Mama. His dancing girl."

She put her hands on her hips. "Oh he did, did he? Well, listen carefully to what I have to say. Dancing is the filth that encourages Satan. Lester knew that. Still he went and taught you dirty. You were just a child, innocent as a lamb, but he knew better." She snapped off the light and spat her words into the dark. "I hope he stays gone."

After Mama left the room, I did what she told me to do: I stopped crying. And in my heart, I said good-by to Daddy and to dancing. I fell back on my pillow and stared at the darkness in the room. I felt completely alone, as if there was no one in the world I could reach out and touch, no one in the world who cared enough about me to hold my hand. I no longer felt like a child. I felt old, unprotected, and fatherless.

I lay there dry-eyed and quiet, like Mama wanted me to, but it was a long time before I fell asleep.

The next time I saw my long-lost father, I was an adult, not only emotionally, but also chronologically. I was a grown woman who knew that crying wouldn't help, a woman who except for one time, in a galaxy far, far away, hadn't danced in nearly twenty years.

I had two children of my own by then, one named after my father (Diego's middle name is Lester) and one—a nine-year-old woman-child—named Suzanne Lucinda Moon, neither of whom were in my care because I was institutionalized for having attempted to commit infanticide.

The year I was nine I lost my father; the next year he lost me. Mama and I didn't stay where Daddy left us. We didn't stay put.

In December, two months after Daddy left home, Aunt Shirley came down with cancer. By the time it was found, it had already divided and spread. Mama and I took care of Aunt Shirley. We owed her our lives. If it hadn't been for Auntie's swift legs and sharp reflexes, neither Mama nor I would have been in this world. That was the God's truth. We knew it and we paid our debt in every way we could.

We washed Auntie's body and we washed her clothes. We cooked what little food she could eat and we cleaned her house. I was the errand-runner. Mama was the nurse; she measured out medicine in the prescribed dosages and administered it at the proper intervals, but it was salve, not cure. During those awful nine months, Aunt Shirley lost almost everything she had.

She lost muscle, one hip, both breasts, her hair and, finally, her eyesight. She kept her faith, though. In fact, it multiplied.

Throughout her illness, Aunt Shirley prayed. She and Mama both prayed and, when they got through praying, Mama took a sip of water, gave Auntie one and then they prayed some more. Their prayers multiplied and became like flowers; they covered the sick room, crowded out the tears.

When Auntie was no longer able to speak, she prayed with her body, with her caved-in chest, her barely beating heart, and her worn out lungs that were fighting for air. She and Mama prayed right up until the moment Sweet Peace walked in, gathered up what was left of Shirley Lee Taborn, and carried her away.

Losing Daddy and Aunt Shirley within one year was too much for Mama and me. Kentucky had become a heavy place, a burden. We laid it down.

We closed up the house Daddy and his friends had built and we moved to Southern Illinois.

# CHAPTER THREE

On a clear day in early September, nearly a year after Daddy left home, a ferry-boat carried Mama and me over the Ohio River. Curious as well as restless during the ride, I got out of Mr. Pete's car and walked around on the boat deck. I looked back at Kentucky and I looked ahead to the new state waiting for us on the other side of the river. I sang a song to Kentucky, low so no one would hear my weak voice. It was a so-long-old-friend kind of song, a song of hope. Kentucky wasn't the same without Daddy and Auntie. I didn't know anything about Illinois, but I hoped that the water churning beneath the boat was whipping up something good, some happy surprise, some comfort. It had to be, I told myself, as I finished my song, wiped away my secret tears, and got back in the car.

I was cautiously optimistic. Mama, as usual, was resigned. She was not curious. Nor was she restless; she didn't get out of the car and lean over the side of the boat to look at any water swirling below. She didn't sing any good-by songs, either, or shed any useless tears. She sat most of the way with her body ramrod straight and her eyes closed like a saint's.

Our family had known Mr. Lovell Pete for decades. A retired schoolteacher who had taught Mama, Daddy, Aunt Shirley, and even Grandma Inez, he gave people rides all over western Kentucky to supplement his state pension. He did it more to have something to do than for the money. He charged a little and talked a lot, but no matter how many times he yanked on his green tie and looked sideways over at Mama, he couldn't get any conversation going with that lady. His car could have been a hearse and Mama a corpse.

Wearing the white gloves she had gotten married in and the navy blue hat she had worn to funerals, including Aunt Shirley's, Mama sat with her back to her birthplace. Facing her new (temporary) home, she was silent the entire trip.

Mama was not purposely rude to Mr. Pete. She respected him—after all, he had taught her to read—and she hated bad manners. It was just that she was in a state of shock. Like Daddy, she had believed that she would live the rest of her life in the house he built. She hadn't dreamed that she would walk out of it, under her own power, either. Unlike Daddy, however, she thought that, at the end of a dreary life, after a proper burial, she would rise out of her grave, dressed in finery, and float above the river in a chariot that had swung low for to carry her home.

She had expected that, when she left Kentucky, she'd rise up through the clouds to Heaven, no stops in between.

Riding shotgun in a Buick, the same color as Mr. Pete's tie, her destination more dry land, more people to suffer, more slings, arrows and heartaches to withstand, more burdens to carry, shut Mama up. She was dumbstruck into silence.

No matter the reason, all that quiet she laid on Mr. Pete wore the poor man plumb out. In the time it took him to get us from our house to Elizabethtown and the Illinois line, he had aged a year—at least. When he picked us up, Mr. Pete had been spry and hopeful, generous and confident that he was doing a good deed. By the time the boat chugged up to the landing, he was deflated, discouraged, and not sure of anything anymore.

"Seems like this trip is getting longer and longer," he said to the side of Mama's face, while tugging nervously on his Christmas-tree tie. "I don't know how many more of 'em I have in me, Claudette. Maybe I should have driven you and Mattie to Paducah where the bus would have carried you across the bridge. Seems like winter's trying to come early. I don't how long the river is going to stay open. I just don't know," he said. "Don't guess anybody does."

He mumbled that last like his lack of knowledge was something he hated for his former pupil to see. By then, the old fellow was probably talking to stay awake. He didn't expect Mama to say anything and she didn't.

When she got out of the car, she opened her mouth long enough to say, "Thank you for your trouble, Lovell." All she said to me was, "Don't forget your bag, Mattie."

Mr. Pete didn't get out of the car, which was not like him at all. He slumped back in his seat and pushed my bag toward me. Then he unwrapped a piece of Juicy Fruit and popped it into his mouth.

I thanked him for the ride, said good-by, and got out of his car. He waved. Halfheartedly. That was a day for poor manners. Everybody was guilty because, since Mr. Pete hadn't bothered to offer me a stick of that yellow-wrapped gum after I had stood in the wind so long my mouth was dry, I slammed his door with all my might. I know I shouldn't have, but I did.

Mr. Pete jumped a bit, but he didn't say anything mean. The last time I saw him, his head was thrown back and his eyes were closed. Chewing his gum, he waited for the ferryboat to back up, turn around like a train, and take him home.

Mama and I left Kentucky the same way Daddy left: unsure where we were going to end up. So we improvised. In small towns. Carrier Mills first, and then Murphysboro and Marion. We rented musty rooms in private homes. We shared a bed and we did housework for food money. We didn't stay in any one place long. Six months after arriving in Illinois, we finally settled down in a place called Eloise.

We weren't exactly a hit. Eloise is an extended-family kind of town—real extended. It's the ancestral home of cousins, cousins of cousins, and their lifelong hangers-on. She doesn't take kindly to strangers in her midst. Not Eloise. Admittedly, Mama and I were stranger than most.

I was lonely those first few years in Eloise. My refuge was the library. I loved that round-shaped brick building standing like a sanctuary in the middle of Library Park. During the summer, the trees were expansive. Green and leafy, they offered a holy shade. Even in winter, when they were bare and brittle, they stood like soldiers, bravely pointing the way in from the cold.

Inside the library in summer, fall, and winter, or, under a tree in spring with a borrowed book, I spent hours reading about the friendships and escapades of others, the happiness and the disasters waiting to happen. Reading helped a lot, but it wasn't enough. I felt isolated in Eloise. Tired of being laughed at and never chosen for games or teams, I finally broke down and asked Mama if we could go back home to Kentucky.

I didn't tell her that my hope was that Daddy would be standing by the tire-swing in front of our house waiting for us, his hat tipped to one side, his harmonica resting in his hand. Just like any other day.

It worried me a lot that Daddy didn't know where we were or how to find us. How could he? We had left neither trail nor clue, certainly nothing so revealing as a forwarding address; we hadn't had one.

We were lost.

When most people think of Illinois, the first place they think of is Chicago. Daddy couldn't have known that we were three hundred miles from Lake Michigan, closer to the Mississippi River, in fact, living in a heartbreak town named after a woman: Eloise.

How could he have known that?

If Daddy had returned to the house he built in Kentucky, he would have learned that even his army blanket and his piano were gone. Mama kept the blanket for herself, but she sold the piano to help finance the move. She had to do something. That's what she did.

The nearest neighbors, who were at least a mile away, couldn't have been much help to Daddy. The only person who witnessed our leaving was Mr. Pete, and for all that old man knew, after we got out of his car and walked up the plank, we might have gotten on a bus or train and gone absolutely anywhere: Carbondale, Peoria, even Springfield, the state capital, would have been a better bet than a town he had never heard of called Eloise.

Mr. Pete, honest as well as chatty, would have told Daddy everything he knew, but he didn't know much: "Claudette sat in the car like it was a morgue, Lester. Her eyes, mouth, and whole face clamped shut. The girl slammed my car door so hard she almost broke it. Nobody's heard a word from them since." That's close to what he would have said.

We were lost. Lost to Daddy and lost to ourselves.

"Can't we please go back?" I asked.

Without an ounce of sympathy, Mama said, "There'll be no turning back. Kentucky is behind us. The Cross before us."

For years, I tried my best to fit into Eloise. I observed the natives, tried to match my behavior to theirs, and smiled until it hurt.

Mama never even tried; she knew she was just passing through. In all her years in Eloise she made only one true friend, a woman she found at Greater Sabbathani Baptist Church named Mrs. Octavia Love. I call her Miss Tavy.

Miss Tavy, a pillar to the community, answers to many names. Her grandchildren and all their pretend cousins call her Ma Grand; the members of Sabbathani call her Sister Love; and, the folks downtown address her as Mrs. Howard Love, because she acts like she doesn't hear them if they don't.

Miss Tavy and her husband, Mr. Love, the first and, so far, the only black councilman in Eloise, are religious and prosperous. They own rental property in three small towns: Eloise, New Baden, and Lebanon. The Loves are generous, too. They tithe. They built the new wing and the Bible Educational Building at Sabbathani. They also donate money to St. Mary's Hospital, to the public schools, and to the Love Life Community Recreation Center on a regular basis.

For a time, until Mama exercised her option to buy, the Loves owned the house we lived in at 301 Elm Street. Mama always said that the Elm Street house was not our home. The day we moved in, she said, "Our home is in Heaven. Until we get there, this will have to do."

Since not even Mama knew when that would be, she grimly prepared for a long unpleasant stay. I helped. We cleaned the house and kept it clean. During the day, Mama kept the house dim, but at night she slept with the porch light on bright. She scrimped and saved for eleven years and finally paid for the Elm Street house, but she never felt like it belonged to her. She was visiting during the early years, hiding-out at the end, with the window shades pulled down the whole time.

Adults in Eloise teased Mama to her face and talked about her behind her back until she became Miss Tavy's new best friend. Then they stopped. They didn't want to have to deal with the woman many of them called Sister Love. It has been said that the line between love and hate is thin; folks in Eloise took care not to cross it.

Mama's friendship with Miss Tavy did not protect me, however. The kids at Logan Elementary School didn't give a damn whose sister Sister Love was supposed to be. If Miss Tavy had climbed out of her car and walked onto the Logan's playground, the local bad-asses would have gotten in her face. They didn't hesitate to take me on. They made fun of my Kentucky accent, my homemade clothes, my skinny legs, and my thick kinky hair.

By the time I reached eighth grade, word was out that I was the smartest student in the class. My classmates stopped harassing me and began asking for help so they wouldn't look quite so bad when they transferred to Eloise High School. As best I could, I helped them with mathematics, reading, and writing. Somebody had to.

At Eloise High, I was placed in the classes with the most promising students and that's where I met my best friend, Theda May, who is my best friend to this day. Theda was an algebra whiz. Two years older than me, she was also a baby-sitter, a checker at Aldono Grocery Store, and a proud lesbian. I thought Theda was the only lesbian I knew. (I learned later that I was wrong.)

Theda couldn't wait to finish high school and start a business of her own. She wasn't sure what kind of business it would be; she just knew that she wanted one that belonged to her alone.

Theda had moved to Illinois from Brooklyn, New York, but she said that before living up north, her family, on her father's side, had owned small businesses in the south. Her mother, who was from Haiti, was self-employed. She worked freelance. Theda wanted to return to her roots.

I had no plans to be an entrepreneur, but I planned to go to a four-year college and then to graduate school. I didn't have a clue about what I'd study when I got there; I just loved the idea of furthering my education. College should have been my way out of Eloise. It was, almost.

I earned a four-year scholarship to the University of Illinois, but on high school graduation day, two months before the time to pack for Urbana, I displayed my previously undetected ignorance for all to see. I got pregnant.

My National Merit scholarship was revoked, without apology, but I got to keep my baby. I named her Suzanne Lucinda.

People in Eloise were shocked the first time I got pregnant. They were merely surprised the second time around. Because they never saw me with a man, they assumed I did without love. I didn't. I had a secret lover.

A woman on the edge of society, one frequently seen walking alone, speaks softly to certain men. These men may not tell anybody, not even their best friends, but they notice a woman who isn't part of a pack; one who appears to be independent and in need of company.

This walking-alone-woman reminds them of someone they saw in a dream, a person (a soul mate?) they can neither recall in the morning light nor quite forget as the day wears on. She's an itch at that place midway down their backs that they can't get to without rubbing up against a wall or a post like a dog. She makes them pant.

Unintentionally, but by example, Mama taught me about these men. Certain men.

For years, they followed Mama home from church on Sunday afternoons, at one o'clock, or two, whatever time Sabbathani finally let out. Certain men who had no wives, and a few who did, men of advanced age, and a couple of the young ones, too, stood at our back door with their hats or caps in their hands, although they knew for certain that they would not be invited inside that house for lunch or fellowship or for any other reason, because Mama didn't invite men into the Elm Street house, not even Mr. Love, who, at least for the first eleven years we lived there, owned the place with his Mrs., Sister Love, whom I call Miss Tavy.

Lining up the way people who know the odds line up to buy lottery tickets—with irrational hopes and both fingers crossed—certain men wasted time instead of money at Mama's back door. Their odd and unrequited devotion, their naked desire, did some good. It taught me a lesson: Certain men are drawn to women with raggedy minds.

These men sneak around. They cherish the hope of getting caught someday, found out and made to pay. When Mama said, "Get away, Merritt," or "Go on home, now, Major," they could barely hold back their smiles. When she blurted, "Mason, leave my door. I only want what's mine," Mr. Tolivor's black diamond eyes twinkled like stars on a clear night.

After Mama double-locked the door, the laughter of these certain men rumbled outside the house like an earthquake along the New Madrid fault. It came from a place down low, where true pleasure lies, and it took a long time to settle. There were aftershocks, tremors, as the men tried to muzzle the sound. Smother it. But they couldn't. Didn't want to, anyway. It's why they had come: to be moved and to move with it. As sure as the next Sunday rolled around, they came back. Some men do. Certain men.

Knowing also that some men never leave in the first place, I was careful how I used my charm. For a long time, I refused to let my little light shine; I kept it under wraps. I walked with my head down, not simply because moving to a new town had made me shy and awkward, but also because I didn't want to attract something—someone—I didn't want. Like Mama, I only wanted what was mine. I wanted Lamarr.

# CHAPTER FOUR

People have said that Suzanne is the offspring of a white man, but that is a lie. Lamarr Robinson is Suzanne's father and he is black, for the most part. The men in his family, however, on both sides, and as far back as anyone can remember, have married the lightest-skinned black women they could find—the lightest skinned.

Lamarr is no exception. He went all the way to the South Side of Chicago to find his alabaster bride. Way before that, though, he was in my bed, all over my dark body and inside it, and he was glad. We both were.

When I became infatuated with Lamarr, he was a senior, three years ahead of me at Eloise High. By my senior year, when he was in college, I was obsessed.

Lamarr was handsome, popular, and good with his hands. His senior year at Eloise, Lamarr was the star basketball player, the go-to guy. I was bookish and clumsy, but at least I had enough common sense and physical coordination to put my books down and make my way to each of his home games at Bobby Joe Mason Auditorium.

From the highest bleachers, I looked down on Lamarr's fine head and shoulders while he played basketball. I knew his every move (I memorized him). He had no weaknesses. Highly skilled, he played a total game.

Lamarr never once looked up and saw me at the top of the gymnasium and, for a long time, he didn't notice me anyplace else, either. When I passed him on the street, I didn't speak to him, because I was too ill at ease, too cowardly, but he was always on my mind. I inhaled deeply each time I was near him. He ran through me like a drug.

I was hooked.

Hours after being in Lamarr's presence, I sat in my room alone and played him in my mind the way Suzanne plays her video games now, over and over. In my imaginary world, I gazed into his eyes and swooned from his kisses. We laughed all night at his jokes and made love time after time in exotic ways.

When Lamarr was on the road, miles away, I felt him right there in my room, so close I could touch him, warm at the end of my fingertips. He was a three-year fantasy of mine, but then one day, when I was a senior and he was a junior in college, he became my destiny.

I walked home from my job at Cohen's Pharmacy one Saturday and passed by Logan School. Lamarr was on the outdoor court practicing his jump shots with some of his teammates. I kept my head down and looked at him from the corners of my eyes. As always when I was near him, my nose was wide open. I inhaled deeply. I was tired from standing all day, making change and being ordered about, but the minute Lamarr hit my bloodstream, I felt glad to be alive.

I perked up and strained to collect any words he might utter to the other players—a few curse words or anything I could replay later in my room. To my surprise, killing me softly, he said, "Mattie Moon."

I kept walking in case I was hallucinating. Then he came toward me. Lamarr in the flesh. I wasn't making him up.

When he stopped in front of me, I jerked my head up and looked into his brown eyes. I felt my heart pounding in my chest, my knees clanking against one another. Then silence. I didn't hear a thing. I had gone stone deaf. I told myself to calm down. Exhale. I reminded myself that I was too healthy for a heart attack, too young for a stroke.

Lamarr's lips moved. I tried to guess what he said. He must have asked me for something. The time maybe. Or perhaps he wanted me to buy a raffle ticket for one of the events his mother, Tanquerey Robinson, was always organizing and presiding over in her highfalutin way. I hoped it wasn't the latter. I was flat broke until I got paid a week from Friday.

Perspiring under my arms, above my lip, and on the palms of my hands, I hoped he would repeat his question. We stared at each other. I blinked first. "Huh?"

"Huh?"

"I didn't hear you."

"I said don't you ever smile?"

His voice was like velvet. His eyes were so soft. I looked away and said, "I smile."

"When?"

"When I have something to smile about."

"Such as?"

He dribbled his basketball on the sidewalk and waited for my answer. The tapping against the pavement matched every other beat of my heart. Every other beat. Lamarr was so close I could have touched him; I could have leapt into his arms.

"Christmas," I said. "I wake up smiling every Christmas."

He raised an eyebrow. "You saying you smile once a year?"

I nodded like an idiot. He laughed; his voice sounded like a bell. I took off.

"I think you can do better than that, Miss Moon," he said, walking behind me.

I slowed down and we walked side by side just like in my dreams. His deep dimples threw off my balance. I dropped my head again and locked my eyes onto the flat, safe sidewalk. Lamarr didn't say much. Even when I stubbed my toe and pitched forward, nearly falling, he concentrated on his basketball. He bounced it until we reached Poplar, the one-way street in front of Logan. Then he stopped, held one hand high and threw the ball to me. Amazingly, I caught it.

"You're quick," he said.

Proud, I threw the ball back to him and missed his head, but not by much.

"Jesus," he said, ducking. "Well, at least you get good grades."

"They're okay," I said, shrugging like an imbecile. "Nothing special."

"That's not the way I heard it," he said. "You're in the honor society. Maybe you can tutor me."

"I guess," I said. "What do you need tutoring in?"

"I'll think of something," he said, heading back.

Poplar Street is the busiest street in Eloise. It's a miracle that I wasn't killed crossing it, because I stepped off the curb without looking either to the left or to the right. I had no awareness of the flow of traffic, no memory of my feet having hit the ground. Nothing. Perhaps I was transported home, borne on the wings of love. My head felt light. My heart was a balloon filled with air.

I couldn't believe my good fortune. Lamarr had actually stopped playing ball—well, he almost stopped—and he had talked to me. I hadn't had to eavesdrop like a spy from another country while he talked to some pretty home-girl. He said my name. He walked beside me and he wanted me to smile.

I smiled the rest of the way home, filled with an emotion I hadn't felt since I was nine years old: joy. My soul was glad. I felt like dancing, but I knew better.

When I entered the house, I found Mama kneeling before her new rocking chair, praying. I bowed my head, sat down on the sofa and bolted my feet together like a statue. With my eyes closed, I prayed right along with Mama. "Thank you," we said in unison and with equal sincerity. "Thank you, Lord Jesus. Thank you. Thank you. Thank you."

A week later, Lamarr caught up with me again. This time he escorted me safely across Poplar Street and walked with me the extra block to Elm Street. I know it happened, because I saw the whole thing out of the corner of my eye. It was better than anything I could have imagined, all the happiness that I could bear.

If strangers had passed by in cars, they would have noticed Lamarr; he stands out. My, how attractive he is, they would have thought. What a beautiful man. They probably wouldn't have noticed me at all.

Had acquaintances seen us, they would have acknowledged my presence, but only briefly and as an afterthought. First, they would have jumped, waved and called out excitedly, "Lamarr! Hey, man! Lamarr!" Then, after savoring their precious reward from him—a glance, nod or pointed finger—they would have looked at one another and asked, "What the hell is Mattie Moon doing traipsing along behind Lamarr? Who does that she think she is?"

Lamarr walking down the street at the same time I was would have been perceived as a joke, a mistake or an insignificant coincidence, but it meant the world to me.

We carried on like that for a few days, walking and talking, basically unseen or unnoticed. And then he called me on the telephone. Although we had little in common, we found a lot to talk about. I told Lamarr that I had felt like an immigrant setting off for a new land the day I crossed the Ohio River in a boat. He told me he felt like his chest was on fire the night he coolly made the final basket that won the Illinois state championship for Eloise High.

I admitted to him that for the first six months after my father left home I cried with the pillow pressed over my head so that Mama wouldn't hear me. He told me that he couldn't remember the last time he had cried. He said he couldn't see how crying helped anything. I told him I had heard that one before.

Although we probably shouldn't have, each of us eventually got around to talking about the other's mother. Lamarr dubbed my mother The Hermit of Eloise. He also described her as a natural disaster, dressed in raingear yet afraid of storms. I reminded him that we lived in tornado and flood country and that Mama wasn't the only person who frantically sought cover from time to time.

I told him that I had seen people cross to the other side of the street, dart into a building, or hide behind a trash can, all because they had seen Tanquerey Robinson hurtling toward them on stiletto heels, waving a stack of raffle tickets or a bunch of campaign buttons in her hand.

We called a truce. No more mothers. But whatever we discussed, Lamarr made me smile. After a couple of months, when he was in town, he came to my window.

I told no one that I sneaked Lamarr into the Elm Street house and invited him into my bed. Not even Theda.

I had fantasized about Lamarr for years. I had thoroughly mapped out the territory in my mind, but when I saw him naked for the first time, I realized that I had a lot to learn.

When Lamarr held me, I didn't levitate as I had in my dreams. We were grounded in reality, locked in each other's arms. Nobody floated.

Lying with Lamarr, bearing his weight, I felt strong, not light or weak. And earthy, not angelic. I didn't glow with desire as I thought I would; however, Lamarr's body warmed me from the outside in. He set my soul on fire.

Everything about my first sexual experience was authentic. The pain was real, but so was the ecstasy. A voice in my head whispered, "I am a woman now." I celebrated my triumph softly, mindful that my "night school" was Mama's temporary, but consecrated house (not home), her sanctified dwelling. No way was I about to holler out and invite Claudette Moon to blow in on us like a category-five hurricane.

I stayed on the quiet side of bliss, teetering, the same way Mama swayed at the edge of the porch without ever falling off. I moaned tenderly.

Lamarr was loud.

"Shh. Be quiet," I instructed. "You'll wake Mama."

"She hears voices anyway, doesn't she?"

"Not human ones. Celestial."

"Trust me, Baby, we're on our way to Paradise."

We went on like that for months. Gladly.

One night Mama went to Sabbathani for fellowship service and Lamarr and I had the house to ourselves. From habit, I was demure; Lamarr was wild. He fell off the bed. Twice.

That was probably the night I got pregnant. The following month, I missed my period. I kept my mouth shut then, too; I didn't tell anyone, but Lamarr knew.

He stopped coming to my window. He watched me grow out of my regular clothes and into wide shirts, baggy jeans and shapeless dresses that had been donated to charity. On special occasions I wore lime, peach, and orange tents.

He knew.

When he saw me lumbering along, he didn't ask me to smile and he didn't follow me home. And later, when he saw me carrying my precious baby in my arms, he didn't follow either one of us. Lamarr didn't come back.

After graduating from Southern Illinois University where he played basketball quite well, but not well enough to make the pros, Lamarr returned to Eloise and began a successful real estate business. That same year his uncles put him in the back of a van and drove him to Chicago where, working quickly, they found him a woman suitable to wed. In the Robinson tradition, she was pale and thin. With freckles. Her name was Rotelle Onay Collins.

# CHAPTER FIVE

"Isn't Eloise a bitch?" Theda asked.

I was sitting in her compact kitchen—sitting all over it, to be more accurate. I was nine months gone with my second pregnancy and, on me, the ninth month looked like the twelfth. I took up one third of all the available space in the room. Theda had to maneuver around me the way she maneuvered around her appliances: very carefully.

She had long insisted that I use her washer and dryer instead of walking eight blocks to the Kell Street Laundromat. Close to delivering my second baby, I finally accepted her offer.

While I put my clothes in the dryer, Theda mixed leaves for her special herb tea.

"Everybody in Eloise wants to know everybody else's damn business," she said. "You know why? So they don't have to do anything about their own messed-up shit. That's why. Your baby's father is nobody's business but yours. If and when you want these people to know, you'll send an announcement. Until then, they can shut the hell up."

"Exactly," I said, with more confidence than I felt.

"You know what people in this town remind me of?" she said, as she filled the water kettle.

"What?"

"A tired-ass married couple. Comatose. Long since through, sitting on the back porch talking about what they used to do. Bored shitless. And to keep from killing each other, they dis' the young folks: "He did?" "Naw, he didn't?" "Yeah.

She did too." Gossiping all day long. Now, if that ain't a bitch, I don't know what is."

Theda is more than my next-door neighbor. She is my ally. She's exactly the kind of friend every woman needs. She's loyal and strong. Serious and funny. She's somebody to laugh with and to cry with, even if the tears don't do any lasting good. Her mind is a fortress. She kept my secret.

Shortly after I found out I was pregnant—for the second time—I told Theda that Jacob Franklin had fathered my unborn child. I told no one else my secret. Not Mama, who upon seeing my abdomen rise, covered her ears and said she didn't want to know ever. Not Suzanne, who assumed it was the same mysterious and absent man who had helped give her life. And not even Jacob.

I didn't tell Jacob. I showed him. He learned through the amazing sense of touch. We were in his car on the outskirts of town, where no one could see us; it was so dark we could barely see each other. I lifted my shirt, took Jacob's hands and placed them on my newly hard belly. The baby moved and Jacob's world shifted.

Jacob, a minister's son, whispered, "Oh, my God."

Jacob and Lamarr learned they were expectant fathers differently. Jacob knew when he touched me, when he felt a human being roll beneath his hands. Lamarr knew when he saw me waddle down Elm Street in a fuchsia tent. But they both knew. The difference between the two men is that Jacob never denied his knowledge. He didn't leave town and drag back a white-looking woman with two children of her own to throw in my face. He stayed right where he was, like a man. Some men do. His emotions, however, were all over the place.

Jacob, an only child, was excited about continuing his bloodline. He wanted to be a father someday, but the timing was off.

Jacob lived at home, in the parsonage, and he worried that his father, Reverend Clay Franklin, who had recently received a warning in the form of a mild stroke, would take the news poorly. Jacob assured me that, in time, his father would come around and welcome a grandchild. He was concerned, however, that Reverend Franklin might become stressed when he initially learned that I was carrying said grandchild. The first few days (or weeks) after getting the news, his father might experience an elevation in his blood pressure (it might skyrocket); his hands and feet might swell; his sugar, which was normally pretty good, could spike. We had to be careful. Stress, even mild stress, could be harmful to a man Reverend Franklin's age, a man who already had one transient ischemic attack under his belt.

Jacob wanted to protect his father. He also wanted to cover his own behind. Jacob was only seven when his mother died. After her death, the Sabbathani congregation had helped Reverend Franklin raise his son. The big women like Sister (Miss Tavy) Love held him to their ample breasts and rocked him when he needed comfort, and the wiry ones like Mama bounced him on their bony knees to distract him when he wanted to play or talk, but couldn't because church is a serious place and his father was the one delivering the serious bad/good news.

The members who were crossing guards watched him until he got home from school safely each day and the schoolteachers, who sat side by side in their special pew, cried and gave thanks the day he was baptized. Jacob wanted to be acceptable in their eyes. He wanted to break the news to the whole church, not just his father, slowly. All he said though was, "Give me time to prepare Dad for the shock."

At least he was completely honest about that part. He didn't say he wanted time to share the glad tidings or to tell of the upcoming blessed event. He didn't say anything about a bundle of joy. He anticipated Reverend Franklin's reaction, chose his words well, and referred to it as "the shock."

He realized that I was so unexpected, so different from what anybody in Eloise, especially a conservative minister, would have dreamed of for his only son, that the mere utterance of my name could disrupt his father's heart rhythms. Kill him dead.

Jacob decided that he would ease up on his father, dropping hints as he advanced: she's not from here, Dad she's from another state. She walks by herself a lot, so she's in good shape. She graduated from high school with honors and almost went to college. She holds down a job and makes her own ill-fitting clothes. No police record, Dad.

The plan was to accentuate the positive and to cushion what, if handled poorly, without great care, could be a fatal blow.

I gave Jacob a tired smile and told him that he could take as much time as he needed to prepare his father and the Church Ladies for the shock of me.

Jacob parked his car two blocks from my house. "Dad will accept you. He just expects me to marry someone like my mother."

"Instead of someone like mine."

"You aren't like your mother, Honey."

"Right. I take after my father's side. We have good sense. Even if we don't always use it," I said, getting out of the car.

Jacob drove away, believing we were a secret. I saw no need to tell him that we were already a well-told story.

A full two months before his world shifted beneath his hands, I had told Theda the details of our relationship and my budding pregnancy at her kitchen table while we sipped colorful herb tea and ate sugar cookies.

The intimacy of women's talk—the trust shared and the comfort given—might have alarmed Jacob, who valued privacy. It was better that he not know that Theda already knew. He needed to stay focused. He had a man's fragile life in his hands.

Theda set a plate of warm cookies on the table.

"I really appreciate you letting me use your machines," I said.

"Girl, anytime," she said. "I only do laundry twice a week now. Miss Rich takes most of her clothes to the cleaners."

"You spoil her rotten."

"Everybody plays the fool sometime."

"Are you looking at me?"

"How can I not, Mattie? You are huge, girl. Too big to be walking back and forth to that damn Laundromat."

"The doctor told me to walk."

"Over hell and back?"

"We do what we have to."

"Well, you don't have to do that shit anymore. Laundromats won't cover their windows. Know why? Because they want everybody to see who has to wash in a public place."

"I'm not proud. But this is way more convenient."

It was more than that; it was a gift. By doing the laundry at Theda's, I got time out of the house and, yet, I was near enough to hear Mama or Suzanne call.

"I hope you're not getting ready to have twins," Theda said, pouring steaming yellow tea into black mugs.

"Don't worry," I said. "No twins."

"You sure? Do they run in your family?"

"Un uh. Cancer and insanity do, though."

"Hell, those are universal," she said, sitting down. "Worldwide maladies. Twins are comic relief. Nature's private joke. I laugh out loud every time I see a set of clones."

The thought of twins cheered Theda so much she sprang up, opened the back door, and unlatched the kitchen windows. The fresh morning air flowed in and made itself at home.

"Call me as soon as you go into labor," she said. "My moms was a midwife. She learned from an old French woman."

"That's Theda's claim to fame," Lilly said, from the kitchen doorway.

Theda's partner had quietly entered the house through the front door. Making a face at Theda, she kicked off her high heels and padded, barefoot, with bright red toenails, to the refrigerator, where she opened the door and took out a dish of peach cobbler. Shapely with everything where she wanted it, Lilly never worried about her weight. She ate when she was hungry, whatever she had a taste for, and she didn't stop until she'd had enough.

"My moms was the bomb," she said, mimicking Theda's New York accent. "A midwife. A carpenter. An accountant. A gypsy. Well, Theda is not her mother. When time comes to have your baby, Theda won't have a clue."

Theda, playing her part, folded her arms and pretended to be offended. She stuck her tongue out at Lilly. Then she turned to me and asked, "Are you sure your due date is right, Mattie?"

"Two weeks," I said

"Two weeks from now, call your doctor," Lilly said, slipping her arm around Theda's waist. "Not Our Miss Fix-it."

Lilly and Theda laughed, but Lilly said, "I'm serious, Country. You will need a certified M.D., not some midwife's daughter from Brooklyn. All Theda would know to do is put on a pot of that nasty tasting tea y'all drink and run around in circles."

Theda May and Lilly Lawson have lived in the yellow house at 303 Elm Street for seven years. Half the people in Eloise are counting. Many disapprove, but Lilly says their opinions must not matter—few of them were considered; none was consulted.

"Damn 'em all," she says, laughing through her even white teeth.

Lilly has always had a mouth on her. The first time I saw her she was talking. Mama had left me in the hall at Logan while she completed the paperwork necessary to verify our current existence and my prior education. Outside the Principal's office, Lilly, a pretty girl wearing purple lipstick, was talking to her friends. All the girls competed to see who could stand nearest Lilly.

Seeing me in my long gray dress, Lilly whispered something to the girls that cracked them up. A few minutes later Mama stepped into the hall, wearing white funeral gloves, her navy blue hat, and black rubber boots as if she expected to suffer forty days and forty nights of rain because Noah had. Lilly said, "Lord, have mercy. What have we here?"

Getting no answer from Mama or me, she came up to me to find out for her-self. "Are you new here?" she asked.

"My name is Mattie Moon," I said, nodding. I had never in my life seen such perfect teeth or shiny lips.

"Where are you from?"

"Kentucky."

"Louisville?"

"I've never even been to Louisville."

Mama said, "No reason to go," as she fastened her coat. "We lived in the country."

Lilly frowned. "Really?"

"Um hm. Outside of Paducah," I said, smiling and hoping to make my first Illinois friend, one with perfect teeth and breasts that already stood out setting her apart from the rest of us.

Lilly looked at my white shoes and my bare legs. Raising an eyebrow, she smirked, "Way outside, huh?" Then she and her friends walked away, laughing.

Mama fastened her coat and left. "Pay attention," she said, hurrying away.

Lilly called me Country from that day on. She often asked how Mama was doing. If I said about the same, Lilly said, "That bad, huh?" If I said Mama was fine, Lilly winked and said, "Sure she is—in her own mind anyway."

Lilly teased everybody. The boys in Eloise were thrilled when she teased them. They felt honored. Throughout high school, Lilly dated, but she didn't hook up with anyone. We thought she would leave Eloise, marry a city man, and live an exciting life on one of the coasts, so when she moved into the yellow house next door with Theda May, she surprised a lot of people. She surprised the hell out of me.

Obviously, in high school, Lilly had kept a secret of her own.

# CHAPTER SIX

Reaching into the refrigerator for Lilly's mail-ordered gourmet coffee beans, Theda said, "We can forget a couple of weeks. You're going to drop your baby in a couple of days." Turning to Lilly, she asked, "Don't you think so?"

"Me?" Lilly cried, loosening her belt to make room for another piece of peach pie. "Honey, I refuse to think about labor pains. Let alone predict when they're going to hit."

Labor. Lord, Labor. I'm convinced that women who say they've forgotten their labor pain are either lying to themselves or to others. That, or they were so heavily medicated that their memories were wiped clean away.

Compared to the equal parts bliss and heartache of motherhood, labor pain pales by comparison, but that doesn't mean it is forgotten. The body remembers. I experienced Labor full-strength, undiluted by drugs, and I'll remember it until the day I die. Nevertheless, I looked forward to the second bout for two reasons: One, the pay-off—Labor's reward is a new human being, someone to love unconditionally, to live for and protect with every ounce of strength you have left. Two, the passion—Labor is proof positive that we are alive. Nothing is more intense, more urgent. Labor is more powerful than an orgasm—any that I've had, anyway—and it occurs spontaneously. One doesn't have to be in the mood for it, nor is one afforded any get-ready time. There is no foreplay.

Labor happens.

Before Labor, I thought I knew pain and handled it well. When my first baby began her mighty descent, I learned that I didn't know pain at all. We had glanced at one another, in passing, but we weren't formally introduced until the day Labor happened.

My first pain felt like a freight elevator was inside me, descending. It was mid-day. I was standing in the kitchen getting ready to make blueberry muffins. The elevator started high, at chest level. I stepped back. Then I reached out and held onto the table for support. By the time the pain crashed down onto my pelvic floor, I was on my knees. I placed my hot face on the cool linoleum, closed my eyes and prayed. "Lord, please help me," I whispered. "Fix me."

When the second elevator dropped, I raised myself into a crouching position and tried to make room for Labor's intensity and power. I didn't cry out or curse. Neither action would have helped. I held on and, at the same time, tried my best to let go, to let loose the pain inside of me. Quite a feat, and exactly the type of thing one tends to remember.

For nine months I had been a safe place for my unborn child, her haven. Then for hours I was the storm-tossed sea. At five o'clock, Mama came home from work and a miracle walked into the house with her. There was an unseen presence; however, it was as if someone had said, "Peace be still." The sea grew calm. The sun came out. I saw a rainbow between my legs. My daughter was born.

For me, Suzanne's birth was unforgettable. For Mama it was a turning point.

Mama had held herself together, uniquely perhaps, but together just the same, from the day we arrived in Eloise until the day I gave birth to Suzanne. Yes, she wore rain gear on dry days. She predicted storms that never arrived. And she chased men from her door with her broom. And it is true that, on her worst days, she stood on shaky ground. However, she stood upright and in one piece, recognizable to me as the mother of my childhood. Suzanne's bright entry into the world changed everything. It knocked Mama sideways, surprised her into someone we didn't even know.

Mama hadn't expected a baby. Throughout my pregnancy, I had hidden my body from her, worn loose clothing and pretended I was hungry all the time. To account for my weight gain, I baked a lot. Mama accepted my girth with a tight smile. Knowing the great sins by heart, she was not surprised that one of the worst of them, gluttony, had taken up residence in our house despite her vigilant watch.

Neither she nor I ever said the word baby. She may not have thought it even as I entered my ninth month with heavy breasts and swollen legs. She may have thought I was beginning to take after my grandmother's half-sister who was the only heavy woman in the family, or that I was developing a glandular problem. After all, I had never openly dated. No shiny-eyed man, laughter rumbling like a quake inside of him, had ever shown up at our back door begging me to take him in out of the cold, rescue him from the safe and ordinary. My own mother may have assumed, along with the rest of the town, that I did without love—until she found me sitting spread-legged on the floor with a miracle between my legs.

Mama rushed to my side, bent over me and inspected me closely. Seeing that I wasn't going to get up any time soon, she removed her raincoat and sat down beside me. She watched while I pulled my gleaming daughter out of my body.

Mama may have believed I was a teenaged virgin (like Mary). Suzanne's rainbow-birth brought Mama scrambling to her feet. She raised her eyes to the ceiling and cried out, "What kind of child is this?"

Mama didn't touch my baby until she was five months old; nearly a year passed before she whispered her grandchild's name. Eventually, she fell in love with Suzanne, but by then it was too late.

All her life, Mama had been thrown away, sent ahead, and left behind. She had been surprised, bereaved, or betrayed by every person she had ever loved, including me. She knew that love was not enough, that it would neither save nor anchor her. In fact, even though Mama loved Suzanne, after my daughter's birth, she ended up in worse shape than Daddy had foreseen (he said he had known exactly how she would turn out someday).

Frayed along all her edges, Mama came undone. She roamed the house for months, singing her own made-up song, "Hear me, Jesus See me. Jesus, it's me."

Mama had a beautiful voice. She was a soprano, but she sang that song in an alto whisper. Her song was a prayer, a desperate request.

Mama was never put completely back together (who ever is?). I maintained her separate parts as best I could for as long as I could. When Suzanne was about three—a miniature woman way before her time—she helped out without being asked. She sensed that somebody had to.

When I left Theda's house, hauling my clean folded clothes behind me in Suzanne's red wagon, I felt caffeine-deprived. Herb tea wasn't working as an acceptable coffee substitute. I wanted mountain-grown coffee laced with cream, dammit, but I was determined to wait until after my baby was born. Determined, but not happy.

As soon as I heard Lilly's brother Johnny Lawson call my name, I felt better. Johnny was a jolt of love and joy. He moved easily in the world, offering kind words, if needed—and a helping hand. Like Lilly, he teased people, but in a gentler way. "Slow down," he said, sprinting up to me. "You gonna hurt yourself. You know what condition your condition is in."

He took hold of the wagon's handle, pulled my laundry around to my back door, and carried it up the steps. I thanked him, awkwardly, knowing that I couldn't invite him inside for drink or a bite to eat, which would have been the polite thing to do, because it would violate Mama's rule: no men allowed.

"I know you'd like for us to spend some quality time together," he said, letting me off the hook. "But I'm going to run on over and get a piece of Theda's pie before Lilly polishes it off. Tell Suzanne I saw her dancing at the school. She's going to kill."

He grinned and strolled back across the lawn as if he had all the time in the world. At eighteen, Johnny had his eye on the prize. He was already working days, going to school nights, and planning to make a good life for himself. I hoped my new baby—I was certain he was a son—would grow up to be like Johnny.

I opened the back door quietly. If Mama had fallen asleep while I was out, I wanted her to go right on sleeping for an hour or so. One look at the room told me that Mama was awake and, worse, she was experiencing one of her spells.

The signs were clear.

Chairs were overturned. Newspapers and towels were scattered across the floor. Buckets had been taken from the closet and positioned around the room. When she was a child, Mama lost her father in a flood. She went back to that night often—the strong wind and the heavy rain, the water rising and rising until it flowed into her house as if no one lived there.

She expected history to repeat itself.

When Suzanne heard me at the door, she ran into the room. Red blotches dotted her cheeks. "Grandma hollered at me," she said, crashing into me.

"I'm sorry, Baby," I said. "Is Grandma in her room?"

Suzanne let go of me long enough to point hard at Mama's room, using the same force she had seen her grandmother aim at the Devil who lurked beneath the floor. "She is now, but while you were gone, she was out here and she hollered at me and said we were all going to die in a flood."

Suzanne threw her voice so that the person who had hollered at her, the mean one she was telling on that very minute, could hear her every word. "She wouldn't listen to me, Mom, and when I told her it wasn't raining she said they don't teach us everything in school. She said she learned from living and I hadn't lived long yet."

"Grandma wasn't really hollering at you," I said, giving my daughter a quick hug, before setting the chairs upright. "It was her fear that made her angry. She wanted her fear to bow down. Not you. We all have times when we're afraid."

"Grandma's afraid all the time," Suzanne said, standing up straighter. "I'm brave."

"You sure are. You are a very brave girl."

"Grandma says the water will be above her head. It won't, will it?"

"Of course not."

"Grandma was wrong."

"She's not so good at predicting. The weatherwoman said to expect dry weather the next two weeks. We need a good hard rain to clean the air."

Suzanne looked up at me with worried eyes. Her lip quivered. The puny confidence she had managed to stir up died out instantly. She grabbed hold of me again and said, "I don't want to drown, Mom."

I held her close to the baby and me and said, "You won't drown, Sweetheart. And Grandma will calm down. She'll be back to normal in no time."

Suzanne gave me a puzzled look. Had I said back to normal? Yes, I really had. We almost laughed, but laughter would have led to tears. We let the moment pass.

After Suzanne and I put the towels, newspapers and buckets away, I went to Mama's room. It was her fortress. She had hung Daddy's army blanket from a rod descending from the ceiling, strung it up as a makeshift partition, a thin green wall that would separate and protect her from a world she could not grasp. She lay on the bed holding a damp cloth to her forehead.

"Mama," I whispered, pushing the blanket to one side.

"You don't have to whisper," she said, staring straight at me. "You're not talking to a crazy person. You think I haven't been in a flood, girl? Who do you think they rowed down the middle of the street in a boat in 'forty-one? Me, Shirley, and Mother, that's who. I was barely able to sit up, but I remember that. I remember how it rained all night long, how the water came into the house, and afterwards how pitch black it was all around us with no street lights or lanterns. No flashlights. We had to depend on folks we didn't know and couldn't see.

"They yanked us out of our beds, hauled us off in a boat, and threw us in the white folks' church like we were slaves. Mother didn't know where we were or what had happened. Shirley Lee couldn't make her understand why Poppa wasn't with us. He stayed behind on the roof of the house to wait for the next boat, which never came. Never came. That was the last we ever saw of Russell Everett Taborn. Poppa drowned at forty years of age because of a run-wild river, a flood that he didn't want us to die in. If you don't believe anything else, Missy, believe that. Don't come in here big as a mountain and tell me there aren't any black heroes in this world. And don't you dare say that water don't rise."

"No ma'am," I said. "There are many thousand. And it does." I sat down beside her and patted her arm. "Worrying about all that now, though, you'll only upset yourself. You've already upset Suzanne."

She yanked her arm away. "Don't pat me," she said, glaring. "All you care about is Suzanne. You treat me like I'm a child, too. I gave birth once, you know. Not on the floor, mind you. In my bed. You wouldn't be in the world if it wasn't for me."

"I only want to help you, Mama. I want to help you feel safe."

"Don't fancy your powers. All my help comes from the Lord."

And then the humming began, the signal that our conversation was over and that, if necessary, she would hum straight through until morning; she had done so before.

I sat there silent and defeated. I didn't give any orders or advice. I barely breathed. After a while, Mama said, "Lester wanted another baby. He always wanted a son. I tried, but I never gave him one."

Hours later, when Mama and Suzanne were both asleep, I lay awake and imagined playing with the little brother I never had, chasing him around in the yard and pushing him back and forth in my homemade swing.

# CHAPTER SEVEN

When my water broke, it sounded like rain.

Getting up once during the night was not unusual. I didn't think anything of it, but as soon as I sat down on the toilet the liquid that poured out of me put urine's anemic trickle to shame and told me one thing: It was time.

I trudged back to the bedroom and opened the closet door carefully, hoping I wouldn't wake Suzanne. The door creaked once and she sat straight up. "What's wrong?" she asked. "Is it Grandma?"

"No," I said, turning on the light. "It's me. My water broke."

Suzanne looked around the room. "Water? What water, Mom?"

"My water. I told you about the fluid the baby's been floating around in?"

"Yes. His own little swimming pool."

"He won't need that anymore. It's time."

"It is?" she asked, suddenly wide-awake.

"Yep," I said, reaching for my overnight bag.

Suzanne got out of bed and whooped with joy. She bounced up and down and grabbed hold of where my waist used to be.

"I'm thrilled, too," I said. "But we don't have time to celebrate. I've got to pack and get to the hospital."

I packed quickly and called St. Mary's. The nurse on duty told me to call a cab and come on out. Knowing there wasn't time to drink a whole cup of Theda's red easy-labor herbal tea didn't stop me from putting the kettle on after I called the taxi company. I figured a few sips of red tea would be better than none at all and it would look pretty in a cup and smell nice, which was probably the point anyway.

Suzanne came into the room dragging my bag with one hand. With her other hand, she held up my flip-flops. "You'll need these, won't you," she asked, flashing those straight-from-Lamarr dimples.

"Thank you, Baby," I said. "You're a saint."

I eased my swollen feet into the sandals. "I won't be gone long. Two days at the most. Theda will come in the morning and help you take care of Grandma."

"The Lord does that all by Himself," Mama said. She entered the room, eye-balling Suzanne and me like we were co-conspirators cutting a last-minute deal behind her back.

It was after midnight. Wearing long white gowns, we faced each other in a semi-circle, three generations of wide-awake black women: Suzanne, cafe au lait; Mama, warm caramel; and me, chocolate brown. We could have been angels of mercy pulling the night shift. I reminded myself, for the fiftieth time, to buy a camera—not to rely on memory alone.

"I'll have tea, please," Mama said, brightly, as the kettle blew. Then she strutted over to the table like she was in a restaurant. "Real tea, black with plenty of sugar," she said, winking at Suzanne, who laughed and said, "Grandma, you know sugar is bad for your teeth."

I turned off the stove. "No time for tea, Mama. I've got to get to the hospital. Besides, tea would keep you awake."

"I hoped it would help me sleep," she said, all gaiety gone. "Every time I close my eyes I see Lester looking just like he looked the first time he walked across my yard. He has his hat on. He's loose-limbed. It's nobody but Lester. He laughs so hard his hat falls off. As soon as I start toward him, he stops laughing. He picks up his hat and backs away. After he's gone that harmonica of his starts up. How am I supposed to get any sleep with that thing ringing in my ears?"

I couldn't afford for Mama to splinter further apart. A stroll down Memory Lane would sink her and, therefore, Suzanne. I sat down across from Mama and held her hand. "You will sleep just fine," I said, giving her hand a sharp tug. "When you wake up, there won't be anything to worry about. Food is in the refrigerator. Your medicine is in the cabinet and Suzanne will be right down the hall."

The taxi horn blew louder than the kettle; Mama and I both jumped.

Mama gripped my hands. "Don't go," she said.

"I've got to," I said, working my fingers loose. "I'm having this baby in a hospital."

I picked up my bag and headed for the living room.

"Will the baby look like me?" Suzanne asked, as she and Mama followed along.

"Of course, the baby will look like his big sister," I said, putting on my coat. "Who else is he going to look like?"

"God knows," Mama said.

I kissed Suzanne and went out the door. Mama came out behind me, but she held up at the edge of the porch, as if those six steps were the only things that lay between her and troubled waters. Tilting forward, she called out, "God knows, Mattie. You may not see Him, but He sees everything you do. Every. Filthy. Thing. He's right beside you."

I looked back and saw that she was tottering a bit. "Be careful," I said. "Go back in the house. Lock the door. Get some sleep."

I struggled into the taxi, wondering whether the driver would have hopped out and held the door open for me if I had been white. Probably.

When I finally got my mini-bag and my maxi-behind into the backseat, I looked out the window and saw that Mama had disobeyed me. She was still at the edge of the porch. Suzanne, my baby-angel, was in the doorway behind her. Like all angels, she was bathed in light. Her hair was her halo and she had someone to watch over: a grandmother who was as fragile as a glass heirloom.

For one second I regretted not having imposed upon Theda, not having asked her to get out of her bed in the middle of the night to come and baby-sit Mama and Suzanne, but the next second my concern was for my unborn child as the taxi driver took off like a wild man. "St. Mary's, here we come," he said, flipping the meter over as he stepped on the gas.

I gripped the headrest in front of me. "Good God."

"Say what, lady?" he asked, looking back over his shoulder.

"Nothing," I said. "I wasn't talking to you."

"Oh, pardon me. I'm the only other person in the car. The only other one born anyway, so I just assumed." He whistled and then snorted. "Women. Pregnant women."

We cut through the night and arrived at the hospital in eight minutes (it normally takes from twelve to fifteen).

At the admitting desk, I signed the necessary papers, wrote down my insurance number, and listed my next of kin. Then an attendant gave me a ride up to the maternity floor in a wheelchair. He wanted me to save my strength (for something people say they forget?).

"I sure hope you aren't getting ready to have twins," the night nurse said, sighing, as if even the possibility made her angry.

"Oh no, ma'am," I assured her. "I want two kids. Total. I already have a girl named Suzanne. I only want one more. A boy."

She watched, frowning, until I rolled onto the bed. Then she said, "You look old enough to know that, in this life, it's not what we want, it's what we get. And you look to me like you might be getting ready to have twins."

She took my blood pressure. "It's a little high," she said. "Lean back and relax."

I took a deep breath. "My water broke more than an hour ago," I said to the nurse's back, "but the pain hasn't started. With my first baby it was the other way around. Without any warning, pain hit me like a freight elevator."

"You bragging or complaining?"

"Neither. I'm just wondering why I haven't felt any pain yet."

"The pain'll come," she said, turning around long enough to pat my knee. "Just wait. Is anybody coming to be with you?"

"No ma'am. I'm by myself."

"You want me to call somebody?"

"No thank you. There's nobody to call."

"All right," she said, going to the door, offended again.

Five minutes later, she returned with a monitoring device and an enema syringe.

"Oh, no," I said, trying to scoot to the edge of the bed. "I don't want that thing."

She gave me a look.

"I don't need it is what I meant to say. I don't need an enema. I don't need one and I don't intend to get one, either," I said.

"You're having a baby, Miss Moon. You're not one," she said. "Roll over."

I came from the bathroom doubled over, holding onto my baby as if I were afraid I'd lose it. Although I hadn't forgotten Labor's pain, it was worse than I had remembered.

I climbed onto the bed and panted while the freight elevator hammered and banged against my spine. "Oh, God," I said. "The pain has started."

"Told you," the nurse said, hooking up the monitor. "One heartbeat," she said, reading the screen. "Wonderful. One. Strong. Steady. Two babies are too many for a woman alone."

I said. "Oh! Oh, God!"

"Um hm. See?" she said. "But it's a short one. It's almost gone."

"You sure?" I asked, grimacing, as the elevator rocked back and forth.

"I'm sure," she said. "Um hm. Yep. There it goes."

Feeling a little subsiding, a little letting up, I gave her a weak smile.

She scowled. "Prepare yourself. They'll get stronger. You ain't seen nothing yet."

Two hours later in the delivery room, when my baby pressed his head relentlessly against my cervix commanding it to yield, I didn't shed any tears, but I called out for the father of my about-to-be-born child. Jacob was nowhere around. But I was not alone. I had a visitor.

A presence came to my side and held my hand. I couldn't see her face, but I knew a woman was there. She spoke to me. "Don't be disheartened, my child," she said. "Hold on. This will pass."

I felt comforted. The woman stayed with me until Diego was born. As soon as I saw that my baby was a boy, whole and breathing on his own, I turned to look upon the stranger's face and to thank her. She was gone.

She had come to me like a Spirit. She left the same way. No farewell; no promise to return.

# CHAPTER EIGHT

Diego weighed nine pounds. Black, silky hair covered his skull. He was strong and impatient to feed. My milk came in fast and Diego became a peaceful baby. While others around him were losing their heads—screaming, Where am I? Who am I? Why?—he slept in a state of grace, snuggled against my breast.

As breakfast was being served, the nurse, who was on her way home at the end of her shift, stuck her head in the door and smiled for the first time. "You done good, Mom," she said. "I'll see you around midnight."

"We might be gone, by then," I said.

She shook her head. "You'll be here," she said.

After attending Sunday school, Jacob came to visit his son. His father, who visited the hospital every morning, had told him that my baby had been born. Hearing the news, Jacob hurried out to St. Mary's and slid along the wall of the hospital like a drug thief, hoping he wouldn't be seen by anyone he knew.

I should have called him a coward, a hypocrite, a dog, but with scrambled hormones and an armful of new baby, I called him darling, honey, and sugar pie.

I was a wreck.

Jacob was a wreck, too, but at least he showed up. He only stayed a few minutes—he had to get back to church—but those few minutes were important. Holding his son for the first time, Jacob grinned, and then he laughed. Lovesick, sleep-deprived, I laughed, too.

"Was that your baby's father?"

Karen, the red-haired, freckled, teenager in the bed next to mine was staring at me from large gray-green eyes.

"Yes," I said, too tired to evade. "He's the proud father."

"He's handsome," she said. "All dressed up."

"He has someplace to go," I said. "He's a preacher, a minister-in-training."

"Aren't they all?" she said, as she concentrated on diapering her scream-ing-out-loud, red-bottomed, red-faced baby girl.

Theda and Lilly stopped by in the afternoon. As soon as Lilly saw my son she ran to the bed. "Your baby's so dark, Mattie!" she said. "He's the darkest baby I've ever seen. Johnny is dark now, but he wasn't dark when my parents brought him home from the hospital."

"He's gorgeous," Theda squealed. "And so big. Look at that skin."

"It's dark," Lilly repeated. "Almost black."

"He's like midnight in the country," I said, smiling at her. "A real brother."

Sitting down in the one and only chair in the room, she said, "He must take after his daddy. Nobody can say this one is mixed. Country Girl, not even the darkest Mexican in Old Mexico or one of these brown-skinned Pakistani doctors running around here could have given you that blue-black baby. This one is a full-blood."

Theda gave Lilly a quick shut-your-mouth nudge. Then she sat on the edge of the bed. "Mattie, what did you name him?"

"Diego," I said, holding my baby close to protect him from Lilly's stare.

"Dee what?" Lilly asked, standing up. "Dee who?"

"Diego."

They both said, "Oh."

Lilly sat back down. "Why?" she asked. "What am I missing?"

"I like the sound of it," I said. "I've always liked Spanish names."

"Sure you have," Lilly quipped. "You heard a lot of those? Way outside of Paducah?"

"No," I admitted.

The truth was that two months before Diego was born I had met a woman named Leticia Valdez at the Kell Street Laundromat. Leticia, traveling from New Mexico to her uncle's home in Detroit and to what she hoped would be a better life, had stopped off in Eloise for the night.

She had three young beautiful dark-eyed children—one too many in my opin-ion—but she treated each one lovingly, and with patience, even as they, happy to be out of the car and off the road, ran from one end of the place to the other, scattering carts, empty soda cans, newspapers, and old magazines as they went.

Leticia's youngest child was named Diego. With his black hair and long, dark eyelashes, he was too gorgeous for this world, but he was tough, too. He kept up with his larger siblings, even overtook them a few times. I liked his spunk and his name. I told Leticia that if she didn't mind I would pass it on.

I didn't tell Lilly all of that. It was too much information. She would have found too much to object to: rowdy children, a family in transit, the difference in culture. Diego's middle name is Lester," I said. "Named for my father."

Lilly laughed. "That's as country as hell. But at least it makes sense."

Theda changed the subject. "Everything is quiet at your house, Mattie. Suzanne can't wait for you to bring the baby home. I'll get back to her and Miss Claudette as soon as we leave here." Then she reluctantly tore her eyes off Diego, turned toward Lilly, and said, quietly, "We sure make pretty babies, don't we?"

"They sure do," Lilly said, crossing her muscular legs tight.

The next day I arrived home in a taxi. Theda, minus Lilly, was the first person in my welcoming party. She walked across our connecting yards, carrying an iron pot. Seeing her, I thought of the women we had known in Kentucky. They didn't think there was any situation that couldn't be made better by a covered dish. Anytime anything went wrong or right, here they'd come with green beans, macaroni and cheese, or a fresh fruit pie. Something warm.

Suzanne came running from behind the house, giggling. Mama watched us from her lookout post at the edge of the porch.

My girls. I was glad to see all three of them.

The driver, the same man who had driven me to the hospital, moved by who knows what—new life maybe—got out and opened the door for Diego and me. After thanking him, I asked whether he was the taxi company's only employee.

His eyes narrowed. "You ever heard of overtime?" he asked, sticking the two-dollar tip in his pocket. "New mothers," he said to himself, as he went around to the driver's side of the car.

As the taxi roared away, Suzanne yelled, "Well, does he, Mom?"

"Does he what, Baby?"

"Does Diego look like me?"

"Give him time," I said, briefly lifting the blanket from her brother's face so she could see for herself.

"Hi my baby Diego," she said, pressing her face against his.

"I made you some vegetable soup," Theda said. "You won't feel like standing over a hot stove for days."

"If ever," I said.

Mama stood stock still until we stepped onto the porch, then she reached behind her, opened the screen door and backed her way into the house. Once inside, she dove into her rocking chair as if it were a lifeboat. She held onto the chair's arms with both hands, rocked, and glared at me like I was the Devil's helpmate, and my son was a demon-child.

Theda, Suzanne, and I sat close together on the sofa, admiring Diego and trying to outdo each other with baby talk. Suzanne won.

When Mama couldn't take any more of our sugar-coated tones, she stopped rocking. "One bastard wasn't enough for you. You had to have two. I blame Lester. He's the one who encouraged you to shimmy and shake. You weren't but three years old and he had you dancing to the Devil's littlest, meanest instrument: the harmonica."

Suzanne looked at me. "Your grandfather loved music," I said, hoping to reassure her. "He played piano, too."

Mama turned her eyes to the ceiling. "Lord, see what Lester's grown-man wickedness did to his child. He'd be proud, too. This time she had a bastard son."

"What's a bastard?" Suzanne asked.

"There's no such thing," I whispered. "Every child on earth has a right to be here."

That answer may have satisfied Suzanne; she went back to memorizing her baby brother's face. But it upset Mama so that she abandoned her rocking chair and ran from the room like it had caught fire.

Theda put her arm around me. "Welcome home," she said.

# CHAPTER NINE

Home.

The Eloise Motel on South Poplar Street didn't even come close, but once a week during the first months of our son's life, that's where Jacob and I had our family time.

We sneaked in. Diego and I arrived first; Jacob came when the coast was clear. Reverend Franklin, who prided himself on his knowledge of other people's business and, in fact, considered it part of his job description to know, still hadn't been told that the moment I became a mother for the second time, he had become a grandfather.

I was disappointed by Jacob's procrastination and his lack of courage, but I empathized with his consideration of his father's feelings. After all, I had to consider Mama's. I also knew that even after Reverend Franklin had received and recovered from his shock, Jacob and I would still have to live apart. There was no way Mama would live in a house with a man, and no way I would leave her alone. She had already been abandoned twice—once by her mother, once by her spouse. A third abandonment, by her only child, was unthinkable.

A white picket fence wasn't even in my dreams so, with eyes wide open, Jacob and I made love and made do at the Eloise Motel.

We had some good times in those shabby rooms. I've had two lovers and, by far, Jacob was the best. He was more patient and generous than Lamarr. He was quiet, too—not for Mama's sake, but for our son's. As a lover, Jacob was a gift. His co-parenting skills left something to be desired. The problem: he was overly sensitive, skittish, even borderline hysterical.

"If I don't hold him tight, I'll drop him," he cried out one night after I tactfully pointed out that the baby seemed somewhat uncomfortably constricted in Jacob's claws-of-life grip.

Jacob acted as if I had accused him of committing the crime of the century. "He's little, Mattie. I can't drop him," he whimpered. "He's depending on me. What do you mean, anyway, constricted? How do you want me to hold him? Show me, if you know so much."

Good grief.

After I showed Jacob that holding the baby confidently, yet lovingly, would work for everyone concerned, he immediately moved on to another worry, another myth.

"I don't think he's getting enough," he said, watching closely as the baby snuggled up to my breast.

My eyebrow shot up. "Enough what?"

"He just nursed. He wants to nurse again. He must not be getting enough."

"Enough what?"

"Milk."

"I have lots of milk, Jacob. Too much. I ooze."

"I know you have milk. Your breasts are blown up like new tires, but maybe Diego's not getting enough of it. Enough vitamins and stuff."

"I know you're not suggesting that my milk is defective or insufficient." I forced myself to sit ramrod straight, perfectly still, as I spoke. I didn't want to start rocking like Mama—without a rocking chair.

Jacob rubbed the palms of his hands down the length of his face. "I don't know what I'm saying."

"Me either. It's late. Maybe we shouldn't talk anymore tonight."

"Maybe you should put him on a bottle. On formula."

"Did you say formula?"

"Isn't that what they call it?"

"They call it that because they made it up. They put it in a can or a box and sell it at the grocery store to people who, for whatever reason, need to buy it. I don't. Right here in my tire-sized breasts, I have the perfect food for our son, designed specifically for him. And Diego likes it. He really likes it."

Emphasizing my point, Diego patted my breast with his tiny hand. He smiled around my nipple, but didn't fully let go of it.

"You're right," Jacob said. "I don't know what I was thinking."

I relaxed.

A minute late, Jacob said, "I just hope he's getting enough."

"He is. Sometimes he nurses from hunger, sometimes for comfort. He knows his own needs. They don't call it feeding on demand for nothing. He demands. I deliver."

Jacob nodded. "Got it. I understand."

He didn't.

As I changed Diego's diaper, Jacob said, "He goes a lot. Seems like everything runs right through him."

I rubbed the baby's brown tummy. "Tell your daddy how things work," I said. "Tell him you use what you need and eliminate the rest. Because you're an efficient baby-machine. A wonder. That's what you are."

To Jacob, I said, "Stop worrying. Take a nap."

He kept at it like a dog with a bone. If Diego spit up milk, Jacob swore he had a stomach virus; if the baby coughed, Jacob reached for our coats. "Let's take him to Emergency," he'd say. "He may have pneumonia."

As pathetic as Jacob was during those first months after Diego was born, I didn't give up on him. He had the potential to become a great father. He was a devoted son. Perhaps he was too devoted, though. Jacob's desire to meet Reverend Franklin's high expectations had left him tentative, afraid to fail. I was sure he would stand up to Reverend Franklin eventually but, until then I was on my own and deeply frustrated.

For therapeutic reasons, I cleaned floors in a big house on Upper Circle Drive, a house that Sherry and Mark Ziegler owned.

Technically, I was Sherry's assistant. We had met in our junior year of high school in typing class. Back then, she was a lower-middle-class girl named Sherry Brady, a roller-skating Dairy Queen carhop turned junior prom queen, who had a crush on Mark Ziegler. Mark was a baseball jock attending Ohio State University. Sherry needed to tell someone about her fixation. I was the perfect person.

One spring night Sherry got lucky. She rolled up to Mark's car with a root beer float and ended up with a date for the evening. She was one thrilled white girl. She and Mark went to a movie and then to his house to make out (his parents were in The Bahamas).

After Sherry graduated high school, she and Mark got married at St. Mary's Church. At that time Sherry was Catholic; Mark was Mark. Their wedding picture is featured prominently on the dining room wall: Sherry, with nearly flat breasts, is dressed in white lace. She is holding yellow roses and Mark's big hand. She looks hopeful. Staring straight at the camera, Mark looks cocky, shrewd.

It's them all over.

After graduating from Ohio State, Mark went to law school. He excelled, passed the bar, and became a partner in his father's law firm, Ziegler, Ziegler and Wolenkramp. Within two years of making partner, Mark became the most successful lawyer Eloise had ever seen and he never let Sherry forget it.

Mark went out into the world each day, but Sherry stayed at home. She wasn't a homemaker exactly—the mini-mansion she lived in was already made, thank you very much. Sherry was more an aspiring artist, home-based. After decorating and redecorating their house exquisitely, she studied ballet. Painting came next, but she gave that all up to become a writer. After Oprah Winfrey established her book club, Sherry decided to write a book about life. There was only one problem: she suffered badly from writer's block.

The plan was that after she had written in longhand, I, her newly hired assistant, would come along behind her and type up. I had gotten a C in typing—my one and only C—but Sherry had gotten a D. I could type her under the desk any day of the week. Unfortunately, many days there was little for me to type; most days there was nothing. Sherry's writing pad was blank and the week was long.

I made coffee, brewed tea, including Theda's colorful herb concoctions, and, on Sherry's worst days, the days she was the most severely blocked, I made her frothy green Margaritas.

Despite all that I had time on my hands, so occasionally I sank to my knees and polished the floors, muttering, "Out, damn spot, damn you!"

My position with Sherry had perks. For one thing, I got to exercise. I walked across town and back each day, at first carrying Diego in a sling and later pushing him in a stroller. I also worked in beautiful surroundings—Sherry's was one of the grandest houses in all of Eloise. Compared to most women in town, who had only graduated high school and afterward worked for low wages in restaurants and factories, I was well paid.

I counted my blessings. The one I cherished most was that Sherry encouraged me to bring Diego to my job. She was lonely. She considered that getting two human beings for the price of one was a bargain.

I fed Diego, sang to him, and rocked him to sleep each afternoon. As soon as he was awake, in a good mood and a dry diaper, Sherry played peek-a-boo games with him and hugged him tight. We both basked in his glory.

"You're lucky," Sherry said, as she danced around the room, holding Diego in her arms like a bouquet of flowers.

"That's what they call me," I said from the keyboard, where I sat, fighting my way through a new computer manual. "Lucky Mattie."

She smooched Diego's neck. "Mark and I tried for six years to have a baby."

"Not every woman conceives easily. My mother had a hard time before she hit the jackpot. It could happen when you least expect it. Don't give up."

"We already have. Mark blamed me. He had a vasectomy last year. Just to punish me."

"Have you considered adopting?" I asked, hoping to distract her, stop her from raining kisses up and down Diego's plump arms.

Kissing away, she mumbled, "I'd be willing to adopt an Asian. They're really smart."

"All of them?"

She paused for a second. "I think so. Anyway, it doesn't matter. Mark would rather die first."

"He might surprise you."

"He would have a coronary."

Without saying so, I agreed. When I tried to put together a picture of Mark with a dark-haired, dark-eyed child, quick or slow, it didn't compute. Mark with any baby didn't compute. He wasn't paternal and Sherry knew it. Deep down inside, women know who and what they're dealing with. We know that—whether the man is a president or a dope dealer, or both. The woman at a man's side knows his character, or its absence. She knows after the first few months, if not the first two weeks. As an infamous wife once said, the only people who know how a marriage works are the two married people. She forgot or chose not include the help. We always know.

I knew about Sherry's marriage, but my job was not to make matters worse by rubbing her nose in it. My job was to help, to assist. Sherry paid good money for my services as a stand-in friend (Mark kept her away from real ones). When she felt like talking about Mark's true nature—the runaway ego, his need to humiliate and control—I listened to her, as a true friend would have listened. I didn't pass judgment. Nor did I try to convince her that she was being too harsh. She knew him as well as I did.

If she was too depressed to talk, or for that matter to move, I simply sat in the room with her the way I sat with Mama, just so she'd know she wasn't alone.

When she tried to nap, I studied Microsoft Word and polished antique furniture. If she couldn't sleep, I served her Margaritas with lots of salt, a preservative, circling the rim of her glass.

# CHAPTER TEN

"I didn't have a choice," Mama said, sitting ramrod straight in her rocking chair. "You do."

I didn't have time to explain my life to my mother. I braided Suzanne's hair neatly, but quickly. She had to get to school by eight. I could get to Sherry's when I got there; we weren't on a clock, but the sooner I arrived, the sooner I would get back home.

Mama continued. "Why in this day and age would a black girl with a high school diploma—a scholarship winner—work as a maid?"

"I'm not a maid, Mama. I'm an assistant."

"Assistant to what? To whom?"

"To a well-to-do woman. A writer."

"What did you say her name was?"

"Sherry Ziegler."

"Never heard of her."

"Her work is going to be published someday."

"When?"

"Any day now."

Mama smirked and eased back into her rocking chair. I dashed into the bedroom to get my coat and, in haste, I made the mistake of looking at Mirror on the Wall.

"I couldn't help overhearing," Mirror said, smugly. "She's right, you know."

"I don't know," I said, putting on my coat. "And neither do you."

Mirror said, "Don't get snippy with me. I have a right to my opinion."

"If I want it, I'll ask for it," I said, closing the door.

Suzanne and I held hands as we left the house. We were running late, but that didn't mean we hurried. We were in the mid-west in winter; we walked carefully down that icy sidewalk. Diego was snug in the baby sling on my back. It was his first snow.

Mama's voice rang out in the frosty air. "When?"

I looked back and saw her standing on the porch in her thin housecoat. Her fist was clenched, thrust high in the power sign. "When are white folks going to start cleaning up their own damn dirt?" she screamed. Her voice contained the rage of three centuries. "When?"

Two boys, wearing baggy pants, Oakland Raiders football jackets, and baseball hats turned backward, walked ahead of us. They pointed at Mama, laughed, and nearly fell down. Teammates, they held onto each other and stayed upright. Then they trudged on in their winter gear.

"When?" Mama repeated. "Answer me that!"

Until the night of the annual Christmas pageant, Mama called out from the privacy of her own porch; on Christmas Eve, she disturbed the peace at Sabbathani Greater Baptist. Suzanne had been named lead dancer in the children's recital. She practiced her routine at the home of her third-grade teacher, Ms. Aleta Woods. Ms. Woods gave her students extra attention and lots of love. Suzanne blossomed in her presence. Mama was against all of it—the special attention, the blossoming, and, especially, the recital itself.

While I helped Suzanne prepare for her big night, Mama watched us in silence with an evil eye. When she saw me attach gold and white wings to Suzanne's dress, it was too much. She spoke up. "You can't pretty this up," she said. "Wings won't sanctify dirty. Dancing encourages the devil. You may not have known that when you were little, but you know it now. Every time Satan hears one heart pound or two fingers pop, he begins his climb. He's a long way down, but dancing gives him the boost he needs. It's the rhythm he's waiting for. The beat and the bounce. He knows that if you'll dance, you'll do anything."

"Miss Woods says dancing is a celebration of life, Grandma," Suzanne said. "She said dancing represents the true joy of man."

"What man has Aleta Woods ever known?" Mama asked, her voice rising. "Joyful or otherwise? Aleta never wed. She wouldn't know Satan if he jumped up and kissed her on the mouth. Dancing is not a celebration. It's an open invitation to sin. Engraved. You don't have to take it to the Post Office. You shake one time, it shocks the devil's hell-hole heart, and he starts climbing."

Suzanne looked at me. She wanted me to say something, but what could I say that would help matters: That the devil is a symbol, not real? That respecting Grandma's wishes, I hadn't danced since I was nine years old? That Mama was wrong and that Suzanne and Ms. Woods were right about joy in the morning? I tilted Suzanne's head down and, concentrating on the task before me, I brushed her hair until the shine popped out.

Mama's disapproval didn't deter us. We set off for the church at seven o'clock. If Jacob had been in town, he would have picked us up on the corner and dropped us off a block away from Sabbathani, but, as a professional courtesy, he had gone to Mount Pleasant Baptist Church in Harrisburg, Illinois, for a holiday revival.

Mount Pleasant. New Bethel. Mount Olive. Saint's Rest. New Caledonia. Shiloh Everlasting. Sabbathani Greater Baptist. Black churches beckon; they call us home. Years ago, black people, hated in every corner of the "new world," decimated by design, and locked out of many so-called houses of worship gathered together in one-room lean-to buildings in which they could feel whole again, places that answered the heart's age-old question: Who loves you, baby?

*Jesus loves me. This I know. For the Bible tells me so.*

Today in some communities, there is a church—an oasis—on every block. Without the church many of us wouldn't have made it. Mama wouldn't have. When Aunt Shirley lifted Mama up out of that pigpen in Kentucky, she had to take that baby somewhere. She took her to Mount Zion Baptist Church in Salem, Kentucky.

The Taborn sisters grew up in prayer. With Vaseline rubbed on their legs and white ribbons swinging in their hair, they went to Sunday School and stayed for church. Doubt, pain, and ostracism, all were banished there. Whosoever will? Let him come. They came. They humbly praised their dear, dear, Lord and sang songs in His name.

We arrived at Sabbathani fifteen minutes later than Ms. Woods had requested, but we beat the first organ solo. The church was packed. Candles were lit; flowers decorated each pew.

I sat near the back in the last empty seat. I was loaded down. Diego, his snow-suit and diaper bag, Maximum Moon (his stuffed bear), my coat, and Suzanne's wool cape were all piled on my lap. I looked ridiculous, but I felt happy. Proud.

My good mood was so good it stayed in my head, even after my eyes settled on Lamarr and Rotelle, who were impeccably dressed and sitting third row center.

Wouldn't you know it? And the only things on Rotelle's lap were her slender, diamond-covered hands, but I kept smiling. I was elated.

Suzanne came onto the stage wearing her white dress and her angel wings, which fit her well. She knelt by the manger. The music swelled and Suzanne rose gracefully.

She danced before the Newborn King.

The audience sighed. Some of us swayed. We might have teared up had we been given more time, but we were not. Before water flowed from anyone's eyes, Mama materialized in the sanctuary like a nightmare. People gasped and blinked.

On a night lacking even a threat of precipitation, Mama stood before us covered from head to toe in rainwear. She wore a raincoat, hat, gloves, galoshes—the works. She marched up the aisle of Sabbathani for the first time in nearly eight years, hoisting a closed umbrella above her head like a sword. She spoke quietly, as if she were alone. "Suzanne," she said. "Not another step. Satan heard his cue. You already got him started. Stop now. Leave him hanging. He doesn't deserve any better."

Barely hearing Mama and not believing what they actually heard, the congregation whispered and moaned. They were stunned; I was worse than that: I was trapped beneath the stuff on my lap. It took me a minute to get out of my seat, cross over numerous knees and feet and reach the aisle. I held onto Diego, but Max slipped from my hand. I bent to pick him up, but Mama took to the stage, so I left Max where he lay and rushed forward, crying, "Mama, no. Please. You can't stay. You've got to go."

On a mission from God, she ignored the likes of me. She grabbed one of Suzanne's wings and reached for the other. Suzanne, equally determined, ducked underneath Mamas' outstretched arm and ran to me. Mama hiked up her coat and came after us.

Ms. Woods, thinking she was in charge, stuck her generous hip out to block Mama's advance. That was her mistake. Mama leaned back and brought the wood handle of her umbrella crashing down on Ms. Woods, who yelled, limped to the podium and frantically tapped a bell.

Four deacons woke up and sprang into action. Louis Coe, the youngest man and the strongest one, overpowered Mama and confiscated her umbrella. Herbert Wilson grabbed one of Mama's arms; Earl Walker grabbed the other. They lifted Mama straight out of her galoshes and escorted her out of Sabbathani, with her feet dangling a few inches above the floor.

Decorum was restored.

The fourth deacon, the oldest, Jerald Bibb, picked up Max from the floor and dusted him off. After that he walked Suzanne and me out to his car and drove all of us home.

Riding along in Mr. Bibb's car, I was as grateful to him as a teenager in love, but not as happy-go-lucky. I didn't giggle or squirm in my seat. I sat still. My heart was heavy; my arms and lap were full holding Diego and our stuff. And my left side hurt. Suzanne, who refused to sit in the back with Mama, sat wedged in between Mr. Bibb and me. Her crushed wing burrowed into me like a knife.

Suzanne's eyes were closed. She held her tears, refused to let them shame her any more than she already was.

Mama held a lot, too. She carried her raingear and a life's worth of disappointments in her hands. Looking out the window at the black moon-less sky, she hummed "Pass Me Not, Oh Gentle Savior." She followed that up with "In The Upper Room."

When we got inside the house, Mama went straight to bed. Her mission had been accomplished. There wouldn't be any dancing at Sabbathani anytime soon.

I sat beside Suzanne while she tossed and turned in bed. "Grandma embarrassed me in front of the whole town, Mom," she said, trembling.

"The church, Honey. One church, and people will forget."

"They won't ever. Why does Grandma have to live with us anyway?"

"We live together. We're a family."

"Tiffany has a mom and a dad. One sister. That's all. No old grandmother showing up making her stop before she gets started good."

"Someday, when you're older, you'll understand."

"I'm never getting older. I'm going to die tonight, right here in this bed."

"When you're a world-famous dancer and actress, dancing in Paris and acting in New York, instead of your embarrassment, you'll remember that Grandma had a hard life. Much harder than yours or mine. She lost her mother to mental illness, her father to a flood. She faced blatant racism. She was poor and she often felt like her only friend in the whole wide world was Jesus.

"You'll look out at the people dressed in their finery; see them jump to their feet and clap their hearts out for you. You'll take your bow and, as sure as I'm sitting here, you'll think to yourself, I wish Grandma could see me now."

She may not have been convinced, but she stopped shaking. She turned onto her side and beat back her tears until, exhausted, she fell asleep.

# CHAPTER ELEVEN

Christmas Day we got up early and tiptoed around each other all morning long. We needed time: Suzanne, to recover from her first public humiliation; Mama, to come down from the high of performing before her first live audience in a long time; myself, to prepare a traditional holiday feast with some of the trimmings.

I had to defrost an eight-pound turkey, roast it, and set it on the table before dark. No one in that house needed or expected company, but that's what we got.

Someone knocked insistently at the door. Mama was rocking and not likely to stop, so, drying my hands with a dishtowel, I went to the door, opened it and there he was—Lamarr Tyrone Robinson, bearing gifts.

I closed the door partway and asked, "Are you lost?"

He said, "Found."

"What is that supposed to mean?"

"I'm here to wish your family happy holidays. May I come in?"

I didn't know what to say. Lamarr had never come into the house through the front doorway like a normal person. He had climbed in through my bedroom window and once, when Mama was at prayer meeting, the night Suzanne was probably conceived, he sauntered in through the back door and acted like he knew the way to my bedroom even though he was heading straight for Mama's room until I tugged on his sweatshirt.

On Christmas, of all days, he was asking permission to enter the house in the customary manner. I couldn't believe him.

I looked back at Mama. To my surprise, she was rocking steadily in her chair, exhibiting no erratic movements. A man had come calling and she wasn't reaching for broom or pan. She must have gotten a lot out of her system when she stormed into Sabbathani, because she stood up and smiled like a Miss Congeniality contestant. "Company," she said, like it was the most natural thing in the world. She walked toward Lamarr, with her dark eyes smiling along with her mouth. I couldn't believe her, either.

I flashed back to Mama opening the door of another house; the new one Daddy and his friends built in Kentucky. She was smiling then, too. Neighbors had stopped by to see it and us. There was laughter, and there were candied walnuts—and corn whiskey for the grown-ups. I must have been four, lucky to get chocolate milk. Five years later, Daddy left, the laughter stopped, and no one stopped by, not even Aunt Shirley, who, struggling to breathe and living to pray, was so diminished she had been confined to her bed.

"May I come in?" Lamarr asked, deep dimples deepening.

Mama was at the door, still smiling. It was if she had never seen Lamarr before. She probably hadn't—she didn't get out much—but after a few seconds of looking at him and smiling, smiling and looking at him, it dawned on her that even if she hadn't seen Lamarr before, she had sure seen someone who resembled him to a T: her first grandchild.

At that moment, as if directed in a play, Suzanne made her entrance. She went to the bookshelf, got a book, and sat on the floor. We rarely had company, but Suzanne, in character, acted as if the only thing of interest to her was the continuing adventures of Nancy Drew.

Mama, who had a front row seat, moved closer to Lamarr. Her come-right-on-in smile fell away. "Dear Lord," she whispered. "I never wanted to know. You don't give us more than we can stand. But I never wanted to see this, Lord. Your will, not mine," she said, talking to Jesus as she went to her room. When she got there, she closed her door quietly, as if might break.

Lamarr, waiting at the door, was letting cold air in. "Oh, what the hell," I said. "Come on in."

He walked over to Suzanne and gave her the larger of the two boxes he carried. "This is for you," he said.

She stood up and smiled shyly, matching Lamarr dimple for dimple.

"I brought something for the little man, too," he said, touched by his own thoughtfulness.

"What's this about?" I asked, placing the gift he gave me on the sofa so I wouldn't hurl it across the floor.

"Christmas," he said. "I dashed to the stores before they closed last night. And here I am. May I sit down?" Miscalculating what my response would be, he sat down on the sofa and spread his legs wide.

"May I open my gift now?" Suzanne asked quickly. Like me, she knew how quickly a mind could change (just like that). She wanted to lay claim to her loot before fate or the gift giver snatched it back.

"Sure, honey," Lamarr said, before I could protest.

"Open it in our room," I said.

"Thanks, Mom," she said, turning to go.

I put my hand on her arm, "It's Mr. Robinson you need to thank."

"Thank you very much," she said, tossing Lamarr his own winning smile.

"You're quite welcome," he said, catching it. He bent his tall frame toward her. "I enjoyed your wonderful dance at the church last night."

The look on Suzanne's face straightened Lamarr up and sat him back on the sofa. As Suzanne left the room, dragging the heavy white box at her side, Lamarr spoke to me in a hushed sympathetic tone, as if he were an invited guest, a friend of the family. "I said the wrong thing, didn't I?"

"Coming here was the wrong thing. Why did you?"

"Because she's mine," he whispered. "Isn't she?"

"All mine."

"I can see, Mattie."

"Since when?"

"Since Christmas Eve."

"And before that, you were blind?"

I moved closer to where he sat, so we wouldn't be overheard, but also because I wanted him to smell my bottled-up hatred, my utter disdain. "I have rights," he said, leaning away from the stench.

I stared down at him. "I don't like your attitude."

"What attitude?"

"The attitude of someone who is used to owning stuff: Space. People. You had that even before you owned anything, when you were in school. I liked it, then. I was lonely and desperate. I don't like it anymore."

Lamarr stood up to me. He had the height advantage, but I backed up, squared my shoulders, and strained my neck.

He winked. "Aren't you still lonely, Mattie? Now you have kids, but no man to speak of. Aren't you as desperate as you ever were?"

I wanted to slap his face, but he would have confused it with a love tap. So I sat down in Mama's rocking chair. How dare he ask if Suzanne was his child? He knew. "Suzanne Lucinda Moon is not yours in any way that counts," I said. "And she doesn't need your trinkets. You can go."

"I may have suspected," he said, sitting down. "When you didn't say anything, I put it out of my mind."

"How convenient."

"I should have checked it out. I'm here now."

"Too late."

He leaned back on the sofa as if he planned to stay all day. "It's late," he said. "Not too late."

My face was hot. Lamarr's arrogance had given me hot flashes twenty years before they were due. I hopped out of the chair and opened the door. I held the door open until the cold air cooled my whole body down. Then, shivering, I said, "We're having Christmas dinner. Our guests will be here soon."

He laughed out. "Who's coming, Lilly, and her man, Theda?"

I pointed my finger at him and started to say that if he couldn't respect my friends and their orientations, whatever they might be, he could let the door hit him in his homophobic ass, but Suzanne ran into the room so I waved at her instead.

She waved back. I closed the door.

Suzanne hit her mark at the center of the room and turned all the way around to show her new suede coat. "Look at my new coat, Mom," she said. "I want to wear it every day."

The coat had a leather collar and cuffs. Lamarr always had good taste in clothes but, damn, suede for a child? One slide on the ice and that coat would be stained and cracked in a million places.

Smiling his and Suzanne's co-smile, Lamarr said, "I'm glad you like it." Then he stood and said, "Mattie, perhaps it's time you formally introduced us."

"Okay," I said. "Suzanne, this is Mr. Robinson. He's one of Santa's helpers. He delivers presents to children in the neighborhood. We don't want to keep him."

Suzanne said, "She's kidding, Mr. Robinson. We don't believe in that anymore."

"Don't grow up too fast," Lamarr said. "I want you to enjoy your childhood."

"I want you to leave," I said, yanking the door open.

Wagging what looked like a manicured nail in my face, Lamarr said, "I'll be back."

"Thanks for the coat. I love it," Suzanne called out. Before he could switch those dimples on high one last time, I shut the door and tripped the lock.

I placed Diego's gift under the tree and went into the kitchen, where I put water on for a cup of that mediciny-tasting chamomile tea that, according to Theda, would sooth my nerves. When Suzanne came into the kitchen, my hands were still shaking. "Is Mr. Robinson our father?" she asked.

There is an art to lying. Tone of voice is important; eye contact is huge. One false move, one slip and the truth can slide out. Standing in front of me, over-dressed in a grown-woman's coat, Suzanne was not giving me enough time to put together a believable lie. More important, she deserved the truth. "Biologically speaking, Mr. Robinson is your father," I said. "He was present at your conception. He's been absent ever since, though, so father is probably not the word we're looking for here."

"Sperm donor?" she said, modern child that she was.

"Now we're getting closer to the truth," I said pouring the water for my tea, which I needed more than ever.

"What about Diego? Was Mr. Robinson present at my brother's conception?"

Tell one truth, may as well tell another. "Mr. Robinson is not Diego's father. Jacob Franklin is our fat boy's father."

Suzanne didn't even blink. "Why did he come to see me today?"

I cupped her chin in my hand. "He took one look at you last night and realized what I've known since the day you were born, that he's a fool."

She frowned. No one wants a fool for a dad. "We all make mistakes," I said, cleaning up. "Mr. Robinson saw you last night and realized he had made a big mistake in not getting to know you. So, he bought you a nice coat to say he is sorry, that's all."

"He's coming back. When he does, do I have to call him Mr. Robinson?"

"Let's not make any decisions today. We'll see what the future brings."

Without being asked, she got carrots, celery and bell peppers from the refrigerator and put them in the sink to be washed. I sighed and blew on my pale tea. Then I screamed, "Take off that coat! You'll get it wet!"

Reluctantly, she removed her coat. "I knew my father wasn't white," she said. "I just knew it."

"Who said he was?"

"Tiffany. Every time she gets mad at me, she says that. She wrong, too, isn't she? My daddy isn't white, is he?"

"No. He's black. For the most part."

When Suzanne, Mama, and I sat down to dinner, we avoided eye contact. We paid close attention to our food. Suzanne was still upset with Mama for embarrassing her by showing up at the church; Mama blamed Suzanne for having called up Satan on tiptoes in the House of the Lord.

There were awkward silences, but no histrionics. No fights broke out. No flood warnings were issued and, after dessert, Suzanne agreed with me that Mama looked pretty in her new, red-and-white Christmas dress from J.C. Penny's.

Mama thanked us and confessed that she wondered if she looked like she was wearing a flag. Suzanne and I laughed with Mama, not at her.

Had someone passed by, looked in our window and seen us, she would have witnessed a familiar scene—a family sharing a holiday meal. The observer could not have predicted the turmoil that lay ahead.

# CHAPTER TWELVE

"Mattie, it's bad," Theda whispered.

I could barely hear her. "What's wrong?" I asked, my heart rate increasing.

"Miss Claudette is down here on the Post Office steps, Girl. Drawing a crowd."

"Are you sure?"

"Would I call you on your job if I wasn't sure?"

"No. What is she doing?"

"Preaching."

"Preaching?!"

"To the white folks at first. The next thing I knew there was a crowd. Kids on their way home from school, black, white, old, and young are gathered around Miss Claudette. Hanging on to her words. You're going to have to come get her."

Sherry drove me downtown. She double-parked her Rolls Royce and waited while I made my way through the crowd. Mama was singing a cappella. Her voice was pure and light.

Where do beautiful voices come from, anyway? Someplace deep in the soul? Or do they drift down from on high? Do human beings really sing that gloriously, or do we the listeners imagine it?

When I was a child the thing I wanted to do most in the world was open my mouth and sing like my mother, but the sounds I brought forth could have come from an alien child. I couldn't carry a tune or hold a note. My inability to sing inspired my dancing as much as Daddy's harmonica did. The more my voice broke, the harder I danced.

I danced because I could.

Mama hadn't sung in public for many years. The Sunday she stepped down from the choir stand, Mrs. Hall, the director and lead pianist, was so upset that Aleta Woods had to fill in for her at the piano even though that meant Ms. Woods had to run back and forth between the piano and organ, which was not a pretty sight.

Special prayers were sent up for Mama's return to the choir for weeks after she left. Some of the same people who made fun of Mama on Saturday as she rushed from the Laundromat to the grocery store to the Post Office to the bakery in her raincoat—rushing to beat the rain that hadn't been forecast—dropped their heads and wept on Sunday mornings, when Mama stood sanctified and still before them in her brilliant blue choir robe.

The prayers were not answered.

The Sunday after Suzanne was born was the last Sunday Mama sang in the choir. After a mysterious falling out with Miss Tavy, Mama left the church entirely, but she kept her choir robe. She remembered the Sabbath, too, and kept it holy. She didn't do any work on His day and she didn't allow me to do any either.

Each Sunday at ten forty-five, Mama marched out of her bedroom, in time and wearing her choir robe. She sat in her rocking chair, read the Bible and hummed her favorite spirituals.

After years of humming at home, there Mama stood in downtown Eloise singing at the top of her voice.

I inched toward the center of the circle of people that had formed around her until I was close enough to reach out to her. She waved at me and then waved me away.

"And now the poem, I promised you, Children," she said to her audience. "This came to me last night in a dream. It's entitled 'Why, Lord? Why' and it goes like this:

> "A hurricane is threatening off the
> Coast of Florida. That modern day
> Hell, Los Angeles, has floated out to Sea.
> San Diego is Venice number three,
> Canals where streets used to be.
> Way north in St. Paul, the Mississippi
> Is mute, frozen shut. It's running toward

New Orleans, though, forcing St. Louis
To soak up the overflow. Alton draws her
Bridge. Cape Girardeau lies low. Eloise?
She's greedy. Dancing. Kicking. Squirming.
Making the Devil lick his bright red lips.
Pull on his climbing boots. Why, Lord,
Why? Won't Eloise hold still? Doesn't she
Know that, if she keeps bucking, a watery
Grave is how she'll get her fill?"

The listeners clapped politely. I took Mama's arm and held it. "Thank you kindly," I said. "Mother Moon needs her rest. Thanks for your time."

A down-and-out old fellow, unshaven and tobacco stained, lying slumped against a lamppost, called out, "Will she be here tomorry?"

"No, Sir," I said.

"Next week, Friend," Mama said, beaming at the man like she knew him. "I'll be here same time next week." When I tugged her arm, she raised her voice to a holler. "Every week until spring." As I steered her away, she called back over her shoulder to the crumpled up man and the others who lingered. "Brothers and Sisters, I'll be here every week until spring. After that, I'm through with it."

As we headed toward Sherry's car, a squad car pulled up. I recognized the driver right away—Sergeant Tom Culver. His daughter Jodie had been in my history and civics classes. He gave the same speech in both classes on Career Day: Join the Eloise Police Department. You won't regret it.

Jodie and I had been friendly until the day our teacher, Olma Callahan, a bigot in black saddle shoes, asked whether the civil rights movement, which brought us affirmative action, lawsuits, and racial preferences, had finally gone too far.

The week before Olma had told our class that Brazil—Brazil!—had the homeliest people she had ever seen, because the races were all mixed up. That stunned. What about the pictures I'd seen in magazines of drop-dead women walking on the sand with fine men and the adorable dark-haired children following behind them? I wanted to ask Olma, but I didn't. She probably hadn't even been to the beach. She probably hadn't ever been out of Illinois. Those angry thoughts about her and her distortions of history ran through my mind, but I didn't give them voice. I knew that no matter how good my course work was, the best letter grade

I would get was a B (pop-eyed Jodie would get the A) and I also knew that a B could be lowered to C+ at the last minute. Just like that.

I felt ashamed of myself for not saying anything, so when Olma asked her question about civil rights my hand shot up. I intended to assert that the civil rights movement had benefited our nation and especially women, like her, and to point out respectfully that negative, discriminatory, and even legally prohibited action still occurred on a widespread basis.

Olma ignored my hand. She called on Jodie.

"My father says if we give them an inch, they'll take a mile," Jodie hissed through her braces.

We stopped speaking after that.

Culver got out of his car, looking just like Jodie in pants and a shirt. He planted his feet squarely in front of me. Tilting his head toward Mama, he said, "Is this old girl running a scam?"

"Not at all."

He looked at Mama and squinted. "You pass a plate out here, Granny?"

"She didn't ask for any money or get any," I answered for Mama. "She recited a poem, sang and prayed. That's all."

"In Eloise, we do our worshipping indoors," he said. "We have some Catholic, but mostly we're Protestant."

"We are too. Baptist. Same as you."

Jodie had brought up the Southern Baptist Conference, without the slightest provocation, numerous times in class.

"I don't care if you're Black Muslims or practice Voodoo," he said, talking out of the side of his mouth. "You assemble, you have to have a permit. Make that crystal clear to this here humming one."

As I ushered Mama down the sidewalk, Culver watched us closely. When I got to Sherry's Rolls and opened the door, he pulled out his Billy club and sprinted toward us.

Sherry got out of the car. "Sergeant," she said, tossing her hair to the left. "Is there a problem?"

Culver pulled up. He was breathing hard from running those few steps and from seeing Sherry flip her hair back to the right. "Mattie's a friend of mine," she said. "I'm giving her, her mother, and her baby a lift home."

Culver looked at Sherry like he hadn't seen a woman for a long time. She removed her shades and stuck her expensive chest out. He took a handkerchief from his pocket and wiped his face. "Nice to see you, Mrs. Ziegler," he panted.

"Sherry, please," she purred.

He blushed like she had kissed him. "I didn't know what to think. We wouldn't want any trouble."

"There hasn't been any. We'll take good care of Mrs. Moon."

He gazed at Sherry. Then he snapped out of it and glared at Mama and me. While he had been drooling over Sherry, we had climbed into the backseat. Under his cold stare, I yanked the smooth-as-silk seat belt, pulled it across Mama's chest, and locked it. I put my arm around her shoulders, so she wouldn't try to escape.

Satisfied that we were leaving, Culver backed up and winked at Sherry. She stepped into the car and we rolled away. Culver's eyes said he hated to see Sherry go.

Sherry eased her car onto Elm Street in full tourist mode. Driving slowly, she admired the well-kept houses as if they were tiny museums, monuments to the simple life. She said, "We never visited each other when we were in school. Isn't that weird?"

"We weren't friends. We were acquaintances."

"I thought we were friends."

"You also thought you wanted to marry Mark."

Sherry groaned. "Mrs. Moon, Mattie is bad, but I don't know what I'd do without her."

Mama leaned forward and said, "When?"

I patted Mama's arm. "Don't pat me, Mattie," she said, "I'm not a child." She reached up and tugged on Sherry's hair. "Tell me. When?"

Sherry rubbed the back of her head. "What?"

Mama said, "W-h-e-n?"

"Look. We're almost home," I said. "You'll have to talk to Sherry some other time."

"Keep your dress on," Mama said. "All I want to know is when her book is going to show up in the stores? I might buy it."

"That's a good question," Sherry said, parking in front of the house. "It's taking longer than I had hoped."

Sherry helped me steer Mama to the door. She kissed Diego and hugged him like she meant it. I thanked her for her time and waited until she hopped back in her European car and drove off to the Saint Clair Shopping Center to buy something she didn't need.

When I got inside, Mama told me her news. "I know what I have to do," she said.

"What's that?"

"Start my own church."

"Beg pardon?"

"You heard me. When you were a little bitty thing, if Lester and me went out in the yard and whispered, you heard every word we said. I know you heard me, close as I am to you. But I'll say it again. I'm starting my own church."

"Where?"

"Outdoors."

"Why don't you go back to Sabbathani? You've missed it, Mama. Bury your pride and go back on Sunday morning."

She hung up her coat, took off her boots. "Christmas Eve was my last time there. I won't go back."

"You loved Sabbathani."

"Sabbathani's the Lord's house. It's the people inside His house that I can't stand. Driving up in cars big as tanks. Falling out in clothes every color in the rainbow. Hats with feathers that will poke your eyes out if you don't jump out of the way. Looking down their noses at me. Gossiping behind my back. The people were the problem."

"Who do you think will show up at your church? People are the same, Mama, indoors or out. Dressed up or buck naked."

"Watch your mouth."

"All I'm saying is you won't like the new people any more than you like the old."

"Maybe not, but I'll guide them. On different corners each week, on rocks, I'll build my church. It will be open to all. No special pews. We won't have to worry about the basement flooding, because there won't be one. My mind is made up. It's what I'll do."

I put food on the table, fed my kids, and cleaned up the kitchen. After that, I went to Mama's room to talk her out of starting her own church.

While I talked, she took Daddy's army blanket down, folded it and placed it at the foot of her bed. She no longer needed a barrier between herself and the world. No matter what I (or Sergeant Culver) thought or said, Mama was coming out of the closet. She was going to spread the word of God in the open air.

That night when Jacob called there was an uncomfortable silence between us. Reverend Franklin fixed Jacob up with a date for New Year's Eve. My feelings were still smarting. Although Reverend Franklin had initiated the crime, Jacob was an accessory after the fact. He insisted that he didn't see anything wrong with sharing a meal with an attractive graduate student from Washington University. "I was polite to her," he said. "What was I supposed to do?"

"You could have declined the dinner invitation."

"It was at my house."

"Your father's house."

"That's not fair. You live with your mother."

"She lives with me."

"Whose name is on the title?"

I was about to hang up, but Jacob spoke fast. "Sabbathani's Fiftieth Anniversary Revival is coming up. As soon as it's over, I'll tell Dad about us. I'll introduce you."

"We've already met."

"This time you'll meet him under different circumstances."

"We'll see. Good night, Jacob."

When I hung up the phone, I spun around a few times. No dancing, mind you. I simply spun around like a top. Church revivals, even the knock-down, drag-out kind Sabbathani threw, with crying and shouting and repenting and baptizing, lasted two weeks, at most. Anybody could wait that long.

# CHAPTER THIRTEEN

The revival came and went. They say it was something to see. Seven souls were claimed for Christ, one woman, marching up the aisle, suffered a heart arrhythmia and had to be taken to St. Mary's by ambulance. Two people, a man and a woman, stood in front of the congregation and agreed to stop cheating on their respective spouses—honest, this time. An older lady was so happy that her grandson joined the church she passed out cold and stayed out for two days. All that, and Jacob still hadn't told his father about Diego and me. Reverend Franklin stumbled upon us by accident.

Jacob and I, believing Reverend Franklin and his ladylove Lela had gone to Mt. Vernon for the day, ventured into Braxton's Shoe Store for our first family-shopping spree. We found the perfect pair of soft crushable leather shoes for Diego. They fit him perfectly.

Seeing our baby all dressed up with absolutely no place to go on a Saturday morning, Jacob and I laughed like school kids. We were laughing when Reverend Franklin walked in the store.

Reverend Franklin looked surprised to see us together, sitting side by side, but he didn't seem alarmed. He walked right up to us. Jacob jumped to his feet. "You're home early," he said, facing his father. "Is anything wrong?"

"Nothing's wrong. We didn't go," Reverend Franklin said. "Lela had a change of heart. She went to a band concert at the high school instead. I refuse to sit through another concert, play, or magic show at that band shell. I've been to over a hundred. No more."

Jacob said, "Are you shopping for shoes, Dad?"

Reverend Franklin said, "No. A car. Of course, I'm shopping for shoes, Jacob. Do you mind?"

Jacob said, "Of course not."

Reverend Franklin looked down at Diego, who was sitting on my lap kicking his feet. "Your little fellow's got a good understanding," he said, sitting in the chair next to mine. He put his hands around Diego's chubby ankles.

Diego held still for a second. He stared hard at Reverend Franklin's gold tie-pin, and then he went back to kicking, or at least trying to.

Reverend Franklin laughed foolishly like men do when they get around babies. Certain men. Keeping a grip on Diego's fat legs, bouncing them hard, he said, "That's what the old folks used to say about people with big feet. They have a good understanding. He's a fine looking boy, too. A fine looking boy."

"Thank you," I said, wondering what Jacob was going to do, what he wanted me to do.

"You know Mattie, don't you?" Jacob said.

"Sure. I know her mother, too," Reverend Franklin said, making wide-eyed idiot faces at Diego. "Claudette used to be a member of my church. That woman could sing. I was sorry to see her stray." He cleared his throat. "Mattie, too."

Jacob said, "This is not the place, Dad, but we need to talk to you. How about dinner?"

"Lela made plans for us tonight. How does tomorrow night sound?"

"Fine with me," Jacob said. "Okay for you, Mattie?"

I nodded.

Reverend Franklin stood up and shook Jacob's hand. "Anytime I can help, you know I am willing," he said. "We'll do whatever we can for Mattie and her handsome son."

Reverend Franklin went to inspect a pair of shoes, but he turned around in time to see Jacob pay for Diego's shoes. He may have thought I was on the verge of being homeless. Heaven only knows what he thought when he looked out the window and saw me climb in the front seat of Jacob's car.

I took extra pains getting ready for dinner at the parsonage. I put on my good dress, the black one with the white collar. I brushed my hair as flat as it would go, parted it in the middle, and shaped it into a ball on top of my head. I was going for a look I had seen in an old photograph of my great-grandmother, Charlotte Moon. She was a handsome, dark-skinned woman with thin nostrils. The Indian in her had grown her hair out long and smooth, but she favored buns and braids. With keen features, she looked formidable. Dignified.

I missed classic by a mile and ended up at the intersection of old-fashioned and matronly.

"Whatever else they say about you, they won't say you're a slut," Mirror on the Wall said, rolling her eyes. "What a getup. A choking collar. Old lady shoes. Who dresses like this? You look fifty."

I turned my back. I didn't have time to trade insults with her. I had to get to the church on time.

When I arrived, Lela was in the kitchen putting the last touches on the meal. Jacob was pacing in the dining room. He was unhappy because of Lela's presence. He had expected a private meeting and, before Lela joined us at the table, he told his father how he felt. Reverend Franklin reminded Jacob that while the parsonage was the Lord's home, he, Reverend Franklin, temporarily controlled the guest list. He made his point. When Lela came into the room, Jacob jumped up and pulled a chair out for her and the four of us ate family style.

Lela served thin slices of roast beef, green beans, and garlic-mashed potatoes. For dessert, she brought out a high-fat, homemade chocolate cake.

After the meal, Lela refused my offer to help her. She went to the kitchen and cleaned up alone, in red high-heels. She kept herself together to impress her man. She was that kind of woman. Reverend Franklin expected no less. He was that kind of man.

Jacob waited until he heard water running in the kitchen. Then he swallowed hard and said what he had postponed for so long. "As you know Dad. Mattie recently had a son."

"I'm not senile," Reverend Franklin said, raising his right eyebrow. "I met the young man yesterday. Remember? He's delightful." He lowered his voice. "Mattie's unwed state is unfortunate, but the Book says let him who is without sin cast the first stone. What exactly is the problem?"

"There isn't a problem," Jacob said. "There is some information you need to have."

"Oh?" Reverend Franklin said, rising. He shook his weak leg a couple of times and walked slowly around the table. "Fill me in, then."

"Well, sir," Jacob said, wiping his upper lip. "I fathered Mattie's child."

Hearing Jacob's words, Reverend Franklin suddenly looked confused. He could have passed for senile. He held onto a chair until he got himself sitting safely and then he turned to me. "What?" he said. "Which?"

Jacob said, "Mattie's son, Dad. The little boy you met yesterday is my son. He's your grandson. Mattie and I have been seeing each other for almost two years."

Reverend Franklin said, "Where?"

"Where we could. That's not important. But we do plan to marry someday."

Hearing that, Reverend Franklin's head bobbed. He steadied himself and a glint entered his eye. For the first time I saw that he wasn't just an old man of the cloth. He was tough. He had hellfire burning in him. He looked like the aging Joe Louis, whose picture hung on his dining room wall opposite the picture of Christ. If my baby had been in the room, I would have held him as a shield, to deflect Reverend Franklin's white-hot glare, but Diego was with Theda. He couldn't hide me from his grandfather's wrath. No one could.

I crossed my fingers under the table and hoped Reverend Franklin's eyes would change and show compassion, but they remained full of reproach. "Diego is a wonderful little boy," I said meekly. "We want you to get to know him."

"I don't even know my own son," Reverend Franklin barked. "Excuse us. Jacob and I need to speak in private."

"I want Mattie to hear anything we have to say," Jacob said. "No more secrets."

"I don't mind," I said, standing to go.

"We know you don't mind," Reverend Franklin said, closing his angry eyes. "You've never minded. With you, anything goes. Anybody."

I headed for the door.

"Mattie, don't leave," Jacob called out. "Dad owes you an apology."

"You owe me one," his father said.

"He needs time," I said. "I'm going home."

Reverend Franklin opened his eyes. "Wait one minute. Has there been a blood test?"

My eyes got real big when I heard that. "Pardon?"

Before his mouth answered my question, his eyes spoke to me. They said, "You, JEZEBEL. You've made trouble forever and who would know that better than a Baptist minister?"

"I'm asking you about DNA," he said aloud, solemnly, as if he were addressing a scientist, instead of the town floozy.

My fight response kicked in, too. "I'm not on trial," I said. "Neither is my son. There haven't been any tests, but Jacob knows who fathered Diego."

Jacob backed me up. "Diego is my son, Dad. Next time you see him, look closer. He's beginning to look just like you. Only difference is going to be his darker skin. I'm surprised you didn't see it yesterday."

Reverend Franklin was one of the few black men in Eloise—three out of five hundred—who had married a woman darker skinned than himself. Diego's skin color came not only from me, but also by way of Jacob's late mother, Marva Franklin. Reverend Franklin had handed down Diego's good understanding, his pudgy hands and feet, and his dark eyebrows.

I felt bad for the old man as he worked to steady his breath. When he called out weakly for Lela to bring him a cup of coffee, "Black, no sugar," I slipped out the door and went home to the people who called me by my real name.

# CHAPTER FOURTEEN

I stood before Mirror to see if I saw what Reverend Franklin had seen: a man-hungry woman who could take a man down and keep him down for the rest of his life—the woman known down through the ages as hussy, slut, wench, whore, and Jezebel.

In the soft light, I saw only me: brown skin; breasts swollen from lactation; kinky hair that, refusing to stand on ceremony, had curled up and wiggled out of the ball I'd twisted it into on top of my head before I went out.

I saw what I always saw: fear, doubt, and pain. I was no Jezebel. Surely, she had had more fun.

In need of comfort, I put my hand on my abdomen and moved it slowly across my pelvic bones and down to the ancient power dome, the plump mound, that warm and secret place both sought and feared by men like Reverend Franklin, certain men. Moving my hand lower, I closed my eyes.

Mirror cleared her throat. "Excuse me. How did prayer meeting go?"

I yanked my hand away from my throbbing body and reached for my robe. "I wasn't at prayer meeting," I said. "I had dinner at my fiancé's home."

She laughed. "So, how did it go?"

"Beautifully."

"Beautifully, my ass. Don't bullshit me, Mattie," she said. "I'm the one person you can be real with. Getting shat on shows. At first it shows around the edges, but, after a while, it shows all over. Get some rest. See you first thing tomorrow."

"Not if I see you first."

"Stop," she said. "You're killing me."

I turned out the light and got in bed quietly, so I wouldn't awaken Diego. He usually nursed once during the night. With luck, I'd get four hours of sleep before he sought his pre-dawn feeding.

"Mom?" Suzanne said, as soon as my head hit the pillow. "Can you hear me?"

"Yes I can. So will Diego."

"Sorry."

"What is it, Honey?"

"My father called tonight."

"What did he say?"

"He wants to see me. He said he has rights."

I closed my eyes. Lamarr was in the house. I couldn't see him in the dark, but I smelled him. I smelled the basketball shoes he dropped at the foot of the bed. I smelled the Johnson's and Johnson's he rubbed on his baby-smooth chest. I smelled the onion on his breath from the burger he'd wolfed down before crawling in through my bedroom window. I smelled his soft fingers probing me. Gladly.

He was back. I could forget about getting four hours of sleep. I'd do well to get a dream-haunted two. A man with dimples as wide as the Ohio River and a behind as high as a Colorado mountain would saunter through my dreams all night long, bouncing a ball as round as the moon.

Suzanne turned over in her twin bed, rearranged her precious body for sleep. "Good night Mom. I love you."

"Good night, Sweetheart. Love you, too."

Love. Stop making a fool of me. Love thy neighbor as thyself. Love is blind. Love is all you need. What's love got to do, got to do with it?

Love? Is that you?

The next day when we awoke the snow was piling high. Mama got up early. She exchanged her rain boots for snowshoes and she wrapped a scarf around her neck to protect her from the chill, but she was determined to head out.

"In this weather?" I asked, groping my way toward the stove.

"I have to spread the Word, before it's too late," she said.

"Are you going alone?"

"No ma'am. I'm going with God."

Even as I tied her scarf more securely and helped her into her coat, I still protested. "Couldn't you wait until spring? That's the time for change."

"I'm not promised spring. Neither are you," she said and then she left. The morning paper hadn't even arrived.

I reached into the cabinet and got a jar of Folgers's Instant. If Mama was going, so was I. She was my mother. I would go. But if I was going to brave the cold and follow behind her ragtag traveling church, I needed something that would jolt my brain.

I would stand off to the side, knee-deep in snow, and watch while Mother Moon spoke of Noah's long-ago ark and the rains that would flood Eloise someday. I would keep a sharp eye out for Culver, say Amen when she finished her song, and bring her home. She would be tired the rest of the day. We both would.

I had found it hard to sleep with Lamarr circling for Suzanne, Mama preaching outdoors, and Diego extracting every ounce of my strength as fast as I produced it. Exhausted, I wanted to get back in bed and sink beneath the covers, but Mama needed me. I would go. But first I had to have a cup of coffee with a teaspoon of cream.

When I left the house, Suzanne was slipping on her dancing shoes. Mama never knew that while she was out trampling though the snow, shivering as she spread the word, Suzanne was at home dancing up a heat wave.

Burning in her heart.

The second time Lamarr came to my front door, he brought Rotelle with him. That stung like a slap, but I kept my head still. "May I direct you folks someplace?" I asked, without a wobble.

"You can point me toward my daughter," Lamarr said. "I intend to follow through with this thing. So does Rotelle."

"What does Rotelle have to do with it?"

"Lamarr and I both want a daughter," Rotelle said. "I can't have more children. You can share."

I moved aside and the Robinsons high-stepped into our lives. I had seen Lamarr skating, tossing footballs, and even fishing once at the park with Rotelle's two reddish-brown boys. Lamarr, who had wanted no part of parenthood when I blew up and waddled past him in Technicolor tents, had since then become a gung-ho Dad. He outdid Mr. Rogers in his sweater and sneakers.

"I brought Suzy some things," he said, handing me a shopping bag. "Leotards, a skirt, and slippers. Rotelle picked them out."

"We know you can't afford the extras," she said, rich sister to poor.

"Is Suzy here?" Lamarr asked.

"She might be napping," I said, going to the bedroom. It wasn't a lie; it was a wish. I chanted, "Sleep, Suzanne, sleep," as I opened the door.

She was awake, of course, and excited to have company.

With Lamarr on the scene, Suzanne became dainty. She laughed a lot and opened her eyes real wide. She basked in the attention she was receiving from him and grew gay, in the old sense of the word. She was falling in love. A young girl's father is her first true love. No contest.

I left the new family alone to blend, until Lamarr called out real loud, "We've invited Suzy to go with us to St. Louis next Saturday. We want to introduce her to the museums, the arts."

"I didn't realize you knew them," I said, coming back into the room.

For Suzanne's sake, I smiled as if I were joking. There were smiles all around. Lamarr's was the biggest of all. Dimples like craters. I took a step backward. Shouldn't dimples close up on a man by the time he is in his thirties? Shouldn't they have the decency to become deep lines—wrinkles—by then?

"We'll take her to the Art and Science Museum," he said. "We want her to see that there is a world beyond Eloise. Surely you do, too."

"Surely I do."

"When the weather breaks, we'll go to the zoo. Maybe we can get her down to Orlando, to Disney World after that. Next year we'll go to Mexico."

My head began to hurt. "She might need to get to know you before a lot of far-flung travel."

"I know him, Mom," Suzanne said, turning on me. I looked at her for what felt like the first time and wondered whose side she was on.

"I can go to St. Louis with him, can't I?" she asked.

"Let me know the time," I said, accepting defeat.

"I want you to meet your brothers tomorrow, Suzy," Lamarr said, patting her on the head.

He took my breath away. "Suzanne only has one brother," I gasped. "And she doesn't like being patted on her head or called Suzy."

Suzanne tugged on my shirt to shut me up. "It's okay," she said.

"No, it isn't," I shouted. "You have every right to set boundaries and to be called by your correct name."

All the smiles went away including mine. Soon after that, our guests left. They went home to all their extras. Disappointed, Suzanne left me, too. She retreated to our dreary bedroom to try on her bright new dancing clothes.

I wasn't alone, though. I had Diego. As I freed my fat boy from his playpen, he laughed with anticipation. He grabbed my hair and shrieked with joy. I held him close. "At least I don't have to share you with Lamarr and Rotelle Robinson," I whispered in his ear. "I don't have to share you with anyone but your daddy and Suzanne."

Shortly after that, I learned that that Reverend Franklin wanted to be known as Papa Clay.

Seven days after insulting me to my face, Jacob's father, bold as day, came to call on us. He had experienced a change of heart. Upon awakening that very morning, instead of blaming Jacob and me for conceiving a child out of wedlock, he said he bowed his head and thanked God for, in His own mysterious way, sending him the grandson he thought he would never live to see, a fine one, too, with a good understanding.

He asked me to forgive him for taking so long to see the light. "Mine is not to question," he said, striding toward the rocking chair as soon as he spied it. "Mine is to start being the best grandfather I can be." Lifting his pants at the knee, he sat down and rocked slowly, like a visiting king. "I do have one request, though, dear," he said.

Here we go, I thought. "Yes?"

"I want the boy to call me Papa Clay. That's what my sisters and I called our grandfather, Wade Clay. You don't object, do you?"

"Not if it will please you."

"I'm sure Jacob wants to be called Dad. That's what he always calls me. There is only one papa per generation in our family."

"He hasn't said anything."

"Give him time. You know he's slow to say what he really wants."

"Wonder why?"

"Well, he honors me and our traditions. He'll do right by the boy, though. As for you, Mattie-dear, I've asked him not to do anything rash. I know that blood throbbing in a man's veins can make him feel like he's in love. Pressure builds. Before a man knows it … *Pow!*" He clapped his hands together so loud I jumped in my seat, "… he's lost. He literally doesn't know whether he's coming or going. I talked Jacob down. He gave me his word he'd stop and take a sober look at his future. If you're in it, I will give him my blessing to marry you, no matter what anybody else says."

"I appreciate that," I said, not knowing what else to say.

Reverend Franklin agreed to stay for an early supper. I brought Diego to him. Then I went to get Mama. She had smiled Christmas morning when Lamarr came calling and had continued smiling until it dawned on her that he was Suzanne's father. I thought that she had lifted her ban on allowing men in the Moon house and that she would especially welcome a visit from a man of God.

I couldn't have been more wrong.

When I identified our gentleman caller, Mama closed the door in my face. She refused to speak to "Papa Clay," let alone break bread with him.

I stood outside her door, whispering. "Come out for just a minute to be polite. We could all be family someday."

"I never wanted to know," she said, opening the door slowly. "Keep Clay Franklin away from me now and keep him away when I die."

I spoke loudly, because she covered her ears. "What do you mean?"

"Don't let him preach my funeral," she said, keeping her hands over her ears. "If that man had anything good to say about me, he should have said it a long time ago. When I needed somebody to speak for, not over, me he was quiet as a snake. I don't want him slithering up to my casket to pontificate after I'm gone. Keep him away." She yanked her hands away from her head so she could slam the door.

Reverend Franklin and I dined alone. He had seconds. Old school, he loved being waited on by women—Lela, me, whoever would, let her come.

Amen.

# CHAPTER FIFTEEN

Mama was stubborn; she never changed her mind about Reverend Franklin, never considered him, even potentially, as family. Every time he and Jacob came to visit, she went to her room and stayed until they left.

She also kept her word about preaching. She preached to, cajoled, and reprimanded folks all over town that winter, until her luck ran out.

In late March, Sergeant Culver shut Mama's grass roots ministry down, just as he had promised. He booked her for violating the city ordinance against unlawful assembly, uncalled-for noise, improper soliciting, and, while he was at it, inciting to riot.

Word spreads fast in Eloise; some folks get it faster than others. Theda called and told me that Mama was incarcerated as soon as she heard the news, but by then Miss Tavy, Mama's estranged friend, had already gone downtown, checkbook in hand, to bail Mama out.

They arrived at the Elm Street house an hour later, with Mama sitting in the backseat like a child. She had her arms folded tight and her mouth was poked out. I couldn't see her feet, but I'd bet they were kicking.

Miss Tavy looked … not happy exactly, but proud. Concern for Mama was written on her face. She knew she had done the right thing: she had gotten an old friend home safely.

I was so happy to see them, I cried. Just for a few seconds, though. I dried my tears quickly before anyone saw them. After I helped Mama out of the Seville's cavernous backseat, I invited Miss Tavy in for coffee.

Mama tapped me hard on the shoulder. "Do you know who you've invited in?"

"Yes ma'am. Miss Tavy."

"Octavia Love," Mama said. "A woman who scandalized my name."

Miss Tavy said, "Please don't, Claudette," as Mama rushed inside.

As soon as we got in the house, Miss Tavy said, "I made an honest mistake, Claudette. I've tried to make amends."

"How?" Mama demanded, hanging up her coat. "By standing up in church and confessing before the Lord that you were wrong? By crawling up those steps out there and asking me to forget your horrible words, your angry face? Exactly how, Octavia, have you tried to make amends?" Not waiting for an answer, Mama sat down and yanked off her boots.

Miss Tavy turned to me. "I'd better go," she said, flustered. "I don't want to make matters worse."

Mama jumped in front of her. "You can't make matters worse. You made matters as bad as they get when you accused me of doing the lowest thing a woman can do to a woman friend: try to take her husband."

My mind raced. "Did that really happen?" I asked.

"I was wrong," Miss Tavy whispered.

"Dead wrong," Mama shouted, her skin drawn so tight across her forehead it looked like it might split.

I looked at Miss Tavy. "You thought Mama wanted Mr. Love?"

"I'm not proud," she said, dropping her head.

"You were," Mama said, trying to drive it lower. "Wrong and proud. All my life I've wanted only what was mine. Lester Moon, who was mine, proved to be too much. I couldn't serve him and God at the same time. Something had to give. Lester gave. He saw the truth before I did. He got out of the way so I could see it. He left me a space. A window. I saw the truth. I'm a one-man woman. My only man is Jesus.

"I didn't come to Eloise to snag a man. Another woman's man at that. In you, Octavia, I thought had found a friend who would be to me what my sister Shirley had been. A sister and a true friend. I was mistaken."

"I was your friend," Miss Tavy said. "I still am."

Mama spoke with a clenched jaw. "A friend lifts you up with the truth. She doesn't tear you down with a lie."

Miss Tavy's head shot up. She put her hand over her heart. "God is my witness. I didn't know it to be a lie at the time."

Mama paced back and forth like an attorney at trial. "Lester Moon was the finest man in West Kentucky. I didn't want Howard. And Howard wasn't any more interested in me than I was in him. That girl who moved down here from Kankakee. Remember her?"

Miss Tavy sank into a chair.

"Do you remember her?" Mama yelled down at her. "Course you do. Ruby. Big legs and short skirts. Couldn't spell, let alone type. No work history. Howard hired her on the spot. Why? You should have asked yourself that question, Octavia."

Miss Tavy looked at the floor. "I trusted my husband. I didn't tell him how to run his business."

"And you shouldn't have speculated about how I ran mine," Mama said, squatting, so Miss Tavy couldn't help but look at her. "I gave Howard the rent. And then the house payment. The only thing he ever slipped to me was the deed to this house."

"I know that," Miss Tavy said, raising her head. "Now."

Mama said, "You should have known it then."

I said, "Well, I'm glad it's finally cleared up."

Mama said, "Be quiet, Mattie."

Miss Tavy stood. She and Mama stood hurt-face to hurt-face. "The Bible says 'Thou shall not covet thy neighbor's ass nor his oxen,'" Mama said, walking over and addressing me like I was a judge on a bench (one not allowed to speak). "She rebuked me," she said. "Scorned me. And scandalized my name."

"No," Miss Tavy said. "No. We had a misunderstanding, but it never left my house. My words never went farther than your ears."

Mama snorted. "The folks at Sabbathani got it somewhere. They whispered behind my back. Clay Franklin egged them on from the pulpit with parables and inside jokes. You threw me off balance. Soon as you saw me slip, you did everything you could to hastened the slide."

Miss Tavy grabbed her purse. "Oh, good grief, Claudette," she said. "Nothing like that happened. Except in your mind."

Mama's eyes got wide. She snatched Miss Tavy's purse and threw it back on the table. "Are you calling me crazy?"

"I'm saying I spoke to you in error, but in confidence," Miss Tavy said. "Gleghorn came by the house selling ball tickets and he told me the truth about Howard's one indiscretion. I knew it was the truth because Gleghorn doesn't lie."

Mama said, "Neither do I."

Miss Tavy got her purse again, took out a handkerchief and dabbed at the corners of her eyes. "I had hoped we could work this out today. I hoped we could go back to being friends, after all these years."

"Because you cry? Because you sashayed into the jailhouse and carted me off like a poor relation, which I am not and never was? We may have been friends once," Mama said. "Now we are nothing at all." She gathered up her umbrella and boots and left the room.

I talked Miss Tavy into staying long enough to drink a cup of coffee and have some cake. She drained her cup, but she ate only a half slice of pound cake, whereas she normally would have eaten two thick portions. When she left the house, she moved slowly like she had lost a great battle. She couldn't have known that her opponent was even more devastated than she was.

In one day, Mama had lost her fresh-air ministry and she had revisited the sorrow of a once treasured friend's betrayal. She was sad all the way to the bone. That evening, she relinquished her singing voice; she gave it up again and hummed until dinner was ready. After the meal, she sat still in her rocking chair while I ran her bath.

I poured lavender salts into the water and helped Mama into the tub. Since taking up roadside preaching, she had pushed herself hard. She was weak; she was tired. Holding her arm, I felt loose skin and, beneath that, fragile bone. Stepping into the tub, she leaned on me as I had leaned on her when I was a child. I held her tight so she wouldn't slip. "I wasn't always this way," she said, easing down into the water. "Remember that, Mattie. I wasn't always this way."

"Don't worry."

"I owe you an apology."

"No you don't. Just enjoy your bath. Have a nice long soak"

"I let you down."

"No, Mama. You didn't."

"People know when they've done wrong, Mattie. Octavia knew today. I know. Even if we don't admit it, we know."

"You have nothing to apologize for."

"Plenty. You had to be your own mother and father. You had to take care of me, when it should have been the other way around. I was nervous and worried. Evil sometimes. Do one thing for me."

"Yes ma'am?"

"Remember. I was better than this, once. I kept moving farther and farther away. I lost myself."

"You couldn't help it, Mama. Don't worry about what you couldn't help."

"When I could have, I didn't. I wouldn't listen to Lester. He got tired of shouting and left me a window. I look out every day. I only see Lester when I dream, but I see my Jesus all the time. No matter where I am, no matter how far out I go, I look out my window and see Him and He sees me."

Mama believed that God's eye was on her, as well as on the sparrow; her belief never wavered. It had, in fact, gotten stronger through the years, multiplied.

I put a clean towel on the chair. "Call me when you finish your bath," I said. "I'll help you out of the tub."

"You've done enough, Mattie."

"No trouble."

"A whole lot. But trouble don't last always."

I went to the door. "Call me when you're ready to get out."

I had washed the dishes and wiped off the stove before I realized that there were no sounds coming from the bathroom. I went to the bathroom door and knocked. There was no answer. I knocked again.

Silence.

I opened the door and saw Mama lying beneath the water. Her feet, higher than her head, rested against the back of the tub. Her hair covered her face. She was gone.

# CHAPTER SIXTEEN

During her lifetime, Mama had been preoccupied with right and wrong. Obsessed with the straight and narrow. I don't believe she considered suicide to be a sin—not an unforgivable one anyway. She moved far away from her temporary home in Kentucky and took a shortcut in Illinois, merely choosing the quickest way to get to Him.

We had a quiet service at the funeral home. I asked Reverend Russell Glen from Shiloh Baptist to officiate. To my surprise, and his credit, Reverend Franklin attended the funeral as an honored guest of the family even though he had not been asked to speak. He and Jacob sat with Suzanne, Diego, and me, which no one thought unusual. Death was an integral part of the Franklin family business. They were always around it. Every few months a series of funerals were held in Eloise. If one person died on Monday, the tight-knit community went on high alert because two other deaths were likely to follow before the week ended.

Had Reverend Franklin been asked to speak, he would have told us what he said at every funeral he presided over: that a train was coming down the track, an equal opportunity train, coming for each one of us, rich and poor, black and white, young and old. A train, Church.

Reverend Franklin, an elder in a former railroad town, a minister for forty years in one church and the voice of his community, stayed in his seat. He didn't issue the warning about a train, but then again, he didn't have to. We heard it rumbling down the track.

Counting Mama, eleven people attended the burial service. Sherry came. She and Theda had a mini-wrestling match to see which one would hold Diego while

I said a prayer and placed a white rose on Mama's casket. Sherry prevailed; she was more motivated. The only white person there, she needed someone to hold onto. Theda had Lilly.

Lilly came solely as a favor to Theda. Her heart wasn't in it. As soon as the dirt fell from Reverend Glen's hand onto Mama's casket, Lilly stepped out of the circle of mourners and headed toward her red BMW. "I've got to get home and take off these black clothes, Country," she said, patting my shoulder as she rushed past. "Girl, I look dead."

Theda came forward with tears in her eyes. Theda knew how hard it was to say good-by to a mom. Six months before, she had buried her own mother, an under-appreciated black woman who could multi-task something fierce, do everything that needed to be done. "Thank you for coming," I said, hugging my friend tight.

She had come to and for me so many times. She'd come the day Suzanne was born. Despite Lilly's teasing, the talented midwife's daughter had helped me clean and dress my first baby, and then she'd helped me put my own mother, who was frayed around all her edges, to bed.

She'd come one monsoon season, when water stood in the street for an entire week. Every evening before bedtime she helped me reassure Mama that the water wouldn't rise more overnight while we were sleeping and that, in fact, slowly but surely, it would run off. Dry out.

She'd come the morning Diego climbed onto his teddy bear, hurled himself over the side of his playpen, and landed on his head. I saw him going, but I couldn't get to him in time to break his fall. Like Aunt Shirley racing to Mama before the pigs could get to her, I moved as fast as I could, but by the time I traveled the short distance from the kitchen to the dining room, Diego was already howling. I picked him up, kissed him and checked his eyes, his head, and his limbs. I calmed Diego down. Then Theda came and calmed me down.

Somebody had to.

So many times, Theda had come. "Don't mention it," she said, running to get to the sporty red car before it left without her.

Someone does it every hour of every day, but to leave a loved one sealed up in a box alone at a cemetery is still an act of bravery. The casket waits politely for us to leave, before it does its vanishing act. Our necessary walk away feels like a betrayal.

Our choices are limited, though. We have only two. We either move along, walk away with the walking wounded without calling any undue attention to ourselves, or we fall out of line and join the ranks of the deranged, the unrestrained.

We can choose the latter, flail around, fall to the ground, pounding our fists until they are raw or raise our arms to the sky and beseech the silent, distant, heavens to spare our loved one, to raise her up, return her to us whole and casket-free with breath and blood flowing through her precious body. We can create a scene, blame fate, the way of the world, and be carted away by family or strangers.

Those are our choices. Most of us walk or ride away quietly and respectfully.

I rode away.

In the old style, I sat in the backseat with my children. Reverend Franklin and Jacob sat in the front. "Thank God it didn't rain," Reverend Franklin said, without irony.

I turned around to take a last look at Mama's final resting place. Something—someone—caught my eye. A woman had appeared out of nowhere. She stood by Mama's grave. We were too far away for me to see her face, but I saw that the woman was dressed in layers of silk.

The second peculiar thing, the thing that actually held my eye, was that when the cemetery workers advanced toward Mama, the stranger did not retreat.

The men worked around her.

The farther away Jacob's car traveled from the gravesite, the larger the stranger loomed. Her silk-clad form got bigger and bigger. She was an Amazon. As the wind rose, the stranger's clothing billowed and spread across the land and the sky. By the time we exited the cemetery grounds, she had blocked out the light.

That night Suzanne slept on the sofa. Jacob slept with Diego and me. After Jacob fell asleep, I lay awake and listened to him breathe.

Just breathe.

He was the first man to sleep under our roof in the state of Illinois. I thought about what Mama's reaction would have been. Then I did as she asked. I remembered her as she had been long before, back when she didn't hate or fear anyone else's good time. Back when she herself had laid nights in the arms of the finest, blackest man for miles around.

It is a warm summer evening. The sun is low in the sky. Mama walks toward the house to get something—supper or clothes or a bucket for water from the well—something always needed to be gotten.

Daddy calls to her. "Claude, wait." He asks her to stay in the back yard with us for a while, to listen to him play the harmonica. Mama squints her eyes, but her mouth is soft and she waits.

Daddy blows on his harmonica and then he says, "Mattie, show your Mama, Baby. Show her your dance."

He blows the mouth organ and I start moving my feet. "Look, Mama," I say. "Watch me dance."

I am three or four. I knock my young self out and shake my thing, even though I don't know that I have one. Mama's reaction falls somewhere between a laugh and a cry. She doesn't say that blowing a harmonica is a sin or that dancing is the first step toward eternal damnation, though. This is before. The way she was. Then.

She is more amused than aggravated and, if she blames my dancing on anything, she blames it on human nature, not the devil or his younger brother, Daddy. She doesn't encourage me by singing, clapping her hands, or patting her feet, but she doesn't make me stop, either. She stands right there and watches me dance.

Eventually Mama turned against lawn dancing, of course. She turned against harmonica playing, card games, drinking, gambling, Daddy, and, after the birth of my first child, she turned against me, too.

Lying in Jacob's arms, I forgave Mama. I remembered her as she had been: a slim, brown-skinned woman standing in the backyard as the sun went down. I saw her beautiful face etched with something between a laugh and a cry—sympathy maybe, probably not for the devil, but maybe for all of humankind. For a few minutes she acknowledges the need for self-expression. Celebration. Not just worship. I'm not sure what she thinks or feels, but her eyes are wide open and clear while a man in a hat plays a jazzed-up harmonica and a little girl dances like her life depends on it.

Five or six years later, when this same woman closed up her temporary home in Kentucky, her face became a death mask, her eyes glazed over, and her features became unequivocally set. Wearing white gloves and a funeral hat, she embarked on her long journey to her permanent home.

The girl accompanying her had tried, but could never forget the feel of the ground beneath her, the wind on her cheek, and the song in her heart as she danced for her parents. She will never forget either one of them.

The night of her burial, I remembered Mama as she had been.

She wouldn't have had it any other way.

Jacob's decision to go to Indianapolis the next week caught me off guard. There was no warning. Unlike Daddy, Jacob had not begun leaving before he left. He made up his mind the Friday after Mama's funeral; he left that Saturday. And he did not have to go.

He was offered an opportunity to serve as a minister-in-training at Freewill Baptist Church in Indianapolis. He accepted. I was skeptical. "A minister-in-training?"

"Yes," he said, eyes immediately going on the defensive.

"Isn't that what you are here? Haven't you been a minister-in-training your whole life? Aren't you Sabbathani's long-suffering unofficial minister-in-training?"

"Calm down," he said. "I don't get paid for what I do here. I have no contract with the church. That's why I go to work at Rockwell every day. Dad wants me to take over when the time comes. But I need to decide if ministering is what I want."

"In Indianapolis?"

"Somewhere. Freewill is giving me responsibilities I don't have here. I'll know if I've received the call."

"From Indiana?"

"From God. I don't want to be like Judas. I have to be sure He can count on me."

"What about Reverend Franklin? He counts on you to be here every Sunday."

"Dad understands. He encouraged me to go."

"Oh. And Diego. Has our son encouraged you to go?"

"I won't be gone long. Six months."

"That's an eternity in baby years."

"I'll come home often. Talk to him on the phone."

"That just leaves us, then. People in Indianapolis don't know about us. Is that why you're going, Jacob?"

"If I don't get my life together there won't be any us. At Freewill, folks won't confuse me with Dad. I won't confuse myself with him. They'll see me for who I am and let me know if I'm on the right track. I have to know."

Jacob was struggling—not with faith, which was bred in his bones, but with understanding his duty, his purpose in life. He had to believe he had been asked to preach by God, not merely by Reverend Franklin. If he had to leave Eloise to find his answer, the least I could do was wish him well. When he left early Saturday morning for Indiana, I stood on the sidewalk. Waving.

Diego, three months shy of his first birthday, was all eyes as he watched Jacob walk to the car. When he saw his daddy open the car and get in without him, he frowned. His lip trembled. "Don't cry," I said. "Wave bye-bye."

Diego opened his hand and closed it, solemnly, without tears. "That's it, Baby," I said, as Jacob turned the corner. "Bye-bye, Daddy."

I went back in the house, half-expecting Mama to be there. Suzanne had been picked up and taken away by Lamarr earlier in the day. Diego and I were alone. My bed was made up. It looked as if no man had ever slept there.

# CHAPTER SEVENTEEN

I had never planned to work in Sherry's home indefinitely, only until Diego was weaned. But when Mama left me funeral expenses and an old house in need of repair, I decided I needed to get a real job sooner than I'd planned—a job with better pay.

The week after Jacob left, I began checking the classifieds.

As soon as I found a few leads, I told Sherry about my change of plans. I didn't expect her to be thrilled, but I was unprepared for her reaction. She was crushed. She opened her checkbook and begged me not to go. "I'll lend you money," she said. "How much do you need?"

"I don't want to owe money. I want to earn some."

"You have earned it. I'll call it a loan for tax purposes, but you won't have to pay me back. We'll consider it a bonus for all you've done for me."

"I haven't done that much."

Sherry's eyes said that I had. She was lonely, with way too much time on her hands, but she was also truly afraid. Although she had never labeled her fear, we both knew its name: battery.

Sherry Ziegler was a battered woman.

When she and her husband had company and when they were out on the town, Mark fronted. He was affectionate and charming, but when he and Sherry were alone, he abused her. He verbally abused her—berated her about everything from the way she walked to the shade of blond she died her hair. Frequently, he hit her. Afterward, he was remorseful.

He ordered flowers.

If Sherry was too sore or too swollen to go the door to personally receive the bright peace offering, I signed the delivery slip and placed the explosion of color on the nightstand by her bed so she could see nature's positive side as soon as she felt strong enough to lift her head.

On mornings after bad nights, I closed the blinds, prepared ice, mixed drinks, and made excuses for Sherry over the telephone. I didn't do much more than that.

Sleeping with her enemy, Sherry was confused, disoriented. She exaggerated my role. "Stay a little longer," she implored. "Please."

"You think a change is going to come?"

"Nothing lasts forever."

Fantasies sure don't. I entertained a fantasy wherein I saved Sherry from Mark. In black and white, it went something like this:

Mark comes home from his high paying, soul-robbing job. He removes his tie, has a drink, and then he starts throwing his fists and his favorite obscenities around. Bitch. Cunt. The usual.

Sherry cowers. I burst into the room, throw down my dust cloth and overpower Mark. Subdued, he is deeply, profoundly ashamed.

He's sorry.

He stumbles to a chair, sinks down low. Lower. Lowest. He wonders how he got so crazy. "How did I get so crazy?" he asks the ceiling. The ceiling doesn't say shit. The whole room stays out of it.

Mark picks up the phone and calls the florist. I, the avenger, rush Sherry to the emergency room and rush her back home again. I feed her soup through a straw.

This heroic fantasy, however, was always short lived. A second picture became superimposed. This one was in color. It went something like this:

I throw down my cleaning rags and intervene, as before, but this time Mark turns on me with a fury that surprises both of us. He beats the hell out of me. "It's my house," he yells, his voice suddenly a boom box. "Sherry's my woman. I bought her when she was seventeen. She was a carhop! Trash then. Trash now. Who the hell do you think you are, anyway, with your uppity black ass?"

Lying on the floor, bleeding, I look over at Sherry and slowly extend my hand toward hers. I expect us to clasp hands in a proud show of sisterhood before the credits roll, but she uses her hands to push her battered self off the floor. She steps over me. Then she fluffs up her hair. She flips it from side to side, forward and back, until she gets dizzy. And then she stops. Stock still, she stands by her maniac.

In real life, I am no heroine. Sherry stayed with Mark. I had to go. I gave her two weeks notice and floors that shone like diamonds.

I planned to spend a few days cleaning Mama's room from top to bottom before reporting to my new job. I wanted to surprise Suzanne with something she really wanted: a room of her own. At first I was hesitant to go into the room, but I reminded myself that the task had to be done. I got my cleaning supplies from the kitchen cabinet, went to Mama's old room and opened the door.

I was surprised by the noise in the room. There was shouting and there were sobs. My first instinct was to turn and run, but I was determined not to let the room get the best of me.

I opened the windows and got to work. I hummed. Mama had hummed for years in that room. Perhaps on some level, I believed that my humming would comfort and soothe the wayward spirits raging throughout the room.

I was wrong. The shrieks and the moans raged on. I launched into some off-key singing to scare them away, but my yelping had no effect. Neither did whistling. I gave up.

When I returned to my room, Mirror looked straight at me. "What are you going to do?" she asked.

"Give it time."

"It's been over two months."

"Mama didn't take it with her. The room is still thick with woe. Time heals."

"If you ask me …"

"I didn't."

"Space is never given, Mattie. You have to make it."

"That room is a sea. If I set one foot in it, I'll drown."

"Control your life and your house, or it'll control you."

When she was right she was insufferable.

I had wanted a real job. The one I got was as real as they come. It was with the electricity company. I had to punch a card going in and punch it again on my way out. I got exactly thirty minutes for lunch and two mean ten-minute breaks. I couldn't be late for work, or, for that matter, early. We worked in shifts. One worker popped up and another sat down before the seat got cold. We responded to complaints and filled orders for corrective actions. We apologized to disgruntled customers.

And we were watched.

Supervisors were Sergeant Culver Clones. They walked a beat; they didn't want any trouble, but they expected some. Strolling back and forth behind us, they stayed as close to our chairs as they could without actually bumping into them. They weren't issued guns, but their eyes were bullets. They kept them trained on us.

At Sherry's, I'd had a bit of variety. I made her a bloody mary one day, a daiquiri the next. I'd type a sentence one week. The next week I might have a whole paragraph to edit.

The real job had a strictly-adhered-to routine and no variations. Diversity was frowned upon, but quotas had to be met. Logs and spreadsheets were required daily. Stress was applied. There was not a drop of liquor in sight.

The worst thing about my real job was that I couldn't bring Diego with me. He had to go to a day care center, where every other child had a runny nose—every other child—and brand new teeth that were used both to attack and defend.

I ran to the center at the end of my official workday and checked my son's face, arms and back for wear and tear. Then I grabbed his stuff, thanked the underpaid staff, and rushed home to my second job.

Suzanne always beat me. Before I arrived, she entered a silent house, completed her homework, and did her chores. She folded clothes, dusted furniture and set the table. A miniature woman, she performed the drudgery females have done forever and ever.

Amen.

My take-home pay was a bi-weekly disappointment. I never got used to it. My new employer, in cahoots with the government, withheld taxes Sherry didn't even know existed. Still, with the third they left me, I fixed the house up, put a new roof over our heads, and made a down payment on a new furnace.

Lamarr was not impressed.

One hot day in June, he showed up at my door. Rotelle clung to his arm. They brushed past me, took their seats and Lamarr announced that they wanted Suzanne to live with them full time.

While he listed his demands, I focused on the heat and humidity. I raised windows as high as they would go, but the air was afraid to come inside. It had been mugged.

I wondered how far back an air conditioner would set me. Too far, I decided. Fall would come and the temperatures would plummet. I'd still be paying for the furnace and someday, before the worst of winter arrived, I'd want to buy a used car. A car, even a clunker, would be a more practical purchase than an air conditioner.

We'd get through three months of sweltering heat, if we put our minds to it. We always had. All we had to do was stay hydrated. And not move too quickly. And when we went outside we would wear lightweight clothes. Light colored, also. And we shouldn't go outside at midday. Fools knew that.

"Fool, did you hear anything we said?" Lamarr shouted.

"Every word," I said, picking up a church fan. "Please. Don't be so rude. Finish."

I stared at him. His lips weren't moving. Oops. Wrong one. Rotelle had the floor.

"Suzy would be better off with us," she said. "She'll soon be a young lady. Go on a first date."

Lamarr shot his wife a look as old as marriage; it said *I'll handle this, wife.*

"You have too much on your plate, Mattie," he said. "A new job. A baby. Except for the afternoons when she does volunteer work, Rotelle is free to devote all her time to our children."

"And I've always wanted a girl," Rotelle said, quickly, when he took a breath.

He patted Rotelle's hand and went on. "Suzy can live with us during the week and visit you every other weekend. We'll take the arrangement we have now and switch it around."

I put my fan down. I was working harder than it was anyway. "Just like that? Disrupt her schedule and her life?"

"Kids are mobile these days. They get used to going back and forth. It'll work."

"Suzanne is not a wind-up toy. You're not going to set her spinning. And she's not the fulfillment of your wife's wish, either."

"Dammit, Mattie. We can give Suzy the things you can't."

"She doesn't need a lot of things. She's not superficial. Besides, she's a fighter. She'll get everything she needs in good time."

"I don't want her to have to fight for anything," he yelled.

Seeing his veins pop, Rotelle put her hand on his shoulder. He flung her hand away and glared at me. "We can give Suzy security. Stability. Sanity."

In that second, I made up my mind to go to Sears first thing the next morning. The payments for the air conditioner would stretch the spending budget to

the breaking point, but better the budget than the last nerve Lamarr was stomp-
ing on.

"Pointless," he said, pulled Rotelle to her feet. "She's not even listening to us."

I followed them onto the porch, not to be polite, but in search of air.

Rotelle looked back over her shoulder. "A girl needs her father," she said.
"Believe me. I know that for sure."

Lamarr reached back and yanked her down from the porch as if what I had
was catching.

"Don't say anything else," he said. "There's no reasoning with the unreason-
able. Suzy will be better off with us and that's that."

"She'd be better off dead," I said, lifting my skirt so that the timid air could
hide between my legs. I hadn't meant that, of course. I was just angry (and
heat-stricken), but seeing Lamarr and Rotelle's eyes go wide at the same time,
hers as pale as a cat's, his dark and deep set—both shocked—made me laugh out
loud.

"This shit's not funny," Lamarr hollered. "Don't think I won't sue your crazy
ass."

Rotelle broke away from him and had her say. "And if we went to court, who
do you think would win?"

They turned away and marched down the sidewalk with their backs straight,
like soldiers. They looked disciplined, boot camped trained, but their maneuvers
didn't scare me.

Six months prior, Lamarr had been pretending he didn't know whose child
Suzanne was, and now, all of sudden, he was the perfect parent, someone
Suzanne should live with on a full-time basis?

I didn't think so.

Judges were obligated to be judicious. They didn't rip children from their
mother's arms, unless the mothers had done something terribly wrong, and I
hadn't. I wouldn't.

Determined to show that I was the perfect mom, I planned to give Lamarr and
Rotelle a sly Claire Huxtable smile, but instead I opened my mouth and
screeched, "Don't come for Suzanne this Saturday. Or next. Don't ever come
back here."

Lamarr opened the door of the Jeep for his bride. He waited until she got her
spindly legs inside, and then he walked back toward me. The whole time he kept
his eyes dead on me like he was trying to scare somebody.

He put his hands on his hips. "Do you know who my lawyer is?"

"Who? Rotelle?"

"Mark Ziegler. The best lawyer in southern Illinois. You won't stand a chance. Mark will mop the floor with your nappy head. That's a concept you understand, isn't it, mopping the floor?"

"There's more shame in Mark's and your work than there is in mine. I didn't do any harm."

"You are now. You're trying to keep my daughter away from me."

"You can see Suzanne as often as she likes. But she's not living with you and Rotor Rooter."

He pointed at me. "That's it. Right there. Rotelle is your problem, isn't she?"

"Actually, she's yours."

"You're jealous of her."

His words gave me wings. I flew down off the porch with eyes as hard as his; scarier, I hoped. "Why would I be jealous of Rotelle?"

"She doesn't have to work, for one thing. I take good care of her. She has long hair, light skin, light eyes, and you're as jealous as you can be. Admit it."

"You've confused your European beauty standards and value system with mine."

"See? You're mad because Rotelle looks white."

"She looks white because she is white. For the most part."

He waved his hands in the air. "Let's just leave my wife out of this."

"You brought her into it when you brought her into my house. When you brought her into town, come think of it."

He shook his head and turned to go. "I'll see you in court."

"Lamarr," I sang out. "Mark can't represent you."

He stopped, but he spoke without turning around. "He's my lawyer. Why can't he represent me?"

"Conflict of interest," I said, running around so I could see his face when the truth sunk in. "I worked for the man. I mopped his floors. Remember?"

He smirked. "You worked for his wife."

"What's the difference?"

"Big Difference. Sherry doesn't count. She never has."

He hopped into his Jeep, like a modern day warrior with chrome wheels and a sidekick, and sped off.

I would have called my own lawyer, if I'd had one. Since I didn't, I went inside, got an ice cube from the refrigerator and rubbed cold water over my face and breasts. Then I called out for Suzanne.

I barely recognized her when she came into the living room. She was wearing a glove, a mask, a helmet, and kneepads, valued gifts from Rotelle's ball-crazy boys.

"I heard you and Dad," she muttered, through her mask.

"Nothing for you to worry about."

"Okay. I'm going outside."

"Wait a minute. We need to talk. Here's what I want to know. Do you like going to your dad's house?"

She nodded her enhanced head. "We do stuff and go places."

"What would you say if they asked you to live with them?"

She removed her mask. "Cool."

I stood up.

She took a step back. "If you and Diego came, too. They have a big house. We'd each have our own room. Rotelle has a maid."

"We aren't going anywhere," I said, moving toward her. "This is our home. Temporary though it may be. I can't believe you'd want to live with those people, under any circumstances."

"I guess not," she said, but she looked cornered.

It was an unfair fight. I let her off the ropes. I sat down, and picked up my useless fan. She got her ball and went outside to play with people her own size.

The sun came up the next morning and Lamarr rolled right back around. He was less angry, but just as insistent.

"I'm going to Sears," I hissed, trying to close the door, but he pushed his way in.

"Just a second," he said, taking his place on the sofa. "I thought about this all night. You never got over me."

"Excuse me?"

"Yes. What should have been a schoolgirl crush, a learning experience, if you will, turned into a life-long obsession," he said. He held his right hand up in a fist. Then he opened his hand slowly. "Let me go. That's all you have to do. Let go. Find yourself another man."

He was amazing. I held onto the pole lamp for support. "Have you forgotten my baby's father?" I asked.

He shrugged. "If you were really into the preacher's son, you wouldn't use Suzy against me," he said. "You wouldn't have the need."

"Unbelievable. You didn't know who fathered Suzanne for seven years, but you knew who fathered Diego before I did?"

"Let's stick to the point. Your father left you when you were a little older than Suzy, right?"

"I was a fool to tell you anything."

"Baby, you couldn't shut up. It was Kentucky this and Kentucky that."

"All lies. I was born and raised in Green Bay, Wisconsin. No, in Canada, by bears. I rode huskies on ice. I caught fish with my teeth. Get out. I'm going to buy an air conditioner."

"I was your first man," he said, ignoring my request. "But you took me way too seriously, Mattie. At sixteen, you latched onto me and never let go."

"Latched?"

"Don't blame me because your father left you."

I sat next to him to keep from falling. "He had to go," I mumbled. "Daddy said he would remember me exactly as I was."

"Maybe he did. Maybe he remembered you for the rest of his days, but I'm not him. I want to be in Suzy's present life. I won't settle for faded memories."

He slid toward me. Our knees touched for the first time in years. "Do you want Suzy to spend her whole life clinging to a dream?" he asked. "Do you want her to be stupid about the first man who gives her some attention? I know I over-whelmed you and it is hard for you to let go."

He put his hand on my knee. I jerked away. "You were never all that to me, Lamarr."

"I still am," he said. "You love too hard. Way too hard. Look in your mirror. It'll tell you the truth."

I jumped up and ran to the rocking chair and set off for parts unknown. "Fuck you."

"You see?" he asked. "Now, do you see what I mean?" He stood and stretched like a cougar. "When you're eighty, you'll be rocking in a chair at a nursing home. The other old women will wonder what you're always grinning about. It'll still be me, Mattie. After all those years. It'll still be me."

"Go to hell."

He sauntered to the door. "You were smart, once," he said. "Don't play dumb, now. Sex is part of life. It's a good part, but when it's over, we have to move on. We can't let it drive us crazy."

He opened the door and peered at the sky. "Rain's coming," he said.

I said, "I hope it floods."

Lamarr had finally scared me. He believed that I still cared about him and, if I did, after he had turned his back on me when I was at my most vulnerable, I was as crazy as he thought I was. More important, if I had a soft spot in my heart, buried beneath years of shame and layers of contempt for that man, I couldn't afford to ignore it. Ignored, the spot could grow.

I read in a book once that the writer, Gertrude Stein, upon returning to her childhood home in Oakland, California, walked around the old neighborhood and declared that she found no "there" there. The cherished place she remembered was long gone.

For Lamarr and me there had never been any "there" there. When I was a teenager, looking at the emptiness, the void, I swooned. I admit that I nearly fell in, but latched on? No way. How could I have latched on when there was nothing there? My hands were always empty, my feet in the air.

And I knew it.

Every woman knows when she's cupping absolutely nothing in her own two hands. Who would know better than she?

Granted, nobody did the nothing better than Lamarr. He was brilliant. Mr. Empty had offered me plenty of nothing and I had been glad to get it. We were both glad. He never said he loved me. I loved enough for both of us. I clasped that emptiness to my breast and filled in all the spaces.

I was an assembly worker, bent over a conveyor belt, shaping my own fantasy world. I worked for free. I never missed a day. My lies to myself came fast and furiously. I scooped them up and believed them. I ran around in circles, chasing a phantom.

At night I pulled Mr. Empty in through my bedroom window and sat on his lap. I lay down with him, but he was never there. I was always alone. What I thought was love was masochism: a quack doctoring her own self-inflicted wounds.

Scary.

Lamarr was right. I had latched on, like a quick-handed magician, to absolutely nothing. He had made me hurt so good that I had gone on hurting for years. I thought I had stopped when I became involved with Jacob, but had I? Had I ever let go of Lamarr?

Of course I had. I loved Jacob. Why, then, so many questions?

How could Lamarr get to me so easily? Why did I scream at him from the edge of the porch? Why was I numb after he left? Most important, would Suzanne be spared my fate? Would getting to know her father better, having a close relationship with him as she matured, keep her from "latching on" to a man who was on his way to Chicago or Indianapolis or anyplace as long as it was away from her? Would some of Lamarr's over-confidence rub off on Suzanne and help her grow up strong and whole, with no soft spots threatening to spread in ten, twenty years down the road?

With Lamarr in her life, would Suzanne, during her teenage years, keep both her bedroom window and her legs closed? If she walked by a tall handsome boy who had a high butt would his skillful ball handling make her imagine him turning her this way and that, or would she stay focused on her own goals, her own talent? Would she keep walking down the sidewalk and walk on to a bright future, or would she stumble? Would she lose her heart, her virginity, and her scholarship all in one month?

Would she latch on?

I didn't have the answers, but I agreed to let Suzanne spend each weekend with Lamarr and his ready-made family.

Just in case.

With Suzanne out of the house every weekend, Diego and I were lonely. Jacob called every Sunday as soon as church let out in Indianapolis. His calls were welcome, indeed, but they weren't stopgaps. Things kept moving in that house; they kept shifting.

Each week, while I talked to Jacob, I kept my eyes on the walls. They had closed in another quarter of an inch. Space was limited. So was time. I didn't have much.

Lamarr was greedy. Despite extra time with Suzanne, he kept up his custody threat. To earn extra money, in case there was a lawsuit, I took a second job with Theda. She had started her own catering business, T. M. Delights.

Theda would have liked to bring her life partner into the business, but that was not an option. Lilly sold Mary Kaye cosmetics and Tupperware dishes when she felt like it and she modeled twice a year, in the Eloise Spring Fashion Bazaar and in the Fall Extravaganza, and she was not going to do one more thing. Not one more. She certainly wasn't about to get the smell of garlic on, or flour caked beneath, her carefully manicured nails.

Johnny, Lilly's brother, helped Theda out whenever he could, but he didn't have a lot of time. Having learned to cook as a child back in Kentucky, I agreed to give it a try.

My specialties were basic foods: mashed potatoes, macaroni and cheese, greens, and roast chicken. I was also pretty good with pie: cherry, pecan, sweet potato, and lemon meringue. But when it came to preparing fancy appetizers and foreign-sounding dishes unheard of in western Kentucky when I lived there, I followed Theda's lead.

I earned the extra money I needed, but I also got more than I bargained for: valuable information about Lamarr's trophy wife. I came upon it by accident.

Growing up, I often wondered why blue eyes meant so much to some people. They are automatically embellished, described as big, clear, beautiful, piercing, ice, sparkling, soft and/or baby blue, even if they are none of those things. Every day someone swoons in print or on television about someone's blue eyes. Brown, gray, and even green eyes are described more simply, if commented on at all. Only blue eyes are breathlessly recalled.

I had asked Sherry her opinion about that. Watching her apply eye shadow and mascara to "bring out the blue" in her azure-blue eyes, I said, "What's up with blue eyes, anyway? Why are they so highly valued?"

She shrugged and brushed on another layer of mascara.

I shouldn't have distracted her. She was already ten minutes late for the annual lawyers' luncheon. She never intended to keep Mark waiting, but she did occasionally, and it infuriated him no end. If she didn't put a move on, there would be hell to pay. Hurry up, sister, is what I should have said. You don't want to have to pick yourself up off the floor again tonight, do you? "Blue eyes are special because they are rare," she said, as she dusted her face with powder two shades darker than her skin to hide a bruise. "Like blond hair. Natural blond."

Later that day, while bathing Diego, I realized why blue eyes mean so much to so many: because we live on a blue planet. When some human beings look up and see blue splashed across a face, they probably feel uplifted. They see reflections of themselves, not as members of a land-locked tribe, but rather a people with unlimited possibility, people who can navigate the waters, float on them, and, if necessary, swim beneath them without drowning.

Even Sherry, who, the night before, had bled on her antique vanity table and tasted the fibers of her own pink carpet as she crawled down her marble staircase to the first floor trying to protect her kidneys from the brunt of her husband's imported leather shoes, even she could stand up straight amid freshly delivered flowers and smile wanly, secure in the knowledge that she had something rare, something special, to bestow on the lawyers and their wives (and the three husbands) at the luncheon when she finally arrived: eyes the color of the Caribbean Sea.

"That's it, Diego," I said. "They are mad about the water because it reflects the blue sky above us."

He splashed the colorless water. Then he laughed and reached for the soapsuds sliding down his dark brown arm.

In Kentucky I knew a woman who had one blue eye. Martina Scott had been poked in her right eye with a fire poker when she was a child. Martina had brown skin, black hair and a graceful neck, but she had mismatched-eyes: one brown, the other blue.

Eloise is a town with all kinds of black folk. We have all shades: we have light-skinned black people who are extremely proud of the complexion handed down to them by the white people they swear they hate; we have dark-skinned people whose white and Indian ancestors bequeathed them thin lips and wavy hair, but otherwise sit quietly on distant branches of the family tree without making a fuss; we have medium brown-skinned people who have dark brown, gold flecked, even cat-gray eyes. But only one of us has blue eyes. Her name is Rotelle.

Rotelle Robinson's blue irises are so light they look like they might disappear. Sometimes she looks otherworldly, as if she is getting ready to transform, to turn into someone (or something) that might bite. Turns out, she does bite.

Theda and I had knocked ourselves out with the appetizers. Despite the air-conditioning, I was wilting in the heat, so I took a break before we began the main course.

Cool air beckoned from the patio. I followed eagerly. Passing a sitting room, I heard two men, one them the owner of the house, discussing a black woman with sexy blue eyes. I stopped. Had I heard him correctly?

"Yes, indeed," the middleman said, to his guest. "Here's her number. She's available for two hours two days a week: Tuesday and Thursdays. Those are the only times she'll talk to you."

"She does more than talk, I hope," said the Buyer.

"And does it well. But she talks first. Introduces herself. Gets you to unwind. Finds out what you need. She plays rough. As I recall, you like that. Spankings. Biting, if you are a bad boy."

"Oh, I'm a very bad boy. Rotelle is an unusual name."

"She's an unusual woman. Nice breasts. Real. A tight ass. She's your type."

"Everybody's type."

"Call her."

"I will. Where did you find her?"

"You remember Lamarr Robinson? Played basketball?"

"Right. We all thought he'd go pro."

"Real estate, now. Rotelle is his wife."

"No shit? Is he in on this?"

"No way. He parades her around town like she's the Queen of Sheba. They make a great looking couple. If she's as diligent at home as she is on her job, he's probably one happy clueless homeboy." They laughed. Clicked their glasses.

The night air felt cool against my skin, but the image of Rotelle providing kinky sexual release to men who laughed at her (and her husband) behind her back while drinking expensive champagne and smoking smelly cigars made me hot under my starched collar. How long had this been going on and what the hell was it anyway? Lamarr had accused me of being jealous, of wanting revenge.

Well, what was Rotelle after?

Confused and angry, I returned to the kitchen and grabbed a knife. I chopped mushrooms, onions, and green peppers into hundreds of pieces. I put plum tomatoes on a cutting board and sliced with precision.

Theda came up to me. "Part of our deal, lady, is that you keep me company while we feed these assholes. Why so quiet?"

I looked at her. "Have you ever wished something bad would happen to some-body and then felt awful when it did?"

"Not really. I usually think, Serves them right. Who did you wish bad luck on and what happened to her?"

"Him. It's happening to him and he doesn't know."

I could have trusted Theda with what I had overheard. She would have kept it to herself, but I decided not to say anything. I didn't know if I would ever say anything. I had always believed that making prostitution a crime only harmed the women and children in the profession by subjecting them to thugs, drugs, and degradation. So what was I going to do now, turn on a dime, make a citizen's arrest, and turn Rotelle over to Drill Sergeant Culver? Or worse, run and tell Lamarr? To my surprise, I realized that I didn't want to hurt anyone, not even Lamarr. Informing him of his wife's extramarital activities might have saved him some future embarrassment, but at a high cost and other people could get burned in the crossfire. I shut my mouth and sliced avocadoes. Then I looked around to see what else needed to be cut.

When I arrived home that night, Rotelle was on the floor playing cards with the kids. Her sons, Taylor and Micah, had indeed become Suzanne's brothers. A woman of many talents, Rotelle was a pretty good babysitter. Mary Poppins after a month in the sun. She kept everybody happy and getting along.

"You're late," she said, studying her hand.

"Sorry. We had an overflow crowd. Last minute special orders from the rich and spoiled."

"You and Theda have to name your hours," she said. "When their time is up, it's up. You're businesswomen. It's a seller's market."

"That depends on what's being sold. Theda and I get paid by the job, not by the hour."

She didn't offer any additional working girl tips, but when she turned her cards over, she revealed that, as usual, she had won the game.

I scooped Diego up from his playpen, hugged him and checked his diaper. He was good, so I set him on the floor and watched him crawl toward the action. "Finally!" his fast moving knees said. "I can't walk and I can't talk, but I'll be damned if I'm not going to play me a game of cards."

When he got to Suzanne, he reached for her Queen of Hearts. She slid her card under her hip and Diego came up with nothing but air. He sat back on his padded bottom. Thwarted again. His big sister grabbed his chubby hands and forced him to settle for another tired game of pat a cake.

Suzanne said, "Mom, I'm spending the night at Dad's house." She turned to Rotelle. "We can go now."

In addition to Lamarr and Rotelle and her boys, Suzanne was also in love with Lamarr's parents. Although she was darker than any official Robinson, darker than any child the Robinsons would have freely chosen, she had won the entire family over. In true Eloise style, the Robinson family included twenty-five cousins and forty cousins' cousins and their hangers-on.

Suzanne was thrilled to have a full set of stable-minded grandparents and an extended family. I understood her wanting to round out our modest circle of three. When I was her age, I so wanted Daddy to stay with Mama and me (I had felt him leaving) and for them to make a baby brother for me to love. I understood why she wanted to spend so much time at her father's house, but it worried me, too. It played into his hands.

"Give me a hug, young lady," I said, holding my arms out. "Then we'll discuss whether you can or cannot go."

She gave me a perfunctory embrace, broke away quickly and began gathering up her things. "Rotelle rented two movies. I'm dying to see them and Dad's going to make strawberry ice cream."

She and Rotelle had their eyes on me. They wanted the same thing: to spend time together. Rotelle (the part-time sex worker) had seemed cold, distant, when we first met. Despite her polished presence and high maintenance, it had been as though a part of her was missing in action. Suzanne found the missing part: Rotelle's kindness. The golden girls connected. They lit each other up.

"Not tonight," I said, disappointing them both. "Friday and Saturday nights with your father. That's the deal."

"Rotelle?" Suzanne said. "Can't I, please?"

"Let's not make a scene in front of company," I said.

"Family," Rotelle said, hugging Suzanne.

Encouraged, Suzanne said, "What if I call Daddy?"

"Wouldn't make any difference," I said.

Looking as if she'd been slapped, Suzanne sat on the couch and pouted. Rotelle put away her cards, took her sons by the hand and left in a huff.

The next day Suzanne made me pay. She failed to come home at the time she was expected. I called Lamarr on his cell phone and he went looking for her. When he showed up at my door empty handed, he wasn't as worried as I was, but he waited with me. We sat on the porch, side by side in plastic chairs like a married couple, watching for our only child.

"I had hoped she was with you," I said, finally, hoping to talk down my rising fear. "She thinks of your place as a castle and Rotelle the resident goddess."

"The goddess went away for a few days," he said.

"Where to?"

"Don't know. Every now and then, she has to get away. She doesn't stay long."

"Maybe she is a goddess. She's worked a change in you."

"What are you talking about?"

"The new improved you."

"I'm the same old me."

"Not. You're flexible."

"I guess. She has to have her own thing."

"She wants what is hers?"

"Her own bank account, car, bathroom."

"My daughter."

"Rotelle loves Suzy like she was her own."

"Suzanne isn't, though."

"I know. So does Rotelle."

"Okay. Suzanne belongs to all of us now in a three-way split. Whether I like it or not."

"Now who's flexible? Rotelle didn't change me. I grew up. I was a kid when I got you pregnant. A man realizes he has something to lose. I don't want to lose Rotelle. So I guess I am flexible. I'm whatever I have to be."

Of all the people he could have talked to about his married love, he chose me. The irony could have knocked me off the porch; that and the realization that he really loved Rotelle, not her lack of color or her straight hair and (sometimes scary) light eyes, but the actual woman. Her essence. He loved all of her, even the part she kept hidden from him.

"You don't have to worry about losing her," I said. "When she's with you, she's where she wants to be. And you said it yourself. She doesn't stay away long."

"Still, I worry," he said. "Life is a bitch, isn't it?"

"I was just thinking that," I said.

Lamarr found Suzanne and Tiffany at the band shell listening to music. They were unharmed. I saw that for myself when they rode up, but I couldn't get rid of the uneasy feeling I'd had that my daughter was in danger.

"We didn't know what time it was, Mom," Suzanne said, talking fast as she climbed down from the Jeep. "We were getting ready to come home. Honest."

Tiffany said, "We knew better than to leave with those teenage boys, Mattie."

"Teenagers?" I yelled, looking at Suzanne and then Lamarr. Suzanne said, "Not yet. Wannabes. I told them not to mess with me. I know karate."

"Since when?"

"Dad showed me."

Lamarr said, "Nothing happened, Mattie. There's nothing to worry about."

I wanted to scream that every second of the day some woman somewhere is being hurt and humiliated because she is female. The ones inflicting the hurt can be any age, even pre-teen. Instead, looking at Suzanne and Tiffany's innocent eyes and brave faces, I said, "You have to be careful. Sometimes it's better to walk away than fight."

"That's what I told Suzanne," Tiffany said, giving Suzanne a sharp-eyed look.

Suzanne dropped her head and waited for part two of my lecture. I surprised her with a kiss. She hugged me tight and I gave silent thanks for the feel of her slight all-in-one-piece body pressed against mine. I also thanked her father for bringing her safely home.

Jacob came home, too, for the Fourth of July. We took the kids to see the fireworks at Foundation Park.

Suzanne was in cotton candy heaven. During her early years, she had made do without a father. Suddenly, in one year, she had two. In the same unselfish way she had shared Lamarr with Diego, she freely helped herself to Jacob's love and affection. Despite the women's liberation movement, Suzanne and I behaved as if Jacob were the sun in the sky. We revolved around him.

Diego, a self-respecting infant, remained the center of his universe. Even when his father came home, Diego's goals remained the same: to eat, sleep, and get hold of something to cram in his mouth—Suzanne's cotton candy, a blade of grass, his bear's stuffed feet. Anything would do.

Jacob was concerned that Diego had not begun walking. I explained that Diego was a human being with a large complex brain, not a colt or a calf. I assured him that our son was not going to take off walking (or running) early and have that be the zenith of his accomplishments, the only thing in life he ever did quickly and well. "There's no rush," I assured Jacob. "Albert Einstein reportedly didn't walk until the age of three. Our genius will walk when he's ready."

Jacob said, "I pray you're right."

I was.

The following week, when Jacob was back in Indianapolis learning the ropes of an official ministry, Diego took his first steps. Jacob missed that milestone. Suzanne missed it, too. She was at the Illinois State Fair with Lamarr and his brood. Lamarr's idea, evidently, of getting to know the arts.

Trapped in that house with walls that moved stealthily, a room on one side of the hall that wailed, and a mirror in a room on the other side that talked smack, I was Diego's one-parent cheering section.

I applauded his wobbly steps alone. I helped him up when he fell. I gave him the thumbs-up sign when he made it from the unstable rocking chair to the solid, yet soft, sofa.

While the walls crept, I sat by the bed and hummed in the dark until Diego fell asleep at night.

# PART TWO

# CHAPTER EIGHTEEN

People say I let myself go. They are mistaken.

As an example, I picked up the telephone one day and heard the sound of heartbreak at the other end of the line.

"What is it, Theda?" I asked. Her voice was thick. She hated what she was going to say so much that she could barely get the words out. She was choked up.

"It's Lilly," she managed to say.

"Oh my God. What happened?"

"Her brother was shot."

"No. Not Johnny. Is he going to be okay?"

"He died an hour ago at St. Mary's."

"Oh, shit."

Not Johnny. He couldn't be dead: the smile cut wide and deep in his handsome face gone; the mischief no longer dancing in his eyes; his swayback, slew-footed stroll across the lawn, down the street and through the park vanished.

Johnny took the time to connect with everyone, to say something to lift a person's load. He was alive in the truest sense of the word. He took pleasure in seeing the world anew each day. And he was a baby. He couldn't be dead already.

"Shot down in the street like a dog," Theda said.

My mind resisted the accuracy of her words. Not Johnny, one of the few young men in town always polite to his elders; not Johnny, who told wicked jokes when none of the elders was present; not Johnny, who dressed as well as he could afford to and was neat and clean, with his pants pulled up to his waist and his shirts ironed. Not Johnny, who had a future all mapped out? Dead already?

Theda said, "He begged them not to kill him. They shot him in the face. Twice. Young boys."

Johnny talked to the younger kids in the neighborhood. He bragged on them when they did well; he set them straight when they didn't. He would have made a good father some day. How could he be dead already?

I tried to pull myself together, but I was shaking and I couldn't stop. I held onto my jaw and asked, "Where is Lilly?"

"In bed. But she's not asleep."

"I'll be right over," I said.

I found Theda alone in her living room. She held a cup of cold tea and a Bible that was closed. She looked like she was going to cry. I hoped not, because before leaving the house, I had made myself one promise: no tears. The last thing they need, I said to myself, as I hurried across the yard, shaking, is for you to fall in the door bawling like an idiot.

No tears. They won't help.

Theda was broken. Her role, the one she had played over and over and knew by heart, was to be strong for others. Working her way through high school, she had, among other things, taken care of children. She had been a natural. With her background—a mother who was a talented midwife, an increasingly rare ability to cook, a good sense of humor and a keen bullshit detector—she made the perfect sitter. For a time, she had taken care of Johnny.

His big sister, Lilly, wasn't the sitting type and she hadn't chosen to pass up opportunities to go out and about to sit at home with a baby brother, not even a funny one like Johnny.

Theda did.

She watched cartoons with Johnny, played basketball with him, and took him to the movies. Theda loved Johnny years before she realized that she had also given her heart to Lilly. And Johnny loved her back. He loved both of them, Theda and Lilly, unconditionally. Their being a couple later didn't bother him one bit. He spent a lot of time at their house, eating Theda's delicious food and teasing Lilly mercilessly.

He told Lilly that no one else, except Theda the Good, would put up with her. He said anybody else would pop her one. Give her a good shake, or leave her over in St. Louis. Lilly usually let Johnny sound off for a while until she got tired of him and asked him to leave.

He came back. They thought he always would.

"She won't talk," Theda said, as I sat down beside her.

She was focusing on Lilly, but it was hard because Lilly wasn't the only one who was hurting in that house. Theda, too, had lost someone close to her heart.

"She'll talk when she can," I said, trying to pull forth some magic words from my trembling throat.

"It's enough to make anybody shut the fuck up," Theda said. "Our men have it so hard. First there was backbreaking slavery, then lynching, followed by laughable wages, nation-wide discrimination, shit-eating jobs, and poverty. Now this bullshit. Hoodlums turning on their own like diseased immune systems. It's one goddamn hard time after another. Decade after decade."

"Without end," I said, gripping my jaw. "I'm scared for Diego."

"Diego," she said, softly. "He'll be one of the lucky ones. One of the survivors."

She set her cup down and wiped away tears before they rolled down her face. "Lilly won't talk to me."

"She needs time."

"Johnny was always there for her. Sometimes it was like he was the older one, the more mature. He stood by her, by us. No matter what, he was there. Lilly took him for granted. Now he's gone. She can't sleep. And she won't talk."

Lilly had always expressed her feelings out loud. For her to go mute, even with grief, was alarming. Nevertheless, for Theda's sake, I repeated what I had already said, "She'll talk when she can."

"She didn't curse the doctors, the police, or the murderers. When Johnny's brain stopped, she walked straight out of the hospital and got in the car. She rode all the way home without saying one word."

"She'll say something," I said, stubbornly. "When she can."

Some neighborhood women stopped by. They dropped off cards, hard-to-spare ten-dollar bills, and covered dishes. Meaning well, they were trying to save Theda, temporarily, from the never-ending drudgery of housework that women have done forever and ever, amen. But having to do the vital things—the cooking, the cleaning, the constant getting something for someone—might have been a blessing in disguise. Theda had worked her whole life, usually two or more jobs. She was used to taking care of business, hers and Lilly's. Idleness, sitting still with a cold cup of tea, was the new hurting thing.

After the neighbors returned to their homes, Lilly came into the living room. She stared at me from mistrusting eyes, as if I had remained in her home not as a friend, but rather as someone there on business: an agent from the insurance company, perhaps, or the police department, or the state government, or the funeral home. She uttered no words, but her sunken eyes said it all: she wanted no part of me, no sympathetic chat. She wanted more silence. Wordlessly, she sat on the floor and placed her head on Theda's lap.

It rained the day of the funeral. The young people took Johnny's death hard. The young men groaned and cried quietly; the young women hollered. Two of them passed out.

Reverend Franklin sought to make an example of Johnny. He pointed out how the good often die young and how violence hurts us all and, of course, he reminded the survivors that a train was coming down the track and that each of us would have to get on board. We wouldn't need a ticket, but we should thank the Lord.

After Johnny was buried (already?), Theda and I went back to the church and fed the mourners, many of whom had bodies that were still growing and needed nourishment. Still shaking, I washed the dishes while Theda drove a group of elderly folks home in the church van.

Lilly passed on the after-burial ritual. She left the cemetery and went directly to bed. She finally slept.

She remained in bed for two days. On the third day, she got up and she spoke to Theda and to me. "It's stopped raining," she said.

She spent the remainder of the day looking out the living room window. Before going to bed that night, she said, "When Johnny was a little boy, he loved to play outside in the rain."

For a short time after Johnny was murdered, although they remained inside the yellow house together, Lilly and Theda drifted away from one another. Lilly talked to Theda, but not much and never about anything that mattered. She quit her part-time jobs and, for the first time in her life, she neglected her appearance. She got to the place where she just didn't give a damn anymore. But she didn't stay there long. Theda brought her back. Gently and with patience, Theda brought Lilly from the brink. They were a team; they regrouped. Lilly rebounded.

I was less resilient. Johnny's murder unleashed something wild in me, something that had been waiting for an opportunity to break free: sheer terror.

Paranoia grabbed hold of me and wouldn't let go.

The safety of my children, especially my son, ran roughshod over my mind. It was all I thought about.

Less than a month after celebrating Diego's first birthday, I found myself obsessing about the day of his death. I had seen too many abbreviated lives, mostly male.

In Eloise, during a three-year period, four young men had died in automobile accidents, their bodies ejected from vehicles, slammed against walls, trees, and, in one horrible case, a train steaming toward St. Louis, Missouri.

Two young men dropped dead in their own backyards; their enlarged, prematurely congested hearts simply gave out. Neither had reached the age of forty. Two others, beardless still, overdosed on drugs. Five died, like Johnny, of gunshot wounds.

I sat up nights and saw my son's future enemies, the men who stood in the way of his long life: the gangs of small, but dangerous and emotionally stunted, boys roaming the town, mean boys who would never mature into men, boys who would live out their brief days picking off their closest relatives on earth, one by one.

I also saw the racist police officers (more Culver clones) who could inflict abuse with impunity, maim or kill at their discretion, and, at the hearing, if one was held, solemnly swear that the perpetrator had resisted arrest.

Who was I to fear more, the predators who would shoot my boy in the back for a boast or a dime, or the peace officers who would shoot him in the head?

It was a toss-up. If one group didn't get him, the other would.

Knowing my tears were useless, I cried anyway. I put my pillow over my head and cried as I had the night I realized that my father was not a train and he was not going to turn around and come home.

My tears were for Johnny and for all the young black men who were dead already.

The thought of Diego's warm limbs, elongated and languishing behind bars, or worse, cooling and bleeding onto the street like Johnny's, kept me awake.

I began walking the streets to keep from beating myself with my fists, to keep from screaming, and to keep from alarming my children.

I'd get out of my bed in the middle of the night and bundle up my children. We'd walk from one end of Eloise to the other. And back again.

Many people live this way, inside this fear. Some of them are trapped in cities, feeling blocked off and oppressed by bad schools, traffic, and drug-related crimes. Some of them try to outrun their lives of despair. They move to the suburbs, or even farther out, seeking open spaces in the country. They often pass people escaping the boredom and the Meth-addicted zombies of their own small towns who are on their way to the city, hoping to get lost in the crowd.

Those of us with modest incomes, poor technical skills, and debt often have to stay put.

I stayed put, within the Eloise city limits. Where would I have gone? What place is safe for a black boy? I often asked myself that question. Where can we go? The answer echoed in my heart: There is no other place. You are already here.

We walked on.

Our nighttime walks were an adventure for Diego. Having the luxury of sleeping during the day, he liked being awake at night. He stared at the darkness and the bright stars around him in pure wonderment.

Suzanne was not amused nor was she entertained. For her, our walks were an imposition and an embarrassment. She didn't go gently. Each night was a battle. Suzanne argued about the distance covered, the direction taken, the fullness of the moon, the temperature of the air, and the dogs barking up ahead.

Friend or foe?

If I said one, she said the other. She fought me every step of the way, balking at the futility of it all, the fatigue.

"Oh, come on," I said. "You need exercise. You don't want to get lazy, too used to your bed."

"People laugh at us," she said, yawning.

"No," I said. "No one laughs. They haven't done that since Mama died."

"They laugh at you now," she said. "And sometimes they laugh at me. But I can make myself not listen."

"How do you do that?"

"Easy. Hear those crickets? I'm going to refuse to listen to them. Okay," she said. "I don't hear them anymore."

"What do you hear instead?"

"Music."

"What kind?"

"I hear drums. And a piano. A horn. Everybody's dancing."

"Are you?"

"Yes. I'm on stage. There are lights near my feet. I'm dancing and I won't ever stop."

We walked on.

# CHAPTER NINETEEN

The time came when I had to silence Mirror. She had always been a know-it-all. Throwing things back in my face was her only purpose in life, the thing she lived for. Because that was her nature, I tolerated her for years. I made allowances. I turned my back on her mocking and smirking. I looked the other way when she was abusive, but one night she went too far.

I came home from work overtired, having walked the night before from midnight until three. I had gotten back up at six, showered, made breakfast and lunch, and rushed off to my job. At the end of what had been a long day, I had no patience.

I squeezed down the narrowing hall, worked my way into the tiny bedroom to change my clothes, and there she was, up against the wall, judging me.

Looking at her was my mistake. I should have kept my head down. The second she caught my eye she rattled off her complaints: my appearance, which she said had gone in recent weeks from careless to outlandish; my life, which she described as unenlightened and backward; my friendships—ship. She pointed out that I only had one. She reminded me that the only person who wanted to have anything to do with me was Theda and that Lilly endured me in short spurts simply to keep peace in their home.

I closed my eyes and put on my robe, determined not to encourage her in any way.

"What have you accomplished with your life?" she asked. "You've spread your legs and pushed out two human beings. That's it. All you'll have to show for that will be stretch marks, sags, and bags. By the way, what happened to your breasts? Where'd they go?"

"I'm not listening," I said. "You can talk to yourself."

"You, too," she said. "You don't have a man."

"Yes, I do."

She looked around the room. "Where is he? I haven't seen him here in months. Once a man knows for sure where you'll be, he moves at least a state away. Or he moves another woman into his life. I'll never forget the look on your face when Lamarr brought his high-yellow whore to town."

That did it.

Had she been the least bit polite, I would have let her have her say. I would have kept her company while she expressed herself. I didn't have anything better to do. But scorn? Rebuke? Oh, hell no. I didn't have to put up with that.

I took a deep breath, went to Mama's room, and opened the door. For a second there was blessed silence, and then the forces gathered rapidly. Before they had a chance to surround me, I snatched Daddy's green army blanket off the bed and fled.

"And another thing," Mirror said.

Then I shut her up for good. The blanket covered her face like a newly laid grave-top. She didn't make another sound, not even a whimper. It was as if she had never existed, never hung around spying on me for nearly a decade.

I went into the bathroom and washed my face. Mirror's little sister, Little M, fronted the medicine cabinet, but she had always been respectful. She posed no threat at all. Each morning when I showered, the moisture in the room kept Little M from seeing me clearly and she wasn't the peeking type. At night, whenever possible, I did my business in the dark, but if I absolutely had to turn on the light, Little M lowered her eyes immediately, disproving once and for all the tiresome myth that it's in the upbringing.

Not always. Siblings are often born worlds apart, different in both character and temperament. In families, there are no foolproof explanations, environmental or genetic, to account for the fact that some members turn out well, others disastrously.

Little M was the polite discreet sister. I never asked for more than that.

Each day I checked my body to see whether any signs of cancer had manifested beneath my skin. I wasn't morbid, but I knew that I was at risk for breast cancer. All women are; some are at greater risk than others.

Death wasn't a great concern to me. People who are bone and mind weary look to Death for the comfort and promise that it is. We fear the unknown, but

Death and I were familiar with one another. Confidants. Many nights as I lay awake, Death slipped into my room.

Death said, "Don't fear me. Pretend I'm not here. If you can."

Considerate, Death never woke my children. It left the light off and spoke to me in the dark. It never called my name; we both knew who it was talking to. Nor did it ever lay a hand on me—that could wait. Death was so very considerate, so relaxed. Why wouldn't it be? Everything went its way. Everybody. Eventually.

It was curious, though. "Can you sleep?"

"No."

"Me either. I like to watch, anyway. After all these years, the thrill isn't gone."

I turned away, not in rudeness, but rather to face the wall. I wanted to concentrate on how Death sounded, not how it looked. Looks aren't everything.

"Since you're up," Death whispered. "What do you want to do?"

"I don't know. What do you want to do?"

"Let's take a walk. Walking seems to help."

Death got my jacket from the closet. I put it on and woke the children from their sleep. Suzanne and I walked side by side. We took turns pushing Diego in his stroller. Death was out front, leading the way.

No, I didn't fear death—my guide and my ultimate destination. I feared the journey, the means to the end. I had seen what the space between here and there, that tortuous tunnel, can do to a person. I saw what it did to Aunt Shirley. The Taborn Family Cancer Road reduced Aunt Shirley by more than half. More than half. It dried her up like a stick doll and left her gasping for air, her whole body praying, "Lord, please help me."

A nine-year-old child, I tried to help, too. I did everything I could to beat the cancer back, but once it began its fateful spread, there was no stopping its advance; it took everything Aunt Shirley had except her faith.

Mama didn't wait for the Family Cancer. She got the jump on it; she made her move quickly, in the dark of night. She swam out before she could be claimed, cut, burned, sustained with wires and tape and tubes, and then, finally, given up for dead.

She eluded the family legacy. Its deep penetrating center eye was fixed on me, watching more closely than Mirror on the Wall ever had, and with less empathy.

My main fear was cancer's ability to take me from my children while they were still children and needed me. So each morning as I showered, I touched my breasts lovingly. Each finger-press was an invocation, an affirmation: all is well one more day. I gave my breasts encouragement, praised them for the sustenance they had given to Suzanne and Diego, not the threat they posed for me.

My morning ritual took longer and longer. I was reluctant to leave home each day. I didn't want to be separated from my son. Once we arrived at the day care center, I held him close until Ms. Harris, his primary caregiver, pried him from my arms and walked me to the door.

Love slowed me down.

I arrived at work not just tired, but weak. I tried to rush, but I couldn't. It was as if I lacked form. My legs were filled with Jell-O, my brain with whipped cream.

I was drifting away.

I constantly searched for stuff: bottles, keys, papers, hats, and scarves. Each morning, after leaving the house, I doubled back to make sure the stove wasn't on, the water faucet was off, and the refrigerator door was closed.

Time is tricky. Although I set my watch to the radio and television, which were within a few seconds of each other, when I got to work time had changed like a mind. Just like that. The office clock was way ahead of me.

One morning I showed up twenty minutes late. Officially. The supervisors were conniving and strategizing behind closed doors, figuring out ways for their subordinates to do more work for less pay, so I hurried to my assigned space and worked feverishly, hoping zeal would make up for the tardiness.

It didn't.

My supervisor, Ms. Lomax, called me into her office and, without any niceties, requested my resignation.

"Please, Ms. Lomax," I begged. "Give me one more chance."

"I can't do that, Mattie," she said. Her voice was a machine gun, rhythmic and deadly. "You were warned. Not only have you come in late on numerous occasions, some days you look as if you had been up all night. This is a place of business. Each of us is expected to arrive on time, looking refreshed and professional."

"I have trouble sleeping. So does my baby. We go for walks at night, but my work doesn't suffer. You've said yourself that I do my job."

"Doing your job includes arriving on time," she said, rat-a-tat-tat. She put her glasses on and wrote in longhand on company stationery.

"God as my witness," I said. "I won't be late again. I'll buy a better watch. Something must be wrong with this one."

Ms. Lomax stood and handed me my walking papers. "These are for your records," she said. "Your final payment will be mailed to you."

"What about health insurance?" I asked. "How will I pay my hospital bills?"

She removed her glasses. "Hospital bills? Are you ill?"

Hope snapped to attention in my chest and saluted. Maybe Ms. Lomax would reconsider, show compassion. "I am at risk," I said.

She put her hand on her chest. "For what?"

"A couple of things. Some I already have and others are on their way."

"Have you seen a physician?"

"Not yet."

"What are you waiting for?"

My mind whispered: Make an excuse. No doctors. Save the worst for last.

Ms. Lomax reached across her desk and pushed her phone within my reach. "If you are ill, make an appointment with the doctor. Now."

Suggest something else, my mind said: Herbs. Exercise. Detox. "Rest," I shouted. "I'll get to bed early every night from now on. I won't be late again. I promise."

Ms. Lomax returned the phone to its place on her sensibly arranged desk. She replaced her glasses. "Good-by, Mattie," she said. "Good luck."

Her eyes held neither compassion nor regret.

Diego's teacher at the day care center hated to see us go. Her eyes were moist as she kissed Diego on his cheek.

"Thanks for taking care of him," I said. "I appreciate everything you did for him."

Diego laid his head on my shoulder. He probably wondered why we made such a fuss, thinking that he'd be right back there the same time the next day.

We left the center and walked around downtown. I was disheartened but not confused. I knew I had to take care of my children and protect them from harm.

When I got home, I called Sherry and, two days later, I was wrestling with her computer, examining her gleaming marble floors for smudges, and getting paid so that I could feed and clothe my children.

Going back to Sherry's house may have been a step backward, but at least it was movement.

Sherry was glad to have us back. That she had made little progress on her novel was not a surprise. Her shift from fruity drinks—tart margaritas and sweet sangria—to Chivas Regal, straight up, was the surprise.

Sherry drank with discipline, though. She drank after noon, at home, and after her workout. She had continued working out religiously and it showed all over. She looked hard, I thought. Regular beatings, silicone implants, and free weights toughen a person up, I guessed. But most people thought Sherry looked fabulous. She caused quite a stir at the Hard Body Gym in the Plaza. Shining like new, she was a living, strutting, Barbie Doll. Everyone said so. Many people envied her. Not me. When I looked at Sherry Brady Ziegler, I saw past the shine, beneath the facade. I saw a fellow desperado, another woman living at the end of her rope.

It takes one to know one.

Despite her appearance and privilege, Sherry felt isolated. All she had was the gym. Before leaving each day, she checked herself in a floor-to-ceiling mirror. Everything was in place: body, hair, face, and expensive workout wear.

Check.

The only thing missing was heart.

"I have to go," she said.

"Then off you go," I said. "Vroom, vroom."

"If I miss spinning class today, I'll pass on Pilates tomorrow. Then I'll give up high-impact aerobics the day after that. One day I'll turn a corner, walk by a window, and see a woman with a flat ass."

"You?" I scoffed.

"It could happen," she said. "A flat-assed, middle-aged woman with a gut."

She looked over her shoulder and saw the way she shined. We both saw that her narrow behind was saddle, lump, and droop free; her stomach concave; her calves muscular. All was tight.

Check.

Now everything was in place, including her determination. "I have to go," she said, opening the door. Before going to her car, she said, "Mattie, to a large degree, we become the women we see in the mirror."

"Ain't that the truth," I said, closing the door.

The next evening when I returned home, Lamarr hopped out of his Jeep like a terrorist. I had seen his hulking imported vehicle parked on the street, but, foolishly, I had supposed he was in the house with his daughter like a normal father would have been, not waiting by the side of the road to ambush me. He nearly scared me to death.

I screamed. He screamed right back. He was pissed that I had lost a job downtown. I hadn't known that he cared where or for whom I worked, so long as I worked, but he cared a lot. "Anytime you take a step back, you pull the whole race back with you," he barked.

I shoved my bag of groceries into his chest, so I could comfort Diego, who'd also been startled by all the screaming.

"We are always lumped together and judged by our mistakes," he said.

"There was one name on my pink slip," I said, going inside. "If I blew it I blew it for myself. I am an individual."

"Individuality is a luxury we don't have," he shouted at the back of my head. "We get screwed as a group. A class. We can't afford to screw ourselves. When we get in we need to stay and bring in the next one and the next."

"If they give us an inch, we should take a mile?"

"An acre. They do."

I set Diego down with his blocks. "Not everyone is hell-bent on getting over. Some of us are simply trying to get by."

"Bite your tongue. I realize you can't accomplish what I have, but at least you could hold onto a half-way decent job when you finally get one."

"Why are you so worked up about this?"

"Because I thought you were finally becoming some kind of role model for Suzy."

"Not all role models work in offices. Some work on farms. In emergency rooms. Some drive trucks over the open road. Some even pull the graveyard shift at factories."

"Suzy's not going there. If she's going to learn how to make her way in the world, she will have to live in my house."

Lamarr's face was so red it almost looked brown. I wanted him to leave me a space. A window. The kitchen was smaller than it had ever been. He was taking up more than his share of the oxygen. "Maybe you should discuss this tonight with Rotelle," I said. "She might have changed her mind about having Suzanne live with you full time."

"Rotelle will go along with me," he said. "We have each other's backs."

Lamarr, I thought, eight years ago we were fumbling in the dark. Now look at us. You have frown lines between your eyebrows, premature gray hair and a mouthful of threats. I'm wasting away in a fun house that is rapidly running out of room and I hear voices; maybe the same ones Mama heard when we were tossing and tumbling in a room down the hall from hers. Gladly.

Where did the time go?

I went out to the backyard and counted to ten. The menacing mushroom shape forming in the east was a cloud, not an explosion, just water and ice suspended in air.

The airplane flying lower was adjusting its speed, preparing to land, not making a nosedive.

The smoke rising in the western sky, over toward St. Louis, didn't necessarily mean that a house was on fire, that young children had been left alone. Again.

When Lamarr came out onto the porch, his lungs were inflated. He looked like the Michelin Man.

"You'd better go," I said. "I'm dizzy."

"Maybe you should lie down," he said. "Do you want me to get you something?"

"I'll be fine."

"You sure you're okay?"

"Yeah."

I called Rotelle before he was half way home. She and I were friends. Sort of. We had something in common, anyway: Lamarr. Our experiences with him had been different, of course. He wined and dined her in a big-shouldered city, brought her home in a van and paraded her around Eloise, as her customer so aptly put it, as if she were the Queen of Sheba. Lamarr outdid himself. He'd married her in an African ceremony, wearing an ankle-length gown. He literally jumped over a broom in Foundation Park to usher a high-toned hooker from the south side of Chicago into one of the most color-struck families in all of Illinois. All he had done for me was escort me across two streets named after trees, sneak into my bedroom and kiss me silly, and then vanish along with my menstrual cycle. Nevertheless, Rotelle and I had both loved him once and we loved his only biological child.

That was something.

Her voice dripped like honey. Mine didn't. "It's Mattie," I said, flatly. "We need to talk."

She invited me to join her at the Country Club. I wore my Sunday-and-every-other-day best: the black dress with the white collar. If Mirror could have seen me, she would have asked if I was going to a barn raising. She would have suggested something more colorful. Fire engine red or deep purple. "Show that hussy you've got some life in you," she probably would have said. Mirror was covered, though. She couldn't see in or out. My own fashion arbiter, I wore what I had; I wore black.

Stepping inside the Club's dark hallway, I blinked. I had prepared meals in the kitchen with Theda for private parties, but I had never been an invited guest. I suppressed the desire to chuckle. I thought, now look who's coming to lunch?

Sitting at a center table in the main dining hall, Rotelle looked perfectly at home. When she stood and motioned for me to join her, the waiter gave me a haughty look.

"Mattie's my guest, Don," she said, taking her seat. "Bring her a glass of wine."

Don sighed and said, "White or red?"

"I'll have Pepsi," I said.

"Coca Cola," he said over his shoulder.

Rotelle opened her menu. "Have anything you want. My treat."

I stared at the menu, feeling confused by the choices. Rotelle became impatient. "How does fish sound?"

"Great," I said. "Don't you want to know why I called?"

"You want something," she said. "We all do. My guess is that you want me to convince Lamarr to leave you alone, let you rear your daughter in peace. Maybe sign something to that effect. Close?"

"Very. In return for your influence, I have something to offer you."

"What would that be?"

"My silence. I won't tell him anything about your volunteer work."

She raised an artificially arched eyebrow. "Are you threatening me?"

"Adding incentive."

We were quiet while the waiter placed a soda can and a glass on the table for me and poured more wine for Rotelle. Then she placed our order and sipped her wine. Finally she smiled at me. "How long have you held your trump card?"

"I got it recently, by accident. I won't use it unless I have to."

The waiter brought a plate of stuffed mushrooms and set it in front of Rotelle as if she were dining alone. She ignored the appetizer. I reached across the table with my fork, speared one and popped it in my mouth. Within seconds my stomach, unused to rich or any other food, cried for mercy.

"It's none of my business," I said, burping. "But if Lamarr tries to prove that I'm an unfit role model, unlike say … you, I'll have to defend myself in anyway I can. Do you understand?"

"You've been quite clear," she said. Her false eyelashes fluttered and that made me sad. Eloise is a lipstick and blush town. Eye shadow on special occasions. False eyelashes are never called for here. There are no cameras, no close-ups. In her own way, Rotelle was as displaced as I was. Coming from opposite directions, she from the city, me from the country, we ended up in the same place, a place that is hard on strangers. Friendships have been based on less.

Pressing my salmon with a fork, checking for bones, I said, "Lamarr has his hands around my throat. He's choking off my air."

She laughed. "You are melodramatic. Which is refreshing, because so many people in Eloise act like they died years ago."

She left a generous tip for the waiter and we took off in her new Porsche. She said that she felt like opening it up and she meant that literally. I gripped my seat and pressed my foot into the floor as we sped down the highway.

There was very little traffic, just the road, the wind, and us. In Lamarr's presence, Rotelle had seemed part of him, an appendage almost. In my mind she was someone who had taken my place, the second wife. Watching her out of the corner of my eye as she skillfully handled her racecar, I saw a complete person, not simply the woman beside the man who was never mine in the first place.

I had to give it to her. Auburn hair flying, matching the reddish-brown scarf at her neck, Rotelle's close-up would have been great. She was, like Theda's mother, a master of many things: a wife, a mother, and a businesswoman. An independent contractor. The Queen of Sheba.

The Queen drove way too fast for my taste. My right foot began to cramp because of my desperate efforts to slow us down. I checked the rearview mirror every few seconds, expecting—halfway hoping—a black-and white would pull us over. "Be careful," I shrieked, as Rotelle crossed the center divide, flew around a lone truck, and returned to the right lane as a motor home bore down on us.

She patted my knee. "Relax. My parents were killed on the Dan Ryan when I was six. I'm living for three people. I'm the best driver you know."

We passed clusters of farmhouses and villages so small ten of them could have set on one side of Eloise. They were isolated places that didn't look like much, but they were home to somebody.

The lights were on.

We rolled past Germantown and Millstadt, whizzed by fields of cattle and horses with their heads bent low. Rotelle made an abrupt U-turn, headed back toward Eloise, and began to talk. "After my parents died, my aunt and uncle took me in," she said. "He was sick. I never knew which attracted him more. Proximity, my tender age, or my color."

"You mean your lack of color."

"Same difference. He was a retired doctor, who had worked at Mercy Hospital. That's not a joke. He shot himself in the head, when I was thirteen. Too late to do me any good. By then I had been hooking for two years."

"Did your aunt know?"

"She didn't want to know."

"Have you had any therapy?"

"I am therapy."

"What do you tell Lamarr? About the money, I mean."

"He doesn't pry."

"Eloise doesn't seem like prime call girl country."

"Men are the same everywhere. Women, too. I'm not the only one."

"Do you know each other? Have a union?"

"I wish. I give some of my money to organizations that help abused girls, if that makes you feel better."

"Does it make you feel better?"

"Who said I feel bad? In Eloise, I'm a little something on the side. A treat. Nobody gets hurt. If I'd stayed in the city, I'd be dead now. Lamarr saved my life."

I wanted to say that he'd nearly killed me, but I held my tongue. We weren't real friends. Just sort of. And it was her trip, not mine.


Back in Eloise, we stopped at Rotelle's house and exchanged the Porsche for the Jeep. We packed up all our kids and went to Eloise Lake for the annual hot air balloon fest.

We arrived at dusk. The place was crowded. People sat on lawn chairs and ate homemade sandwiches from picnic baskets. There were cold drinks for sale and live music. It was better than the Fourth of July.

Diego reached for the huge balloons as soon as he saw them. They were high in the sky then, but as they drifted toward us, he jumped up and laughed as if they were coming down just because he wanted them to. The balloons hovered above the water like multicolored clouds, then fell to dry land and collapsed softly around us as though they were exhausted from the trip.

Local officials made speeches and congratulated themselves and us for making the event bigger and better than the year before. We applauded the officials and each other and then the balloon people got ready to take to the sky again.

Fire makes me uneasy. I flinched each time a pilot was lit. There were eerie, untamed sounds in the air and the light was odd, which made me remember: fire will end the world.

The wind picked up, fanned the flames, and drove the anxiety deeper into my mind. I would have left, but I was riding with someone who was in no hurry to leave. Rotelle was having as much fun as Diego was.

The balloon people made me feel uneasy. They reminded me of carnival folks: transient, working quickly, doing whatever had to be done, and laughing at one another's jokes, all the while seeming dangerously free. I held Diego close and kept a keen eye on Suzanne. I saw when her hand shot up.

One of the bearded longhaired men offered the children a free ride. Suzanne responded by waving an arm wildly. She stands out in a crowd, so she was among the chosen ones. I refused to let her go. I insisted that she stay on the ground.

Stepmother Rotelle objected. "Let her try things. That's why we're here."

I was not persuaded. "Maybe next year."

"I won't ever get to do anything," Suzanne said, as the bright carriages lifted off without her. "I'll always have to stay with you. Never go anywhere or do anything."

I didn't apologize to her or pick up the guilt trip she dropped. She was angry with me, but at least she was safe. Later, riding back to Elm Street in the Jeep, I knew for sure that we were not alone in the universe. A long line of the big balloons glowed above us like planets close enough to touch. They made me homesick—lonesome for all the places I had never been.

# CHAPTER TWENTY

The following week Jacob came home. "I should have warned you," he said, as he entered the kitchen. I wondered if he noticed how small it was.

"No warning necessary." I said, grinning as he kissed Diego lots more times than he had kissed me.

I toasted some bread and made Jacob an avocado, cucumber, and tomato sandwich. I had stopped eating meat, among other things. Vegetarian sandwiches taste better than people think. Jacob ate two.

When he finished his meal, he told me that he had spoken to a stranger, a mysterious woman, early that morning. "Weird," he said, rising to rinse his plate.

"What way?"

"Every way. Her attitude. Her aura."

"She had an aura?"

"Sure did. It had a strong effect on me, too."

"Jacob."

"I knew you'd say that. But it's the truth. I kept blurting out stuff. Things I usually keep to myself."

"Such as?"

"Mistakes I've made. Goals I haven't met and may never."

"To a stranger?"

"I'm saying."

"Was she from Indianapolis?"

"Somewhere else. She was passing thorough."

"What did she look like?"

He chewed on a fingernail. "Dark smooth skin. No lines. Penetrating eyes. That was the main thing. Sitting all the way at the back of the church, as still as a post, her eyes drew me to her. She almost put me in a trance."

"You think she was a black magic woman?"

"She moved me."

"One time I wanted to say magic words—not to move someone, but to stop him in his tracks. Couldn't do it."

Jacob sat down and I rubbed his hand. "The woman you met sounds like someone I saw right here in Eloise after Mama's funeral. A stranger. A woman who could change shapes."

He shook his head. "If this lady had been in Eloise, I'd remember her."

"Maybe there's one in every town."

I poured him a glass of iced tea. He drank it down and wiped his mouth. "I felt like I was talking to my mother today. The stranger knew my whole game."

"I don't even know it."

"Yes you do: Procrastinating. Playing safe. Trying to do the right thing. Most of the time doing nothing."

I poured more tea, set the pitcher down, and touched Jacob's face. "Did you talk to her about your calling?"

"She already knew."

Jacob stayed two days, and not once did he mention my appearance. I had been losing weight and I was losing still. My hair was braided, not fashionably, but haphazardly in fat clumps twisted at the ends and it hadn't seen a comb in a long while. There were dark circles under my eyes from lack of sleep. Jacob didn't acknowledge or confront the wreckage he saw. Despite his eye-opening conversation with the stranger, he went right on being Jacob.

He left the next day, looking Hollywood handsome in a gray suit and tie. If I hadn't known better I would have thought he was on his way west to become "the new Denzel." Instead, he drove back to Indiana to finish what he had started at an oasis called Freewill Baptist Church.

"Does Franklin come and go as he pleases?"

Lamarr had no shame. He was sitting in the dark talking to a woman who was turned away from him, rocking in a chair.

After he and Suzanne went swimming at Fairview Park, he had come inside to talk to me. Rotelle was good. She had insisted that Lamarr drop his custody threat and, for a time, he had left me alone, but, Lord help me, he was back.

I didn't answer his question. I thought silence would do the trick (the dark and turning my chair away from him hadn't).

"What's up with him?" he asked.

"Now you see him. Now you don't."

"What about you? What are you doing at Sherry's these days?"

"I write."

"You mean type?"

"There isn't much to type, so I'm writing. I've completed an outline for my own book."

He laughed. "Your own book. That's funny. What's it going to be called?"

*"How White Is The Black Woman You Married?"*

He stopped laughing. "That's pitiful."

"They say write what you know."

"Is it about me?"

"You're so vain. It's about the slave mentality among displaced people. Color prejudice in the world, mistaken identity, and the inaccuracy of the American census count. It's going to be a big book with lots of pages. Not one about you."

"You're sick, Mattie."

"And tired."

I got up and held the door wide, so he could fly back into the night. He stepped onto the porch and stood under the light. He looked genuinely concerned. I felt bad for everybody, including him. "Remember one thing," I said, as he flapped his wings. "I wasn't always this way."

I tossed and turned for hours before falling asleep. When I finally slept, a dream rolled through my brain like a major motion picture.

Mama swam in the river in the backyard. As she waved and swam toward me, she looked as she had when she was alive. Her hair, her face, and her skin were the same. Her nails had grown long, though; they curled over her fingertips like shields, blunting her sense of touch and her ability to defend herself. "There's no need, nothing to fear," she said, splashing in the water like a child. "Come."

Afraid that I would be pulled into the river, swept away, I cried out, "I can't. I've got to stay. Suzanne and Diego need me."

"Come," Mama said, as the water rose. "Come."

She slipped beneath the water without causing a ripple. The river kept running. On the other side, Stranger Woman sat atop the Gateway Arch with a shawl over her face. The river rushed to her. It surrounded her, but it did not rise above her. The water stopped. Then it bowed down and waited for her command. She raised her hand, turned the water around and walked it back toward me. I wanted to run away, but I couldn't move. My body was full of holes. The night air blew right through me.

When I opened my mouth to let out a scream, my tongue fell into the river and dogpaddled away. My brain unraveled and floated off in the opposite direction. Empty headed, I began to sink.

The entire time, I was aware that I was dreaming about my ineffectiveness, my loss of self, but I couldn't stop. I kept dreaming my own death.

When morning came I was drowsy. Sleep, the dream carrier, was at my side. It spooned me. "Want some more?"

I fought sleep off, got up, and put on my robe. I stumbled into the bathroom and turned on the shower. When I raised my left arm over my head and touched my left breast, I felt a small knot, no larger than a pebble, above my ribcage. I was not surprised.

"It's probably nothing," I said out aloud. "A clogged milk duct. Hormones change, breasts thicken, especially when in use, and mine are workhorses."

I still breastfed Diego twice a day. When he was at the daycare center, I pumped myself like a cow. After a day of resistance, my fat boy gave in and drank my milk from his bottle, but as soon as we were back at Sherry's, he took juice or water from a bottle, but no milk, thank you.

If I poured soy, cow, or goat's milk into a cup and pretended that I liked it, licking my lips and rubbing my stomach like a fool, he laughed at the show. When Suzanne or Sherry acted as if they were sneaking up on a bottle of milk meant for him, he played along, reached for the bottle as if it were a prize, but as soon as they brought the dripping, rubbery nipple to his lips, he slapped it away with both hands. Diego liked pretend games as much as the next waddler, but, seriously folks, he insisted, the only milk that counts is Mother's.

I wiped the fog off of Little M. "I'll call the doctor, but he will take one look and send me on my way," I said. "Right?"

Little M, unable to say something nice, said nothing at all. The only voice in the room was mine. "It's nothing," I said. "Nothing. Or everything."

# CHAPTER TWENTY-ONE

Without asking for any explanations, Theda agreed to watch my kids while I went to see Dr. Day. Before leaving the house, I picked up the phone to call Sherry and tell her that I would be in later than usual, if I made it in at all. A police detective answered the phone, identified himself, and barked, "Who is this?"

"Mattie Moon."

The man called out, "Sergeant. Mattie Moon?"

Sergeant Culver's flat voice came from somewhere in the background. "The help. Tell her not to come in today."

I spoke quickly, before the detective could hang up. "May I speak to Sherry?"

"There's been an incident. A police matter." He sent the dial tone into my ear.

Heart pounding, I ran up the street to Sherry's house. Two police cars, a fire truck, and an ambulance were parked in front. A stretcher was being taken from the fire truck. It wasn't as if no one knew that somebody in that house wanted somebody dead. I knew that Mark was a hater. He hated women in general, Sherry in particular. Females are usually killed by their partners or their johns. Men who hate and harm women switch on and off like lights. I love you; no, I hate you.

Maybe the hatred develops because their mothers beat them when they were too young and too trusting to fight back, or maybe their grandmothers, mothers, or sisters got dressed up and walked out with strange men and left them frightened and alone at night, or maybe they saw their fathers beat their mothers and, unable to prevent it, years later they projected their pain and sense of degradation on the entire female race.

Maybe it's genetic, or cultural. Maybe there is no reason, but I knew that if Sherry was dead my silence had betrayed her as much as Mark's hatred had. I prayed that she was still alive.

She was.

Despite all the commotion around her—police officers and technicians were at work—Sherry was sitting on the sofa, calmly drinking a glass of orange juice. Freshly made bruises were on her forehead and at her throat.

Our eyes met, but when I stepped inside, a baby-faced detective blocked my path and called out, "Sergeant."

The wizened veteran Culver, came forward, looked me up and down, and shrugged. "The maid," he said. "Let her in."

The boy-detective let me pass.

"Mark is dead," Sherry said, reaching for my hand. When they brought the stretcher in, neither one of us shed any tears. The only person who cried was Mark's devoted secretary, Dana, who leaned against the wall and sobbed like she had lost her best friend. Or her man.

The coroner and the criminologist were highly professional. They wore gloves, followed up on clues immediately, and obtained fingerprints. They covered the body with plastic. No blankets were taken from the linen closets, although many were stacked there in color-coordinated piles.

"If I hadn't killed him, he would have killed me," Sherry whispered to me as the late Mark Ziegler was lifted from the floor and placed on the stretcher. "I had no choice," she said, as they rolled him toward the door.

"You chose yourself," I whispered back, as Mark's lifeless body crossed the threshold for the last time.

That scene made her cry. She wept softly for what could have been, but wasn't. Then she dried her face and finished her juice like it was the beginning a new day, because it was.

Sherry had stopped believing in the photographs on her wall, the exquisitely framed representations of a happily married couple, the mementos that Mark knocked to the floor every time he became enraged and that she carefully hung back up the following day so that she would have something to show and, more important, something to believe in.

She finally stopped.

Mark had done what he said he would do: beat some sense into her. If she hadn't acted, he would have done more, reduced her to trace and fiber. DNA.

Sherry understood the concept. On the days writer's block had blocked her so bad she couldn't think of a word much less a sentence, she had gone into her den, drink in hand, propped her feet on her olive burl wood coffee table and watched Court TV.

Sherry learned that the blindfold on Lady Justice was a joke: she saw who came calling and she was as biased as anyone else, as easily bought. If a defendant had money, charm, and good looks, which Mark had in abundance, a jury of not necessarily his peers, but somebody's, could ignore, disbelieve, and dismiss all the incriminating evidence against him—circumstantial, scientific, and otherwise.

In one trial, Sherry saw prosecutors bungle the presentation of a strong case by confusing the obvious and highlighting the hard to believe. The overwhelmed judge kept a sequestered jury waiting for hours, day after day, while the attorneys in the courtroom turned cartwheels and took turns performing like clowns at a circus. The judge was the weakest part of the show.

Another judge reduced a jury's murder conviction to manslaughter and (figuratively) tongue kissed the accused (the convicted murderer!) by not even imposing probation.

She also saw cases that were efficiently tried by dedicated attorneys and patiently deliberated by thoughtful jurors, but she didn't like her chances. She knew what she was up against.

She chose herself. She killed Mark—before he killed her and got away with it.

Knowing that every "good-bye" ain't gone, Sherry didn't write a good-bye note saying that all she had ever done was love Mark. She let the facts and Mark's cold body speak for themselves. She didn't attend the candlelight service that was held the next day to commemorate Mark's short life or the private funereal that was held the day after that. She didn't have that much nerve.

Sherry, who was brought up Catholic, is no longer religious. She didn't say Mark was better off, just that she is. To date, she hasn't said anything about being reunited with him in Heaven. She believes that, when it's over, it is, and that it ended for Mark and her the day she picked up his gun. She said she knew they were through the second she pulled the trigger.

I didn't let myself go. Sherry let me go.

In Sherry's mind, for more than a year, I had been an imaginary buffer standing between Mark and her. With his death ruled a homicide, she needed real buffers, costly buffers of renown: shrewd men and women who make their living testifying in criminal courts on blood splatters, ballistics, defensive wounds, and the battered woman's syndrome. Experts in their fields.

The Saturday after Mark's funeral, I got up before dawn, put on my black dress and sat at the kitchen table with a pen and a writing tablet. At the top of my list, I wrote: What shall I do?

Thoughts bumped into each other and disintegrated upon impact. Letters slid across the page. The room was so small it felt like a closet. Perspiring, I clawed my way to the living room and sat in Mama's rocking chair.

I wrote down the names of my children. First, Suzanne Lucinda Moon: if anything happened to me, Lamarr would at long last become the full-time parent he threatened to be. Having circled for years, he would swoop down and grab his prey. He would overcompensate for the missed years. He would send her to an expensive college and, if necessary, help her buy her first home. He would guide her away from boys like the one he had been. Lacking all the facts, he would try to turn his "Suzy" into a miniature Rotelle. My daughter, a fighter, would survive both of them. She would miss me, but she would be okay.

Next I wrote: Diego Lester Moon. My fat boy's name appeared in a shakier script. Diego wasn't really fat anymore. Getting around independently, he had lost a lot of his plumpness, but he was still nicely round. What would happen to my baby? His father was, in Mirror's cruel but accurate words, a state away. I was not sure when, or if, he would return.

Therefore, moving down the page, I wrote not Jacob's name, but his father's. Were he able, Reverend Franklin would care for his only grandson, but that was the problem. He wasn't able. In Jacob's rush to get back to the church in Indiana, he failed to notice that his father was growing increasingly frail.

Lela, an attractive companion and an attentive nurse, had all but moved into the parsonage. She was resigned to the fact that she would never receive a marriage proposal from Reverend Franklin. She knew that, in his heart, the Reverend was forever married to his deceased wife. He was definitely the staying kind. Reverend Franklin kept Marva Franklin alive in the round tower of his heart. He would have no other bride.

Lela had staying power, too, though. Reverend Franklin would have a hard time getting rid of her. She cared for him with absolute devotion and she did what she did for love, expecting nothing so showy as a public license or a wedding ring. She wanted exactly what she got: the gratitude and companionship of a good man.

At sixty, Lela wore high-heeled shoes, fancy cologne, and nail polish every day. She had no desire to raise another woman's child.

I crossed Reverend Franklin's name off the list. In its place I wrote Theda May? She was a good friend. If something happened to me she would want to take Diego into her home. Theda loved my baby, but she already had a baby of her own—so much baby, in fact, that she worked two jobs in order to support her grownup baby, Lilly Lawson.

Lilly wasn't heartless. She loved Diego—in her way. She had loved Johnny, too, but she hadn't taken care of him. Theda had. And Theda couldn't handle any more. I drew tiny circles over her name until it was hidden from view.

I didn't write Miss Tavy's name down, didn't think to, knowing she was over-booked, taking care of a house, a husband, a business, grandchildren, and their hangers-on.

I balled up the paper, threw it away, and forced myself back into the hot kitchen, where I prepared a lunch of string cheese, fried green tomatoes that came from my garden, and apples that had, allegedly, been shipped direct from the state of Washington. I packed a box of animal crackers and a bottle of water in the diaper bag for Diego. To keep him company, I threw in Max the Bear, too.

The lunch was for my kids. My own appetite hadn't returned; nausea had taken its place. As I wiped down the kitchen counter, it occurred to me that if liver, stomach, or colon cancer had slipped in the door while I was at the window keeping a look out for breast cancer, the joke would be on me. The hard place in my breast hadn't grown harder or larger, but it also hadn't gone away.

When I left that house at seven o'clock in the morning, I had no plans. The important thing about leaving was not to arrive at any particular place or to do any specific thing once I got there; the important thing was to get away before my kids and I were crushed to death.

Who wouldn't have fled a place that had one room as treacherous as the sea, a mirror that mocked if given the chance, walls that moved in on a weekly basis, a kitchen on fire, and doom swimming around in the backyard like a week-end guest.

We had to go.

I walked away as fast as a woman can walk with two sleepy children in tow. I glanced back at Theda's bright yellow house and saw someone at the window. Lilly probably. Theda had a rare day off. She'd planned to sleep in. Lilly had probably climbed out of bed at first light and showered. Over-dressed, she would wait as long as she could stand it before she woke Theda and dragged her to St. Louis, shopping store to store.

After Johnny's death, Lilly had become hyper. She couldn't sit still, always had to do something, buy this and eat that. It was as if, like Rotelle, she was living for more than one person. She was living for herself and Johnny.

We walked past the Tates' house. Mr. and Ms. Tate were on the porch enjoying the clean morning air. He nodded. She smiled.

The Tate family is small; there are only two of them. They stick to themselves, which is rare in Eloise, a town of families who can't get through a single day without a mini-reunion, an impromptu gathering of the clan.

The Tates used to live outside of town—way outside. They lived in the country, where they were the only black people for miles around. They probably got lonely out there, avoided and isolated as they were, looked down upon and perceived as different by the very same country folk who have been thought of, historically, as ass backward—marginal—for centuries.

Perhaps Mr. and Ms. Tate were pushed, too, if they are, in fact, over the line. There have been rumors of incest.

People say Ms. Tate is Mr. Tate's mother, that he is her only son. Adopted or biological, no one knows for sure. Details are unavailable, facts sketchy, but people in Eloise believe what they want to believe and this one is too good to totally discount.

All I know is that when I was a girl, the Tates used to come into town on Saturdays to have a few beers at Leon's. They socialized with themselves, never mingled. To be fair, they weren't invited to join the locals. They didn't act as if they felt slighted, though. They whispered to one another, drank their beer and watched the young people dance.

She smiled. He patted his foot.

When they left the club and walked to their truck, the second-guessing began and continued for the remainder of the day.

Five years ago, when the Tates moved to Eloise, they settled in the white house on Homer Street. They got a good deal; the last white family on the street, the Agars, highly motivated to flee, sold to the Tates for way below the asking price. Way below.

Once the Tates were residents of Eloise, the rumors about them died down, but not out. People still wonder. I wonder.

The Tates don't look alike. She is short and solidly built. He is tall and lean. They both have dark skin and, although she looks somewhat older than him, their ages are undeterminable—somewhere between forty-five and sixty would be my guess, for both of them. He has the manners, the chivalry, of an older man. She has the smile of a satisfied young girl.

They mind their own business. Usually, when out in public, they do not touch and, while walking, they keep a respectable distance: she walks slightly behind him or a few steps ahead. At home, they sit on their porch and drink coffee or beer. I saw them hold hands once on their porch and I've seen them sitting close, side-by-side, in their truck numerous times. But that's it. Not much to go by.

The Tates seem content with their secluded lives. In addition to her downcast eyes, she has her youthful smile. He has his silence, his formal nod, and a woman (his?) by his side. In the face of their unity, their rock solid stability, I felt adrift, eternally unwed.

We walked on.

When we reached Lincoln Boulevard, we met Carmelita Dixon, a high-functioning alcoholic who walks more than I do, and she walks faster. Carmelita works in Doctor Day's office. Competent and responsible, she always shows up for work on time. Her clocks must match.

Although her drinking is heavy, she confines it to weekends. On Saturdays she drinks off and on all day and at night she dances at Leon's. With no partner in her way cramping her style, she kicks her powerful legs high and wide. Occasionally, uninvited men dance near Carmelita. They dance around her, but they don't dance with her. She dances alone.

Leon's used to have a big dance floor. Although minors couldn't buy or even go near the liquor, which was kept under lock and key in the front, we could hang out in the back. We could dance. At no time was I ever asked to dance, but sometimes, after Baptist training union and without Mama's knowledge, I helped hold up the wall. I watched the more fortunate others dance.

Carmelita's dancing made my mouth drop. She was almost Mama's age but they were lifetimes apart. Carmelita was Mama without the temperance. Mama without the church.

Carmelita stomped, hunched down and shimmied across the floor until she made me woozy, nearly drawn into her orbit. I wondered whether I would have turned out like her if I had kept dancing after Daddy left Kentucky. Would I have turned to liquor, too, I wondered, or would I have still hated the taste and the smell? What I wondered most, though, and secretly feared, was whether the Devil was working his way up through the middle of Leon's dance floor, whether he was being called up like a snake by Carmelita's fast moving feet.

I had never stayed long enough to find out if the devil put in an appearance. I got my behind home before Mama got suspicious. Kids don't hang out at Leon's anymore, but Carmelita still dances there. In the summer, when she's overheated as well as high, she takes her dancing outside. Suzanne has seen her dancing in the street. She's even tried out a few of Carmelita's moves, but they are tricky, they require a drinking woman's hard-boiled technique. More fight than not. Suzanne is a fighter, but she doesn't have Carmelita's sense of defeat. A miniature woman, Suzanne doesn't have that much pain yet. May she never.

Carmelita's white dog Tiger ran along beside her the day we walked. Tiger is short and snappy, Carmelita's perfect partner. She loves him. Tiger and work are all she has. Excuse me. She has her legs. They are toned for days. At forty, she had the legs of a twenty-year-old and nearly two decades later her legs didn't look a day over thirty. What genes that woman must have inherited.

She strode past us, wordlessly.

Carmelita doesn't speak to anyone but Tiger on the weekends. On weekdays she speaks only when she has to. At Dr. Day's office, she points out chairs to sit on and slides papers forward if they need to be signed. She takes frail patients by the arm and leads them to the scale, to the blood pressure cuff, and to the examining table. She'd rather walk with them than talk to them. She didn't even glance at us. She walked on.

As we walked across Foundation Park, we saw Obedego M'bedela meditating on the grass. Obedego is a native son; he was born and reared in Eloise, where he was formerly known as Charles Grant. Chuckie for short.

He recently returned from Africa, after eight years, to care for his aging parents. The Grants don't understand Obedego. They don't understand the ancient language he speaks. They don't understand his frequent meditating, his pillbox hats, or his name change. They are totally mystified by his insistence that he is African, not African American, and certainly not a person of color, just plain African, black African. He instructs them, patiently, lovingly, but they just don't understand.

The Grants savor Obedego's presence, his herbs, and the soothing oils he rubs into their dry, sensitive skin. They deeply appreciate his abiding respect for them, which he had even before he left home, but they wish they understood him better (they may never have).

Obedego didn't open his eyes as we walked by. He sat as dark and still as the tree he had camped under.

I used to find it disconcerting to stand in front of Mirror and see West Africa looking back at me, while all our memories (hers and mine) were of Illinois and

Kentucky. Obedego is lucky. He has walked in the Motherland. He has touched the ground on which his ancestors stood, smelled the fragrances, and tasted the spices they cooked with. He doesn't talk much about what he saw and did in Africa, but he must have pictures he can run though his mind like a movie, even when he is wide awake and sitting beneath a tree in the United States of America.

We didn't disturb him. We walked on.

We sat down near the edge of the park. My children watched the ducks, ate their lunch, and gave Max some love. When they were refreshed we went on, past St. Mary's Hospital, Diego's birthplace, and then on past Eloise Cemetery where Mama's body lay. I didn't stop to pay my respects. In hindsight, I realized that I didn't betray her by leaving her there. I carry her with me.

We kept on going.

When we reached the Interstate, though tired, we did not turn back. We continued, walking off the shoulder of the road, facing traffic. Somewhere miles ahead there was cool gray water. But if it called to me, I didn't hear it. By then, I was deaf to the world.

I held my fat boy every way I could, high and low. We had started out with him on my back and stayed with that until my shoulders cried out. When we came to the end of the road, to Eloise Lake, he was riding on and sliding off my hip.

I looked out at the water. There wasn't a thought in my head.

I was weak and exhausted. The same cannot be said for Suzanne. Tapping into an inner reserve, the strength that allows dancers to dance through pain, prize-fighters to stumble back into the ring, and runners to finish marathons, she skipped—skipped!—off to play and rejoice in the clearing.

I moved slowly toward the water, not thinking about it, but knowing we had a history. Water had swept Mama's father from the roof of his house before a second boat came to rescue him (if there was a second one), and, later, water had covered Mama's head in the bathtub, mercifully allowing her to stop being a person that even she no longer recognized. Water carried her back to her original self, to a place that is worry and pain free.

I didn't think about that, I just walked. When I got to the water, I kicked off my shoes and stepped all the way down until my feet touched the cold scratchy earth. The water was cold even though sunlight bathed Diego's face.

Squinting, he smiled at me, his protector. His solace. The person he had trusted since before day one. We could have been in paradise. To him, any place was safe as long as we were together.

I waded out, carrying Diego like an offering. The weight of the water worked against me. Pushing and pulling, it lapped against my thighs and circled my waist. I might have bent forward and let Diego go, if I hadn't heard a voice say, "Mattie Moon."

I half turned and saw Stranger Woman, dressed in black from head to toe. She was standing on dry land, halfway between Suzanne and me. Light shone all around her. Gold flashed at her wrist. "He's awful young for swimming, isn't he?" she said.

Her voice was like a rope thrown out across the water. I grabbed it.

"He can't swim," I said. "He's only one year old."

"He's got plenty of time to learn, then," she said, holding tight, preventing any slack. "I can see him now. Swimming at the Olympics in Barcelona. Diving in Costa Rica. Splashing around in the Hawaiian surf. Won't Mr. Diego Moon have himself a time in this world?"

Her eyes were as black as the night; they drew me to her. I waded back.

"Hand the baby to me," she said, as I climbed out of the water.

Stranger Woman held Diego easily. He could have been her child. He was safe with her. As Stranger Woman wrapped a thick towel around us, Suzanne ran up, saw that I was soaking wet, and she immediately checked to see if Diego was drenched, too. Finding her brother mostly dry, she opened her mouth, but before she could ask her question, Stranger Woman bent down and asked her one. "You the dancer?"

Suzanne's eyes went wide. "How did you know?"

Stranger smiled.

Suzanne looked at me and whispered, "Do we know her, Mom?"

"It's high time you did," Stranger Woman said. "As soon as we get your mother some solid food, we're going to take ourselves a trip. This is a great big world and we're going to see some of it today.

# CHAPTER TWENTY-TWO

Stranger Woman led us down a path through the woods to her shiny car, which was in the middle of the road as if it had landed there (we soon learned that it had). She opened the trunk and took out a dress that looked like a dream. It was the dress I would have worn to the prom had I been Lamarr's girlfriend instead of his secret.

The dress was pink with sheer sleeves and an uneven hemline that was waiting to swirl. It wasn't my great grandmother's dress; it was mine and I wanted to wear it.

I discarded my old dress as fast as I could. Stranger Woman and Suzanne helped me put on my new one. Seeing my reflection in the side of Stranger's car, I smiled. Mirror would have loved the way I looked.

"Black is beautiful," Stranger Woman said, holding the door open for us. "But even I can't wear it all the time."

When we got into the car, Stranger Woman gave us bread and sweet fruits. Then she turned on the car's ignition and we drove east. We rode past trees and streams, but before we reached the interstate, the car lifted gently from the road.

I wasn't even surprised. It had been that kind of day. When Stranger Woman brought me out of the water, I'd felt as if I had been baptized for the second time. Rising through the air in a car that could fly seemed like the natural way to celebrate my rebirth. After months of being afraid to live in my own house, I felt no fear whatsoever as we headed toward the clouds, just a child-like wonder and that rarity, pure delight.

At first the car was like the hot-air balloon Suzanne had wanted to ride away in. Only better—there was no open flame. We floated gently without hitting any air pockets, but then, when we were above the clouds, we flew rapidly.

The engine didn't roar; there was no sound at all. I couldn't even hear anyone breathing, so I forced my gaze from the horizon and looked at my children to make sure they were with me, and real, not dream-children in a fairy tale. Diego was asleep, but he was warm, fully present. I felt his heart beating. Suzanne was the most awake she had ever been. She scrutinized the open space all around her.

We flew over continents. I, who had never been to the seashore or flown in an airplane, looked down and saw blue over green over white, two great oceans at one time—the Atlantic and the Indian. Meteors flew by us, shining their way across the sky. Upon entering the earth's atmosphere, they burned and left the colors of the rainbow in their wake.

We flew on.

The sky became blacker than any black I had ever seen, blacker than a starless night deep in the Kentucky country where I grew up. There was blackness and then, as we sped by, the sun shining so bright we had to look away. Light flooded the car like a spotlight. And then the contrast again: the great black sky on one hand, the universe shining on the other.

Home, the planet Earth, looked fragile, unreal and yet so familiar it broke my heart.

I wished that everyone I had ever loved—my parents, Aunt Shirley, Jacob, Theda and Lily, even Lamarr, Rotelle and their boys—could see our magnificent planet, whole and from afar. I wished that the car had been packed with people clapping, craning their necks to see more, shouting for more. Bravo! I wished that every man woman and child who felt despair and sadness and futility could see what I saw and know what it felt like to have a mind suddenly on fire.

There were only four of us, though: Stranger Woman, Suzanne, me, and Diego, who was fast asleep and missing everything except the silence.

"Isn't this world big, Mattie? And glorious?"

Stranger Woman's voice startled me.

She said, "It's bigger than you and Illinois, isn't it? Bigger than your biggest fear. And mysterious, too. Take a good look. They'll never figure this out, though I admire them for trying. You can't control this. I can't either. We have to let things be. Look and learn. I didn't bring you out here today just for the ride. We came for the perspective."

"This ought to be enough perspective to last me a lifetime," I said, my own voice echoing in my ear.

"That's the point. A whole lifetime. Don't give out mid-way. Remember that you are a part of this glory."

I didn't want to cry about all the glory that I saw, but I had to do something, so I hummed a few bars of "How Great Thou Art" and then I launched into "In the Upper Room"—two of Mama's favorites.

Suzanne tugged at my arm. "Why do you always hum, Mom? Why don't you ever sing out loud?"

"I can't sing. Never could."

Stranger Woman said, "You may not be Leontyne Price or Jessye Norman, but you can sing, Mattie. Everybody can sing, because everybody's got a song."

Suzanne said, "I sing and dance."

Stranger Woman laughed. "You sure do, Miss Suzanne. Your mother used to dance. Didn't you, Mattie?"

"Yes ma'am," I said, feeling ashamed, because I suspected that if she knew I used to dance she also knew the rest—how much my dancing had meant to me, the moment it came to a stop, and the reason.

Stranger Woman reached across me and opened the door. The car didn't even rock. "Don't be shy," she said. "Step on out there. You won't fall. I won't let you fade away."

I got out of the car and entered the silence. I felt my heart racing. Astronauts had walked where I was. Wearing helmets, boots and oxygen tanks, they were weightless. What did I look like, I wondered, wearing a prom dress and floating beside a car that could fly? Could anybody besides Stranger Woman see me?

I threw my head back and howled. Fresh blood pumped through my veins. My feet moved to the silence, until the music began.

Miles Davis and John Coltrane were on horns; Donny Hathaway sat at the piano. Ella Fitzgerald, Nina Simone, and Sarah Vaughn provided vocals. Calvin Simmons, who floated from Earth too soon, conducted the divine orchestra and I danced.

For the first time since the day Daddy left home, I felt free. Nothing held me back or down. For the first year after Daddy left us, I'd held myself tightly, so I wouldn't burst into tears and worry Mama. Then I held onto Mama, so she wouldn't come apart. I latched onto Lamarr, even though, for the most part, he wasn't there. Then I held Suzanne and Diego and, when he was there, Jacob. For the first time in a long time, I wasn't holding anybody. The universe was holding me.

I danced above the darkness. I danced in the light.

As we came down, the moon passed us on the left, rising like a silver balloon, flat at first and then fully inflated. We landed, not in the California desert or at a space center, but exactly where we had taken off, in the good old Midwest. There was no threat of fire; no emergency equipment was on stand-by. And not one person ran out to meet us. When the neighbors saw the car rolling down Elm Street, a few of them gathered on the sidewalk, but they stood still. They didn't run.

At first, they didn't recognize us. Whispering to Ms. Tate, Mr. Tate said, "Wonder who that is sitting behind those tinted windows?"

Ms. Tate answered shyly. "A rock star, maybe, or a politician selling lies?"

To think it was I, Mattie, with my children and Stranger Woman who was visiting Eloise. Inside the car, we held our tongues. Mostly people speak about small unimportant things, the day-to-day occurrences: He said. She said. Girl, I should have said.

The trip we had taken was huge, too big for the words we knew.

# CHAPTER TWENTY-THREE

Stranger Woman helped me put my children to bed, and then she went to the kitchen to make lentil soup. I laid down and drifted off. I dreamed that a man was peeping at my window. His face was familiar, but I couldn't name him. I had seen him go door to door every summer selling ball tickets—chances to win money on Major League games. I had seen him cutting grass, selling watches, pumping gas, and hauling paper in a truck. I remembered his face, his industry, but not his name.

Eventually his face floated away like one of the orange balloons he twisted into animals and sold at the park on the Fourth of July. After he left, I didn't see anybody, just miles and miles of sky and sunlight shimmering on a white, blue, and green sea.

When I awoke my children were still asleep, the kitchen smelled of garlic and onion and Miss Tavy Love was in the house. She was talking to Stranger Woman. At first their voices sounded warm to me, like the conversations Mama and Aunt Shirley used to have in the kitchen when I was a child. They made me smile. After a few seconds, I realized I was mistaken. One voice was cold, accusatory. That was Miss Tavy's voice. She sounded highly offended; Stranger sounded amused.

The conversation ended and Miss Tavy entered my bedroom cautiously like she was a stranger, too, rather than the former owner of the house and Mama's ex-friend.

Standing near the door, holding her purse like a basket, she said, "It's me, Mattie." Then, as if I had lost my memory as well as my way, she said, "It's Octavia Love. Miss Tavy, you always called me. That always sounded so sweet. You remember me, don't you?"

"Of course I remember you, Miss Tavy," I said. I hadn't remembered her being so weird, so tentative, but I simply said, "I'm surprised to see you."

She looked down at the silk bows on her leather pumps. "I deserve that. I should have come sooner. I feel awful about what happened today."

"Who told you?"

"Gleghorn told me."

"Gleghorn," I said. "That's who it was."

Gleghorn was the man at my window. I tried, but I couldn't bring the face back. It kept right on floating away. "Who told Gleghorn?"

"Gleghorn knows everything," she said. "And he never lies. When he told me what almost happened at Eloise Lake and that now you were in bed and a stranger was cooking in your kitchen, I knew it meant trouble. I got in my car and came straightaway."

"Why?"

"Why?" She took a few steps toward me. "Somebody had to."

"Well thank you. I've got plenty of help, though."

"That stranger? Gleghorn doesn't even know who she is and he makes it his business to know. He has some ideas. He thinks she's one of the Before People."

I sat up. "The who?"

"He means the ones who came before. Before Adam. Before Eve. The original people, he believes, who came up out of the water or down from the trees. The people who were here before other people came up with the name "people." Before People, the pure, undiluted ones that roamed Africa and walked out of it, walked the whole world when it was whole, millions of years before we were sold and brought here as slaves. Before we were lynched, lied to and lied on, stolen from, and told we didn't have anything worth anything anyway. The first ones who will also be the last ones, Gleghorn believes. I don't agree with that kind of talk myself. I go by my Bible."

"I thought you put a lot of faith in what Gleghorn says."

"I do. Unless it goes against the Good Book."

"Why do Gleghorn and the others say the Before People instead of the people who came before or the first people, the original people?"

"Why does anything get turned around? Everything does in due time. Gleghorn says we were people way before other people started calling themselves that and us something else. However you say it the meaning stays the same. I understand it, but I don't condone it. I don't like to think like that. The first people were Adam and Eve. Adam and Eve."

Miss Tavy finally walked up to my bed. "Whoever that stranger is or isn't, you don't need her. You need somebody who knows you personal, somebody who knew your mother. Somebody you can count on."

"Stranger says I can count on her."

Miss Tavy sat at the foot of the bed and made sure she had my attention. "She doesn't have any manners. She still hasn't introduced herself. The first thing I do when I come upon somebody new is extend my hand and say, "How do you do? I'm Mrs. Octavia Love. Wife of Howard Love. Pleased to meet you.""

"I said that to her and she just smiled like she had been expecting me, like she had talked to me yesterday. She stood there stirring a pot like a witch. Dressed head to toe in black. Had on everything but the pointed hat. Had the nerve to ask me if I recognized her and I hadn't ever seen her before. Had you?"

"I saw her twice, once in a dream. And I heard her voice and felt her hold my hand. But today she called my name."

"Did she tell you where she was from?"

"Here and there."

"Here? She certainly is not from here. I know all the blacks in town and most of the whites. She's from there, somewhere else."

"She said she is from all over."

"Sounds like she may be a games player. I'll keep an eye on her."

Miss Tavy slid her feet out of her pumps and sighed so loud she made me wonder if good shoes hurt as bad as cheap ones do.

Then I remembered. "She took us for a ride in her car, Miss Tavy," I yelled.

"What does she drive, one of those ugly vans?"

"No ma'am. A sleek car that can go anywhere. Everywhere. You have got to ride in that car."

She waved the thought away. "I'm happy with my Seville, thank you. And I wouldn't ride with a stranger nohow." She patted my shoulder. "I realize you weren't yourself."

"We flew above the clouds. Saw the stars, the sun and the moon. All the planets."

Miss Tavy grabbed her chest. "Lord Have mercy. I should have come sooner." She clasped her hands and took a deep breath. "Well, I'm here now," she said. She set her purse on the floor and stepped over to my closet in her stocking feet. "Let's find you some decent clothes to put on. You can't lie around here half naked all day. Gleghorn said you didn't even have a robe on."

"This is my new dress. I'm not ashamed, Miss Tavy."

"Don't be proud either. You need to wear more than a slip."

"My black dress got drenched. It's gone. Stranger Woman gave this one to me."

"Funny. She's overdressed and gave you not much more than a scarf. We might have to turn on the heat early this year. We had a heat wave in January and cold in July and smothering in August. They send one more rocket out in space, no telling what weather we'll end up with on God's green earth."

I took advantage of the opening. "We went into outer space."

Miss Tavy closed the closet gently, but she came back to the bed with tears in her eyes. "The notions that must run through your mind. Poor thing. No wonder you ended up at the lake."

She opened her purse and took out her Bible and a Kleenex. She blew her nose and wiped her eyes. "The Lord is still on the throne. He's still in the healing business. We'll take this to Him in prayer."

"I used to pray every night. I stopped."

"Today is the day to start back."

"After what I saw today, you may be right. It's enough to make us all bow down on our knees."

She put her arm around me and rocked me like a baby. "I should have come sooner. When you started walking. Back and forth. Day and night. A woman walking that much is walking away from something. I should have come when Claudette passed. The last time I saw her she made me feel so ashamed that I refused to attend her funeral or bring anything to the house. I stayed home and felt sorry for myself, instead of you. I acted ugly. God don't like ugly. I pray He forgives me my wicked ways. Claudette was my friend and I let her down."

"Don't be too hard on yourself, Miss Tavy," I said, growing drowsy from the swaying. "Mama always said she didn't count on anybody but Jesus."

Miss Tavy teared up again. I changed the subject. "Were you surprised when I got pregnant the second time?" I asked. "Or were you shocked?"

"Neither one," she said, blowing her nose. "In the first place, Miss Tavy don't shock easily and I wasn't surprised because you're a woman, too. We all have needs and, Lord forgive us, we face temptations. Especially when we're young. We're human. Entitled to make a mistake. At least one."

She left the room and came back a few minutes later, carrying Mama's red and white Christmas dress. "This dress is nearly new, Mattie," she said, shaking the dress like a rug. "We'll let some air blow on it and you can put it on."

"It's not mine," I said. "I don't want it."

Miss Tavy said, "I got it from Claudette's room. She'd want you to have it."

"That room is a sea," I said, making the sign of a cross with my forefingers. "You shouldn't have gone in there."

Miss Tavy slapped my hand. "It's just a room," she said. "Don't give it power. Power, like glory, goes to God."

I pulled the sheet up to my chin. "The walls in this house walk like men," I said. "And at night the backyard turns liquid. One night a flood rolled through here."

"This will cover you from neck to knee," Miss Tavy said, handing me the dress. "I'm glad I finally came. Something told me to."

"Wonder what?" Stranger Woman asked. She had come into the room and sat on the floor, legs folded like a Buddha's. "Wonder what told you to come, Mrs. Love? Woman's intuition?"

"Something far greater than that," Miss Tavy said, without looking at the stranger. Her eyes stayed on me. "What about shoes, Mattie?"

I shrugged. "Ruined."

She picked up her purse. "Then I'll get you some new ones at the shopping center."

"Octavia throws money around faster than she throws insults," Mama said.

I saw her the minute she floated in, but I wasn't go to say anything if she didn't. When she spoke, I pushed the covers aside and sat up to see what would happen next.

Stranger Woman stayed right where she was on the floor. She was the picture of serenity.

Miss Tavy, on the other hand, was shocked. She started backing up and she kept backing until she banged against the wall. "No," she cried out, in a high-pitched voice I didn't know she had.

Mama said, "Yes, Octavia. I'm back."

"What do you want, Claudette?" Miss Tavy shrieked. "Why have you come back here?"

"Mattie wouldn't let me rest."

"I never thought you'd come back just because I was lonely, or lost, Mama," I said.

"I asked you to remember me," she said, with tears in her eyes. "Not conjure me up."

"I don't have magic words."

"You don't need magic. I hear your cries. You have two children. You know how it works." The tears ran down her cheeks. "Don't I deserve my rest? Didn't I earn it?"

Feeling bad for the trouble I caused, I whispered, "I'm sorry. I won't dream about you anymore. You can go."

Miss Tavy eased off the wall and held her head high. "I don't believe in ghosts."

"You're doing a lot of talking for a nonbeliever," Mama said, giving her a look.

Miss Tavy took a step toward Mama. "I don't believe in ghosts, Claudette, but I felt something as soon as I walked in this house today. I felt it when I saw that stranger stirring. I didn't want to let on to Mattie, but I felt it too when I went into your room. I've prayed that you forgave me for what I said to you about Howard. For what I believed even though I should have known better."

"You knew better."

"Have it your way. Just say you came back to forgive me."

"Forgive yourself, Octavia. I'm dead."

"Then why are you here? What do you want?"

"I only wanted what was mine. Now I don't even want that." Mama went to the window. She looked out on her old neighborhood and then she turned and looked at Miss Tavy. "Did your daughter, Violet, get what she wanted? Did she make it to Hollywood?"

"A thousand got there ahead of her," Miss Tavy said. "When Gleghorn went out there to see Mickey Mouse, he saw Violet too. She was walking on that street with the names lined up in a row so you can look down and point to your favorites."

"The whole place is a snake pit," Mama said. "Hollywood Boulevard is the main walkway to hell."

For Miss Tavy's sake, I chose to look on the bright side. "Do you think Violet's seen that big sign on the hill that spells out the name of the city where dreams come true?"

Miss Tavy sat on the bed. "Violet might be looking up at that sign this very minute. It would kill Howard if he knew. And if he found out that I've known for months and kept it from him he wouldn't be the only one dead.

"I should have gotten on a plane and gone to get my Violet. I used to say I wouldn't ride in something that had a built-in slide and a seat that floats, something where they had to read you your rights and strap you in before it took off, but now I have to fasten my seatbelt soon as I start the Seville and if I stop too sudden a balloon will blow up in my face. I should have gone straight to the airport and bought an airplane ticket to Hollywood. Instead, I stayed on the ground and prayed to God for my girl's deliverance."

Miss Tavy closed her eyes, bowed her head and prayed. "Jesus, who loved Mary Magdalene, it's me, Octavia Love. I'm speaking to you on behalf of my own Mary, Violet June. She's standing in the need of prayer. Spare her body, Lord, and consecrate her mind. Wash her feet, Lord. Please wash her feet. Don't let her forget she has a home to come home to, Lord. You, who were once part man, understand all things. Forsake us not. And another thing, please don't ever let Violet's earthly father learn about Violet. It would kill him. And he wouldn't be the only one dead. He'd take me with him. And I can't go yet. I've got to stay. I've got to raise Violet's daughter Ce Ce and help Cressie Jean raise her children, too. Amen."

When Miss Tavy finished her prayer, I reached for the silver lining again. "Violet is lucky to have you and her daddy right here in Eloise," I said. "The last time my daddy laid eyes on me, I was nine years old. That's how he remembers me."

"In some ways, we're children all our days," Miss Tavy said, dabbing a handkerchief at the corners of her eyes. "That's why I let go and let God. I put it in His hands."

Stranger Woman arose from her lotus position. "You don't have to put things in God's hands, do you, Mrs. Love? Aren't they already there?"

Miss Tavy looked at Stranger Woman with eyes that were hard and dry. "I lean on His everlasting arms. And so should you." A look of displeasure passed across Stranger's usually serene face. "Why refer to God as him? Might be a her."

Miss Tavy jumped to her feet. "I know my Bible," she said, in a deep voice.

"Then you know it was written by men," Stranger said, gently.

Miss Tavy yanked her Bible open to Genesis One. "So God created man in His own image, in the image of God created He him," she read, emphasizing each male pronoun. "These words were written by inspired men. Watch yourself, Stranger."

"Men, nevertheless," Stranger Woman said, with a slight bow. "God gave birth to the universe. What man has given birth?"

Miss Tavy's eyes narrowed. "What woman ever gave birth natural without a man, other than Mary, who He chose, which proves my point. Right, Claudette?" she said, looking around for Mama to back her up. "Tell this stranger in our midst that you've seen His blessed face."

There was no response; Mama was gone.

I had seen her go and my feelings were mixed. She would finally get her rest, which was overdue and well earned, but I would probably never see her again. I told her I wouldn't dream her up anymore and I was going to try hard not to.

Miss Tavy's feelings were not mixed; she was flat out distraught. She ran from the room, calling out in a voice that was dragging on the ground like a wounded animal, "Claudette! Claudette!"

When she got no answer, Miss Tavy came back and glared at Stranger Woman as if it was all her fault.

Stranger Woman held up her hand, "Peace," she said. "I realize that people think and speak the way they were taught. Years ago, men walking across the desert said to themselves, "Men, we're men, therefore, God's a man." It made perfect chauvinistic sense. They couldn't give birth, but they were determined to define and boss everything born from that day until the day they died. I respect tradition, but, honestly, if I hear one more modern woman say "The Man Upstairs," I'll scream. God is all. God is everywhere, alive in all of us, male and female. Don't you realize that by now, Sister Love?"

"Get back," Miss Tavy said, slicing the air with her Bible. "I hate to say it, but you are no sister of mine."

Stranger Woman didn't argue any further. That's not her style. She simply got out of the way. She bowed once more to Miss Tavy and then to me. "Namaste," she said, stepping into the hallway.

"What did she say?" Miss Tavy asked. "Something about nasty?"

Miss Tavy might have thrown her Bible, but Stranger Woman quit that house faster than Mama had. Even I didn't see her go.

Miss Tavy ran to the window, still clutching her Bible. "What kind of car flies, but doesn't have any wings? Who goes but stays? Who is from here, but nobody saw her black tail before this morning at Eloise Lake? I tell you, Mattie, that woman is a games player."

When she was satisfied that Stranger Woman was not coming back, she came from the window and examined my feet. "What size shoes you wear, dear? Seven? Eight?"

"Nine," I said, with embarrassment. "Everything shrunk but my feet."

"I remember when I could squeeze into a nine," she said, reaching for her pumps. "These are tens." She pushed her feet into her well-made shoes and left for the shopping center.

I took a bath and then, for old time's sake, I read a story to Suzanne. The sleep she had missed while we were out walking at night caught up with her big time. After I read but a few pages to her, she slept for the second time in one day.

Not taking any chances with my milk, I fed Diego a carton of strawberry and banana yogurt. He smeared it everywhere: across his face, in his hair, and all over his time-traveling—thank God, machine-washable—teddy bear.

When Miss Tavy bustled back into the house, she had four shopping bags. She took two shoeboxes from one bag and handed them to me. "Don't start," she said. "These are yours. And I got clothes, books, and toys for your children. I owed your mother. The Lord intends for me to pay you. That's what I think Claudette wanted me to know."

My new shoes were the finest I had ever seen. One pair was red leather; the other was black suede. Miss Tavy must have figured my walking days were over, because the black shoes were sitting-around-in shoes with a high tapered heel. And the red ones were showing-off shoes, happy shoes.

I loved both of them as much as I loved my prom dress.

"We can get you some knock-abouts later," she said, reading me the way Daddy used to do. Then she laid her Bible on my lap and said, "Read this."

I said, "Yes, Ma'am. I will."

She went to the closet, took out my suitcase and put it on the bed. "You need time to heal. You're coming to my house. You'll stay until you get well." With that, she went to packing my raggedy underwear and nightgowns and my loose-fitting tee shirts.

I tried on my shoes and chose the red dancing ones. "What will Cressie say?"

Cressie, Miss Tavy's older daughter, lived at home. As pretty as Violet, Cressie had never sought a glamorous career on stage or screen. Her focus had been on settling down in a happy marriage with the right man. Cressie's problem was she had difficulty telling a do-right man from a do-wrong one. Misjudging her prospects, she had left her parents' house and returned three times in the past seven years.

When her first two marriages ended, she hauled her stuff across town in Mr. Love's truck and was back in her old bedroom before the sun went down, but when the marriage to Toby Palomino washed out on a beach in South Florida, she rode Greyhound for two days before she got home.

She had only been back a few months; she was probably still grieving her loss. I didn't think she'd welcome sharing her childhood home, her sanctuary, with my kids and me.

Miss Tavy folded a pair of faded jeans. "If Cressie can't find it in her heart to share with you and yours, she can move out. Gleghorn is honest, works hard, and has a house waiting for her to move into. She's done worse. But if that doesn't suit her, she can get a job and support herself. Cressie has options. You don't."

"Will it be alright with Mr. Howard?"

"Howard takes care of the businesses. I run the house. He's not stingy. That's what got him in trouble that one and only time. He shared too freely. Now he over-understands that charity begins and, in his case, ends at home."

Secretly thrilled at the thought of getting out of that cave-house, I offered one last half-hearted protest. "I don't want to be a burden," I said.

"You won't be. You'll be a member of the family."

Miss Tavy is rigid about some things, like God's gender and His Holy Word. She adapts easily to other things. For example, she doesn't stop loving her children or other people's simply because they've done something wrong, or something stupid. She loves unconditionally. She forgives with a heart as big as Jupiter, a spirit as wide as the Ohio River. Two places I have seen with my own eyes.

We left that house that evening, as we had planned; however, I didn't go home with Miss Tavy. My destination changed.

Just like that.

# CHAPTER TWENTY-FOUR

I had prepared carefully for the trip to Miss Tavy's house. I wanted to make a good impression. I put on Mama's dress. I corralled my hair and filed my fingernails into oval shapes. I was going to give Mirror a reprieve and, at the same time, take a look at myself, but someone knocked at the front door.

I turned away from Mirror, stepped into the hall, and peeked around the corner. Doctor Day stood in the living room with Levi Gates, a social worker, Sergeant Culver, and a woman who was dressed like a man. She wore a gray suit, a tie and black shoes laced up tight. She had a handkerchief sticking out of the top pocket of her jacket. Everybody but Culver had a briefcase in hand. He was packing a gun.

Who sent for these folks, I wondered, knowing that Miss Tavy and I hadn't and that Gleghorn sure hadn't.

Guided by the words of a sister-poet, Gleghorn speaks true, but he doesn't tell everything he knows. In pursuit of the heart and hand of his dream woman, Cressie Jean Love, Gleghorn is involved in one or two endeavors that, technically speaking, are illegal. His endeavors don't harm anyone, but he steers clear of people who are sworn to enforce, interpret, regulate, or in any way uphold the letter of the law—folks like Sergeant Culver and his back-up team.

So if Gleghorn didn't tell, who then, I asked myself. I tipped to the window and peered out. Was Lamarr our there? Had Lamarr reverted to his old ways?

No one was there. I looked in the closet and under the bed. Nobody lurked there either, so, figuring I would be better off in the living room with people I could see rather than alone in a room with someone I couldn't, I hurried out.

When I ran into the room, everyone jumped, except Miss Tavy. The others recovered, smiled, and took turns asking questions. They listened without changing facial expression, until I told them about my trip with Stranger Woman and then they frowned, cleared their throats, and looked at the floor or up at the ceiling.

Mr. Gates opened his briefcase. "Elvis is a trainee," he said to Miss Tavy, not me. "She's observing."

Like at the zoo, I thought, while nodding politely. I couldn't afford for them to think I was uncooperative or, Heaven forbid, disgruntled. Mr. Gates took out a tape recorder, but before he had a chance to say anything about or to the recording device, Miss Tavy said, "That won't be necessary, Levi. Put it away. If I had come sooner, Mattie wouldn't have felt desperate and alone because she wouldn't have been. I'll fix this."

Mr. Gates put his tape recorder straight away. He knew that Miss Tavy knew the mayor and the governor personally. Sergeant Culver nodded, too, and he didn't call Miss Tavy Granny or accuse her of practicing the ancient rites of voodoo. He knew exactly who he had sworn to protect and serve.

Dr. Day asked Miss Tavy, not me, if he could take a look at Suzanne. Miss Tavy gave me the go ahead.

When I returned, holding my daughter's hand, I couldn't keep the smile off my face. If anyone expected to see scabs, dirt or dead eyes on my Suzanne, they were disappointed. She was clean and well rested, deeply dimpled and wavy-haired. Dr. Day checked her pulse and excused her from the room without asking her any questions about her day.

Then he and Mr. Gates advised Miss Tavy, not me, that a voluntary hospital stay for me would probably be the best thing for my kids. I didn't protest. Suzanne and Diego's safety meant more to me than it did to these people.

They were just doing their jobs.

Miss Tavy didn't like the suggestion much, but when I asked her to, she agreed to drive me to the hospital herself. Sergeant Culver, Levi Gates, and the cross-dresser left, but Dr. Day stayed behind. He phoned the hospital and made arrangements to meet Miss Tavy and me there.

An hour later, we left that house and stepped into the middle of the nightly newscast. A woman wielding a camera jumped in our faces. Lights flashed. A helicopter flew in circles overhead. People shouted my name.

Miss Tavy told me to keep walking and that's what I did, but the camera woman, wearing a Cardinal's baseball cap and fatigues, stayed with me, step for step, while the reporter fired questions. "Will charges be filed? Was anybody helping you? Who or what stopped you? Did you leave a note? What about the father? Where is he?"

I stared blankly into the camera lens. I meant to answer all the questions and say: "I was alone; the Stranger called my name; I didn't write anything down, because my mind was blank; and whose father, mine, Suzanne's or Diego's?"

My mouth opened, but no words fell out.

Miss Tavy nudged the reporter's microphone away with her Bible. She glared at the camerawoman, who was black like us. "You should be ashamed of yourself," she said, quietly. "This ain't the only job. There's other things you can do beside taking pictures of people's trouble. If you put on a dress, my husband would hire you."

The woman pulled her camera back a notch, but the reporter kept pace with Miss Tavy, who was really moving for a woman that far along into her sixties.

Speaking quickly and distinctly into his microphone, the reporter said, "Are you Mattie Moon's mother?" Then, when he held the microphone in front of her face, she had a mouthful for him and all her words fell out. "I am a mother and a grandmother," she said, proudly. "I'm the wife of one of Eloise's top black businessmen. The top businessman period, if the credit due is given. Howard Love is his name. I'm Mrs. Howard Love.

"I was a close friend of Mattie's mother, who can't be here today, which is why I am. I'm also a lifelong citizen of Eloise, a God-fearing, church-going woman. Good day."

The reporter skipped—skipped!—alongside Miss Tavy. "Were you with Mattie at the lake?"

Miss Tavy said, "No. I came late, but at least I came."

He asked, "Who told you what happened?"

"Gleghorn and he speaks true." With that, Miss Tavy snapped her mouth shut and pushed on through the small crowd gathering around us. Carrying Diego in her arms, Miss Tavy shielded Diego from the camera like a celebrity mom who had given birth that day in Santa Monica and didn't want the wrong publication to get the first pictures.

Mother-henning a path straight to her car, she signaled for Suzanne and me to follow. As we scrambled into the car, the reporter tried to keep Suzanne from closing the door. She gave him a swift kick. The reporter howled. Still, I didn't reprimand my child because the circumstances were extraordinary and my girl is a natural-born fighter.

When we were all safely inside the Seville with the doors locked, Miss Tavy shook her tightly permed head. "Privacy is a thing of the past. Self-respect died first. Then shame. All that's left is dog-eat-dog. The smell of blood and pain and they run wild." Looking at the man's long face pressed against her window shield, she sighed. "Two-legged pack dogs chasing after the next ugly thing."

She turned on the ignition and the anxious face receded from the window, but the man's mouth kept working, begging for a morsel, a scrap. Miss Tavy drove slowly so she wouldn't run over him. She let him live.

He ran after us a few steps and then he gave up. The camerawoman, crouched low, kept running, filming the back of the get-away car.

"You don't ever have to come back to this house unless you want to," Miss Tavy said, as we moved on down the street. "Memories can be awful things."

Memories I could have handled. It was those wayward walls I couldn't abide. I looked back at that unpredictable house. It looked big on the outside, but I knew that the interior was the size of Diego's fist.

Within forty-eight hours an official report had been filed and a psychological evaluation had been completed. A brief hearing was held the following week, and then I was transferred from St. Mary's to this place for rest and recuperation. Rehabilitation.

# CHAPTER TWENTY-FIVE

People say I let myself go. They are mistaken. I was driven away. I was lost. My father found me.

I recognized Daddy the minute he walked up the hall. I recognized him by his hat. Most men have long since given up the habit of wearing a well-made hat, but not Daddy. He still wears a hat and he wears it the way he always did, turned to the side, slanting over his right eye. The hat he wore today looked more expensive than the ones he used to wear. It had a ribbon around it, a snap-brim. He looked like some dandy, but I recognized him: the man of my heart.

In this place, we don't get many visitors. Family mostly, and the extensions: the friends and neighbors who feel especially close. The dignified man who came up the hall wearing a hat had an attendant at his side. They paused before entering my room.

We had been in some of the papers—all four of us: Miss Tavy, Suzanne, Diego, and me. There were two pictures of me: one where I was standing on the sidewalk in front of that house, staring into space, and another one of my children and me getting into Miss Tavy's car. He said that he told himself that the woman shown in the picture, the woman standing on the sidewalk, with a blank stare, couldn't be his daughter. She had to be some other Mattie Moon, he figured, but when he saw the other picture of me the red shoes caught his eye. He thought they were the kind of bright shoes a dancer might wear. A certain dancer.

The next day he read in a Chicago newspaper that the Mattie Moon being written about had been born in Kentucky and migrated to Illinois; that's how he knew that I was his own girl, all grown up. After twenty years and a near miss, he had found me.

He came to Eloise the same way he left Kentucky—via the railroad tracks. This time though, instead of walking between them a good part of the way, he rode on top the whole way, as an overnight passenger on an Amtrak train.

Miss Tavy picked him up at the train station, took him to her house to freshen up, and then she drove him out here.

We had been apart so long that, at first, we were like strangers. There was white hair under his hat, white in his neatly trimmed sideburns and in his moustache. His face was thinner—he is all eyes, cheekbones, and hollows now, but his skin is still dark and smooth.

Daddy's hair wasn't the only thing that had aged. His joints had, too. They were stiffer; he had slowed down, each movement was thought through. Still, he had me beat. I had stopped moving altogether. Not yet thirty, propped up in an institutional bed, I felt like an old woman about dead.

I held back my useless tears, though. Sometime tears help, but they hadn't brought my father home; red dancing-shoes had. I hated for him to see that the shoes were all I had and how much I had changed. My hair was uncombed, thick white socks covered my feet (instead of party-steppers) and a blue uniform passing for a dress was draped across my grownup body. "Sorry," I said. "For everything. I don't know what happened to me."

He put his hand on my shoulder. "You are still my daughter," he said. "That business at the lake is over. The past is a cave-in waiting to happen. Don't look back. Keep steady moving."

"Not much moving around room in here," I said.

"In your mind," he said, removing his hat. "Keep moving in your mind. Walk around in the present. Claudette got ahead of herself. She lived for heaven, for the future. She left before I did, if you can understand that."

"Oh, I can. You felt her leaving."

He nodded. "I was standing between her and Jesus. I got out of the away."

"You left her a window."

My mind asked: what did you leave me? I may as well have said it out loud, because after all the years, Daddy can still read me.

"Claudette not wanting me was one thing," he said. "But you needed me. Maybe I should have stayed. I felt I had to go. I treated you and Claudette like a package deal. Leaving you to take care of Claudette was too big a burden for you."

I felt like he had put his fist in my chest. "We managed," I said, trying to defend Mama and myself at the same time. "Mama asked me to remember her the way she was before she got sick. And I did." Wanting to land at least one punch, I looked at him and said, "You broke Mama's heart. She missed you real bad."

"She missed me when I was there, too," he said, looking out the window.

He sat down and we listened to the sounds in the hall, the footsteps and the carts being pushed in and out of rooms. There was some weeping and some wailing, but mostly there was the lack of sound, the eerie quiet of people who have no place to go and nothing much to do.

"We can lose perspective," I said, finally.

"You don't have to tell me," Daddy said. "I've had ups and downs. Sitting on the train today, though, seeing the sun come up and the land rolling by, I was thinking what a great thing a life is. One is enough. And what a wonderful place this is to live that one."

"I've seen it all, Daddy," I said. "The whole world at one time."

He chuckled. "Have you now?"

"I sure have," I said, hoping he'd believe me, but not counting on it. "How is Uncle Rob Roy doing?"

"Bragging day and night. But he can back most of it up. He has his own business. Auto repair. He told me to say he'll come see you real soon. You may never lay eyes on him. Then again, he may show up next week."

"Do you have a car?"

"Of course I have a car. I've had three total. This last one I bought new from the factory. I left it with my boy."

My heart lurched. His boy? I had always wanted a brother. Never knew I had one. I looked down at the floor. "What's his name?"

"Sam. Samuel Lester Moon."

I smiled. "We're getting a lot of use out of the name Lester, aren't we?"

"Sure are. Mrs. Love told me that was Diego's middle name. Thank you for that. I count my blessings. Sam's eighteen. Works. Going off to college next year."

"So you've got a new wife, then?"

He nodded. "Three must be my number. Three cars. Three houses. Three wives. Sam's mama, Rita Lasky, was wife number two. When Sam was one, she took off and went to Chicago. Haven't seen her since. She thought she could do better than me. From what I hear, she didn't."

The words "serves you right" rattled around in my head. Daddy heard them as soon as I did. He shrugged. "Who am I to judge? At least she gave me the one thing I wanted more than anything else in the world. A son."

My mind went quiet as a tomb.

"Now I have two children," he said, standing to stretch his legs. "The perfect number, to my way of thinking."

"Mine, too," I said, grinning.

"Sam is going to study business. But he hopes to sing on the side."

"Did he get his voice from his mother?" I asked, since I didn't get one from mine.

Daddy nodded. "Rita was a singer. She put me in mind of Whitney Houston. That was the trick she used on me. Singing in my ear before I fell asleep at night. After she left I was lonely for a long time. Didn't trust myself with a woman until I met Patty two years ago. Patty Moon. She took my name. Rita insisted on keeping the name Lasky. That should have told me something right there. But I convinced myself that she wanted everything about me except my name." He put on his hat and tilted it like he was leaving, but he didn't go anywhere. "What a fool believes," he said, laughing out loud.

Hearing the sound of his laughter, remembering its timbre and depth, made me realize how much I had missed the man sitting in front of me, the man I barely knew who had my father's laugh rising in his throat.

The new/older man in my hospital room and the remembered/younger man who played the harmonica behind our house in Kentucky could have been father and son. Same laugh, similar hats—different men.

The man sitting beside me was not simply older and more experienced, he was also sadder, despite his laugh. My young father set off walking down a railroad track, suitcase in hand, asking only that the future wait until he got there. The man who returned was resigned. Circumspect. His laugh said, "What the hell? What a fool believes ... But we all have to believe something. Life isn't so bad. It's better than no life at all (has to be) and a lot of the bad we bring on ourselves. At the very least, we end up with something to laugh about."

I wanted him to stop laughing and tell me the truth about his life; how it felt to be left twice, the first time for Jesus and the second time for Chicago; the humiliation of growing up poor (shoeless!) in Kentucky; his fears, if any, of going deep into the belly of a mine each day, with only a lamp and the man in front of him guiding the way. I wanted to know what he thought the first time he looked up and saw Mama, and why he married her even though he knew himself how things were going to turn out.

He didn't speak of any of those things nor of the aches and pains his body had absorbed over the years, the dreams he had seen die. He didn't even talk about the good times he had when he first hit the Motor City, or give any details about the stops he'd made along the way.

He didn't say anything about our missed years. Neither man, the younger nor the older, had ever given me a curfew or a driving lesson, sent a card congratulating me for graduating from high school (almost going to college), or giving birth (twice!), told me to braid my hair or sit up straight, or, more important, advise me away from the kind of boy who can dribble a ball and make it match a girl's heart-beat, bounce for bounce. He had never given me praise or punishment. Time and I had gone on without him.

When he went to the window, I took a long look at him. I had a lot of looking to make up for—twenty years plus. I wondered whether we'd have another twenty.

"If my health holds up," he said, as always on the same page I was on, "I believe Patty and I will help each other make it through. Neither one of us wants to waste time making anybody feel bad."

"I hope your third time is lucky."

"Some people say we make our own luck."

"Always?"

"Not always," he said, turning to look at me. "It matters what hand we're dealt. You got a bad hand when I left."

"At least you came back."

Daddy came over and put his arm around me. He hugged me tight. "I'm staying two days. Mrs. Love insists that I stay at her house so I can spend time with my grandchildren."

"You can call her Miss Tavy, Daddy. Or Sister Love, if you want."

He frowned and shook his head. "Mrs. Octavia Love is the way she introduced herself to me. Mrs. Octavia Love she is." Then he smiled. "Your boy is a kick and Suzanne—well, she got her dancing from you."

"Mama used to say she got it from the devil."

"There was a time I didn't believe in the devil. But I've seen him too many times not to believe. I've seen him in Kentucky, red-faced, in a pick-up truck with a gun and a dog in the back. I see him every day in Detroit in a big sports truck with a gun on the floor. I've seen him in the White House, at the police station, on television, and at the grocery store. Everywhere I go I see him and he sees me."

"Are you religious? Will that help?"

"It might. I do seem to be going that way in my old age."

I wasn't sure how to respond. Religion is a sore subject for me. When I was young, sitting beside Mama, church was the best place to be. I loved the music (doesn't everybody?) and the praying. I loved the crying, the shouting and the calming down before we hugged each other and went home to live out the week just like everybody else in Kentucky, the saved and the unsaved, confident that we would we gather again the next Sunday to be renewed.

It has been a long time since I've been to church for anything other than a recital or a funeral. When I listen to Yolanda or Kirk or Sweet Honey In The Rock it is as if I am right back there, warm and safe in the church, the oasis, but I'm not sure if I ever will be again. I wonder whether I saw the face and work of God as we spun through the universe in Stranger's car. Is there something more somewhere? Anyone who cares whether or how we suffer? Whether we live or die?

"Stranger Woman says there are hundreds of religions in the world," I said. "But only one love."

His eyes twinkled. "Stranger? I've known three Majors, two Preachers, and a Brother, but Stranger's a new one on me." He laughed, but then he turned serious. "Mrs. Love said you gave her credit for bringing you out of the lake. I hope to meet her one day and thank her."

"She says no thanks necessary. She'll be back, though. She said she would."

"So will I," he said. "When you're better you can come visit me."

You once told me when I got big I could come, I thought to myself. It didn't happen.

"I'll leave my address and my home and work numbers with Mrs. Love," he said. "You'll know where I am. Where to find me."

"You're still working?"

"I still have a hand in it. The day a man stops working is the day somebody starts measuring him for that suit. And before long they put the suit on him. It doesn't matter that it doesn't fit, because where he's going he won't need it—or shoes or a hat."

"Your suit can wait."

"Yours, too, Mattie. Let it."

"What kind of work do you do?"

"The kind somebody around here does. Laundry room at a hospital. A regular hospital. Not much, but it beats sitting around waiting for the suit."

I said, "I wish you could stay longer."

Same old baby. Same old love. But Daddy left when he said he would. A man his age can't afford to stay away from a job too long. He didn't have a three-week vacation with pay; he had three days of unpaid leave and a weekend that was all his own.

Before he left, he said the things visitors always say: The rest sure is doing you good. You're getting stronger every day. In no time, you'll get out of here and put your life back together.

I felt like screaming. He had been lost for so long and when he was finally found we only had a minute and then he was gone again.

It is good that I was here, in this place, when he left. This place is not a rock, a cleft; it doesn't hide me, but there are benefits. There is space, room to breathe, and I am given calming medications here—anti-panic pills twice a day. I get regular examinations, too. If the family cancer comes calling, I'll be one of the first to know.

Here comes the doctor now.

He is old. His hands shake. His teeth are as yellow as gold. He has ears down to his shoulders. His hair is white and thin across his pink scalp. So many hours, so many years of his life he has helped people like me—held our hands, comforted us, and, when necessary, relayed the bad news. Nearly decrepit, he carries on. He wears his white coat proudly, even though it falls from his shoulders like a drape and is as stained as his teeth. No matter. At least he eludes his funeral suit.

When he stands too close and hits my knee, I kick him instinctively. He leans toward me and nearly falls when he places the stethoscope on my chest. His breath rattles when he peers into my small (compared to his) ears.

I hold out my hand to help support him.

When he tells me to, I lie down. He kneads my breasts. Before, I had a scare. Nothing malignant, yet. He finishes, smiles and sighs because I have been spared, again. I don't tell him we are both about gone. Some things are better left unsaid. I do the polite thing. I sit back up and take a deep breath. Another. One more. Just like he tells me to.

His model patient, I stare into the light. I smile. Of all the doctors who free-lance here, he is my favorite. He asks the fewest questions. He relies on his experience, his five senses, especially the sense of touch. He is interested in my body, not my mind. The others are after what's left of my mind. They are in search of the tipping point. We go back from the lake, through that house, across the river into the woods, and down the hills of Kentucky. Each time we meet, they sit in one chair and I in the other, but we arrive at the same place and we never find what we're looking for: the switch to turn my pain off. This one, the one I like, is more helpful. We're getting somewhere. He comforts me. I give him something to do.

Some women with family histories of cancer take drastic measures. They have preventative surgery, double mastectomies and complete hysterectomies. They are called pioneers—daring women who fight to extend their own lives by any means necessary. No one locks them up. They are free to come and go. It has been decided that I experience obsessive thoughts, catastrophic fixations, which require me to reside here a while longer, in this place. I am not free to go. However, I am allowed to write. Today, after my favorite doctor examined me, I wrote a note to Sherry Brady, a few words to cheer her up, one inmate to another.

Sherry is in the county jail awaiting trial. She uses her original surname now, her father's name. I write her preferred name in big letters on the envelope— B-R-A-D-Y—hoping it will be delivered to her. Most everyone stubbornly still calls her Ziegler, saddling her with her tormentor's name, even though so far she hasn't got his money. It's tied up.

Mary Stokes, one of the more communicative women here, talks frequently about Sherry's case. She insists on saying Ziegler no matter how much it hurts my ears and my feelings. She believes Sherry should be convicted on the top count: murder in the first degree. We disagree, Mary and I.

Late afternoon. We are sitting side by side in plastic chairs in the so-called recreation room—sitting so close I can smell the bergamot in Mary's hair. We share yesterday's newspaper. I tell Mary that Sherry is not guilty of a cold-blooded murder, that she is not guilty of murder at all. "She was beaten. She acted solely in defense of herself," I try to explain. "She was backed into a corner."

"A lot of men beat their wives," Mary says, "but that doesn't mean they would kill them."

"Maybe not," I say, turning to face the wall. "But if a man beats his wife regularly, he wants her dead. Maybe not all the time, but often. When he's beating the shit out of her, at that moment, yeah, he wants her dead. He may want to die, too, miserable and debased as he is, but he's beating her, not himself. If anyone ends up dead, she will. Sherry Brady decided her death could wait. She chose herself. Her original self."

I listen for Mary's response. All I hear is a squeaking chair. Soft footsteps. I turn around and see Mary walking out the door, and she is pissed. I can tell by the way she is swinging her good arm, the one her husband, Tom, broke in two places, not the arm he scalded and cut off below the elbow.

With Mary gone, I feel very alone in the rec room. I have no one to talk to and nothing to do. For the next few days, Mary probably won't say anything to me, not even, "Go to hell."

Despite the harsh opinions of the women like Mary, many of whom have repeatedly felt their own partner's pain in the form of crushing blows and fiery slaps lodged upside their well-meaning but stubborn heads, Sherry's situation is not hopeless. Sherry is not doomed. Her fate is not in Mary's hands and, with luck, there won't be any Marys on the jury that decides her fate.

She may be acquitted. Her lawyers are clever. Two of them came all the way from Manhattan. The man and woman from New York City aren't simply experts in the field of the battered woman's syndrome, they are crusaders. Zealots. They aren't charging Sherry a dime (if she inherits Mark's money she will make a contribution to the Battered Women's Collective). The city lawyers are doing it for the glory and a how-to book that will be published later. They have assured their client that everything that can be used will be, including the truth. They intend to show that Sherry was a fragile teenager when she married Mark, that he damaged her and that he would have extinguished what little was left of her, her half-life, had she not chosen to survive him when and where she did.

I would be willing to testify on Sherry's behalf, but I won't be called to the stand. Concerning any testimony that I provided, the jury would be advised to consider the source. I'll send moral support. Notes of encouragement.

Although they'll be instructed otherwise, the male members of the jury may be swayed by Sherry's upturned nose, by her Caribbean-blue eyes, and her blond hair. It took forever, but I finally understood the deal with blue eyes. I'm pretty sure the obsession with blond hair has something to do with light shining in a predominantly dark universe (I've seen how miraculous that is). Light would be especially important to people who lived far from the equator for tens of thousands of years, before trekking down from the mountains to take over the world. White (or yellow) on top of a head probably reminds some folks of the snow-capped mountains of yore. Even if the only peaks they've seen are on the pages of *National Geographic*, race memories are triggered. A sense of snow recalled. If blue eyes remind people of water and their ability to swim, light hair must remind them they can cross the water, climb out of their rickety boats, and rule the natives when they come ashore. We are the direct descendants of Vikings, Celts, and Germanic folk (the master race?) they must think. They may not go that far and this theory doesn't explain why so many dark-skinned women, black and Asian, are bleaching their hair, but what obsession makes sense?

None of mine have.

Anyway, Sherry has other weapons in her arsenal. The large implants and rigorous exercise classes Mark insisted upon should pay off nicely; and, in addition to her show-stopping body, she has a cover girl smile. With no new bruises to hide, she can wear less make-up, work that fresh-faced angle. Every angle.

Appearing in court each day, she will resemble the woman she was before Mark's beatings aged her soul and splintered her heart. She will be renewed: Sherry Brady restored.

She can look the finders of fact in the eye and tell them the truth: that she loved Mark; that his cruelty came at her full blast; and, knowing that there was only one way to eliminate that cruelty, she chose herself.

The jury may render a unanimous decision that, rationally or not, in her own mind, Sherry believed that she had to end Mark's life to save her own. She could be found to have suffered diminished capacity and be declared not guilty, which is not the same as innocent.

I hope Sherry prevails. She is not a cold-blooded killer. She was created, unintelligently designed. Monster by Mark.

However it shakes out, she found her voice. She is writing every day on yellow legal pads provided by her attorneys. She says the words are pouring down, falling like fat nourishing raindrops. She lost her home and her garden, but she has a well now. And she can keep going to it until she has completed her book about life.

# CHAPTER TWENTY-SIX

Suzanne was going to live with Lamarr and Rotelle until she decided that Diego needed her. Lamarr was devastated; he would have taken his daughter to court if he hadn't known how capable she was of arguing her own case. By the end of her opening statement, the judge would have been on her side. Lamarr gave up. He's amazing. He gets more flexible by the day when it comes to the women he loves.

Jacob understood right away, without Suzanne having to tell him, how important it was for her and Diego to live together under one roof, with a woman like Miss Tavy. Jacob admits that, although he had no siblings, when he lost his mother he would have loved to have had Miss Tavy take him to live in her big house with the exquisite Violet Rose and the incredibly friendly Cressie Jean.

Jacob wasn't that fortunate, but Miss Tavy checked on him every week at the parsonage, the same way Theda checks on Suzanne and Diego now.

Theda visits me often, too. Lilly came with Theda once and she said then that she would come no more. She said she wouldn't take the chance on having some kind of post-traumatic/re-surfaced, always-threatening-to-break-her-down episode of grief about Johnny's death and end up trading insults with one-armed Mary for the rest of her life.

Jacob moved back to Eloise. He missed Diego's first step, but he heard his first word and called it a miracle. "Da Da," a miracle? For sure, Jacob says. For sure.

A true believer, an ordained minister visiting the shut-in, Jacob sits by my bed each day, offering encouragement. "It won't be long, now," he says. "You'll be home, soon, Darling."

I almost reach out and touch his beautiful face. He looks handsome with the sun at his back, still young in that way some men manage until sixty-five or seventy, right up until the time they get sick and die on you, leaving you feeling, oddly, that they were cheated somehow, cut down in their prime.

I want to touch Jacob, but I don't. Touching him would bring up feelings that I am not allowed to express in this place.

Jacob believes that faith is a bridge that we can walk out on and not fall. His faith has been tested and found strong, strong enough, he thinks, for both of us. It is difficult to explain to him that, while he was away, my own faith did not simply erode or weaken, it disappeared. Vanished. I felt completely alone.

I try to form the right words to help him understand how I ended up at the lake, but my mind is a regular wall. It doesn't budge. "I felt under siege," I say, working my thoughts like stiff clay. "Jobless. Frightened. Afraid you might not come back."

"You knew I would."

"I knew you were gone."

"Your mind played tricks on you."

"What mind?"

"You're not insane." Jacob insists that I was never insane. Grief-stricken, spiritually challenged maybe, and suffering from postpartum depression or an anxiety disorder, but not insane. "Not you," he says.

"Mama was. So was her mother. Why can't I be?"

"Because when we created Diego, we started something that we have to finish. That's why. You'll recover."

"What if you have to venture farther east to search for your calling? Say to Ohio or New Jersey?"

"I'm not going anywhere," he says. "I felt my son's first kick and heard his first word. God willing, I'll see him become a man. All we need is faith in God to make this thing work."

"Jacob, it's Saturday. Don't preach."

He laughs. "I preach every day. I was born to preach. I know that now."

"You always knew. Deep down inside."

"I have faith in us, too."

The smile spreading across Jacob's face makes something stir inside me. The will to live, perhaps, a literal hunger for a life on the outside with him, the freedom to lie close to him in a room far away from this restrictive rehabilitative place.

Young Pastor Franklin is as strong-willed as his father and as stubborn as his own son. "Wouldn't it be wonderful if life were simple?" I say, "If all we needed were love and faith?"

Jacob's smile dies. "I know life's complicated. Even unfair. But faith is not simple-mindedness. It's knowing deep down that we are loved. That we have purpose. It is what gets me through."

"I wasn't belittling you. I sit in awe."

"Promise that if things go wrong, if you are in pain, you'll talk to me. Or to Dad."

I look into Jacob's deep brown eyes. "I can't promise anything. Until I understand why I went to the lake how can I promise never to go back?"

He takes my hand. "We'll understand in time."

"By and by?"

"Sooner than you think. You're getting the help you need here and when you get out we'll build a life together in the church."

"What church would have me?"

"The Church of the Living God."

In this place, I am allowed to think, and my thoughts are these: What a beautiful black man Jacob Franklin is. Maybe I had to go through Lamarr to get to him. Some day I hope I do something to deserve him. I can already think of a few things. Seeing the silly look passing over my Moon-face, Jacob pats my hand and says, "Love you, too."

I entwine my fingers with his, lower my eyes and think thoughts that make me smile. "Did you hear me?" he asks.

"Of course I heard you," I say, shifting my gaze so I can see the world outside my window, the trees and their golden leaves waiting to fall. "Broken-down Mary can hear you in the next room and she has a busted eardrum."

"It's not my fault that these walls are thin and I have a baritone voice. You'll be out of here soon and I can say what I want to say. Loud as I want to say it."

Jacob's crazy. He knows as well as I do that I may never walk out of here. I may ride out of this institution the way Mark Ziegler left his mansion: stretched out on a cooling-board. Still, Jacob makes plans. He saves money for a house; he keeps the faith. He reads ornamental passages from the Bible to encourage and enlighten us both. He doesn't give up, so neither will I.

Sometimes when I close my eyes I see myself free, not simply free of this place, but truly free. I see all of us—Jacob, our fat boy Diego, Suzanne and me. We are running toward our new house. I'm wearing a white, loose-fitting dress—no more black with a choking collar. Suzanne is as beautiful as she has always been, and as brave. The sun is shining and the breeze is gentle, but strong enough to make the grass sing. Jacob opens the door to our new house, to our new lives and we enter.

Sometimes when I close my eyes.

Jacob is gone and I am alone. I am relatively at peace. I don't like this place, but that doesn't mean I haven't gotten used to living here. I've gotten used to waiting. That is what most of us do here. We are the true waitpersons. We don't serve meals; our meals are served to us and we wait patiently for them. We wait to receive visitors, to bathe, to be weighed, examined, analyzed, and, at the end of the day, we wait for night to surround us. If we wake up in the middle of the night, we wait for the dawn. Most of us have gotten very good at what we do: wait to get better or die trying.

The smart ones, however, the truly successful among us, don't wait at all. They've stopped. They simply exist. They ask no questions of anyone. They don't write. They don't call or send up any smoke signals. They don't hope to make sense here or after they are released, if they are. They don't expect to be. They hold out no hope. Their only preoccupation is with their breathing. Inhalation. Exhalation. They've reached Zen.

I, on the other hand, an optimistic fool, am waiting and hoping like mad. I hope Daddy and Jacob are right. I hope I walk away from this place, my third home, also. I hope that Jacob and I will be able to make a safe place for Suzanne and Diego. I want them to feel what I felt in my original home, before Mama first got sick and Daddy began leaving: secure and protected.

Back then, like my father, I was a lover of our land. I had green grass to roll around in and red hills to run up and down. I smelled flowers in bloom and picked ripe berries from the trees as I walked (and skipped!) home from school. I marveled at the clouds in the sky and never felt afraid of them. Every day I spoke to our neighbor's bull and understood why he didn't speak back.

I had an aunt who was one of the bravest people in the world and, best of all, I had a dance I performed that was all my own.

In my second home, I lost my sense of safety. Fatherless, and essentially motherless, I lost perspective. I misplaced my values and latched on to nothing at all. I became stuck.

I lived without faith.

On my trip with Stranger Woman I saw the majesty of the universe and I danced again. I don't dance here, but my time with Stranger Woman was not wasted. I relive it whenever I need to. With her help, I learned that I still believe, somehow and some way, in God. I don't quote things that were written long ago, chapter and verse, but I give thanks for my blessings (Jacob, rainbow-born Suzanne, and my fat boy, Diego Lester). I can't explain why I've been "blessed" when so many others have not been. All that I can do is pray that widespread human suffering ceases, that hunger, illness, war and desperation cease to exist. I know that they have always been with us and that perhaps they always will be; nevertheless, as I sit and wait, I pray. I also try to respect others and judge not, lest I be judged. I try to love my neighbors. Including one-arm Mary.

Tonight, when Stranger Woman dropped by—no one heard her coming—we talked about faith and the lack thereof. Stranger acknowledged that, although she goes everywhere sooner or later, she isn't always in more than one place at a time. Sometimes she is, sometimes not. It depends. She regrets that she cannot do more. She is the first to admit that, although she does as much as she can, it is never enough. An emissary, she relies on others to take up the slack. She doesn't apologize. That's not her style.

Stranger Woman told no fairy tales this evening. She doesn't believe in fairy tales, yet she understands why people tell them to one another: to teach each other lessons and provide what comfort they can. She, however, prefers grown folks talk. "Suffering is part of life," she said. "The greater part. All the more reason to rejoice and dance wherever you can. In the street. Wherever you find yourself. Embrace the universe. We can't change it. Things were set in motion long ago. There's no turning back, now. You remember our trip?"

"Of course I do."

She laughed. "Wasn't that the big picture? What more could you ask for, child? Who would have wanted to miss that? We all face hard times. We suffer losses. We can't just love people though. We have to love life. When you need a reason to go on living, you have to make it up as you go. Meaning comes from doing, from sharing, from giving and from forgiving, from loving and learning, from both grief and joy.

You have to make it work. That's your challenge and your reward. Work it. Wear your crown. It's yours. Don't fear the dark. Everything came out of darkness. To darkness everything will return. In the meantime, while you live, shine your light. Fight for yourself every day. You can't expect somebody else to fight for you. Not even me. You have to make up your own mind to endure."

Strictly grown folks talk.

That's her style.

I have no idea where Stranger Woman went when she left. This I do know for sure: she'll come back around this way, even if she can't stay long. She will be who she will be.

As I washed up and got ready for bed tonight, I thought about Mama. When she lost faith in herself and her life on earth, she called on the power she had witnessed as a young child, the awesome power of water. She created her own flood.

Which brings me back to Susan Smith. I often tell myself that I'm different from Susan. There are differences I can cite: I didn't lie and blame a nonexistent member of a historically maligned race of men for my actions. Unlike Susan, when they stuck that microphone in my face I didn't say one word. My mother, not my father, committed suicide (Lester Moon has no suicidal tendencies. He will fight off that funeral suit as long as he can). There was never a hypocritical stepfather stalking my house, feeling me up with one hand, pointing toward God with the other, and sending me off in a misguided search for love. I was not a frustrated child bride (or any other type, for that matter).

My story is different from Susan's, but there are similarities. We are both women and we were both drawn to water. We turned to it, perhaps as Mama had, hoping it would wash our troubles away.

Susan Smith drove to Long Lake in the dark of night. No one called her name or the names of her children. None were saved.

I walked to Eloise Lake in broad daylight, but behold! Stranger Woman was there.

She called my name.

I am not better than Susan Smith, Andrea Yates, or any of the other desperate and distressed mothers who've committed infanticide. Just luckier. My life was saved. My children were spared.

People said I let myself go. They are mistaken. I went, but I came back. And even if I never get out of here, Suzanne and Diego are safe. That is the important thing. They are surrounded by love, a love that will exalt them, not one that will frighten them, smother them, or weigh them down. They won't get stuck. They will soar.

My children will fly through the universe like stars in the night. They will be something to see.

That is my story. Suzanne and Diego are my song.

978-0-595-40608-1
0-595-40608-4

Printed in the United States
98273LV00003B/27/A